THE GIRL IN THE PINK SHOES

BOOKS BY STACY GREEN

THE GIRL IN THE PINK SHOES

STACY GREEN

bookouture

Published by Bookouture in 2023

An imprint of Storyfire Ltd.
Carmelite House
50 Victoria Embankment
London EC4Y 0DZ

www.bookouture.com

ISBN: 978-1-80314-929-5
eBook ISBN: 978-1-80314-928-8

Dedicated to the millions of children whose voices are ignored.

ONE

I'm not a killer. Or a savior. I'm just one person trying to repair the broken scales of justice one jagged crack at a time.

The crack I planned to eliminate tonight sat ten feet away eating nachos. His short, pink tongue darted out to slurp the gooey cheese off the chip before shoving the tortilla into his mouth. He smacked his lips when he ate. Licked his fingers and started over again, like a pig fighting for its mama's teat. This coward wouldn't be the dominant piglet. He's the sort who would be shoved aside to starve. The only way for him to feel powerful is to prey on the weak.

I flagged down my favorite waitress. Another drink was essential to the evening's success. She grinned and started navigating her way between crowded tables.

Famous for its microbrews and restored tin ceiling with golden tiles that cast a warm glow over the entire restaurant, Chetter's Bar and Grill was a hallmark of the historic Old Kensington area of Philadelphia. If I were in my twenties and still naïve, I'd probably love the place. But it's too noisy, too full of people who can't see what's right in front of them.

A few tables to my left, a pair of middle-aged women tried

to corral two hyper boys who were old enough to know that shaking salt on the wood floors was unacceptable. In between telling the boys to quit, the two women competed for shittiest day and sucked down strawberry margaritas. The bigger of the two boys had a red bouncy ball, one of those cheap things bought in any gas station. He took great delight in how the ball sprang back up from the hard floor. I waited for him to toss it at Chetter's prized ceiling. Instead, he miscalculated his bounce and slammed the ball off his foot. It rolled three booths down and into the foot of the man positioned in the corner.

Nursing his beer, the man picked up the ball and examined it as if it were a rare gem.

One of the women—I could only assume it was the kid's mother—snapped at the boy and ordered him to fetch the ball. Chin against his chest, he trod down the aisle and muttered something before sticking out a chubby hand.

The man, who looked like any other Joe Schmo off the street, smiled obligingly and gave the ball back. The middle-aged woman waved appreciatively and fluffed her hair. Brat boy shuffled back to his own table. Supposedly kids are more attuned to the things adults don't want to see. Did the boy sense the evil he'd just encountered? Perhaps not, since the child was the wrong gender. He and his margarita-loving mother would go on about their lives, peacefully oblivious to what might have been.

The waitress finally reached my table. She wore stonewashed denim shorts with carefully constructed rips in them—the kind I wore in my youth because we were too poor to buy new ones. She had the Bettie Page vibe right down to her jet-black hair and the pin curl in her bangs. The men loved her too. Their eyes glazed over whenever she walked by, and I didn't blame them. She never messed up a drink order, and her tables constantly smiled, even if the women who watched her strut away did so with wistful jealousy in their eyes. I liked her because she didn't ask me how I was doing every four minutes. "What can I get you?"

"Martini, dry, please."

"Your fingers cold?" She squinted at my hands.

"Circulation problems." I flexed my fingers. Beneath the wool, the latex clung to my sweating hand. "Plus I'm a bit of a germaphobe. Gloves solve both issues." Not to mention they were an essential part of my toolkit.

Tipping the glass made the liquid swirl beneath the bar lights. It sparkled. Dry. Two olives. Boisterous laughter came from several tables down. Twenty-somethings on a date, chowing down on potato skins chased with one of Chetter's microbrews. I envied their youthful ignorance as much as I detested them for it. I wondered what they would do if they knew a monster was sitting just a few red booths down from them.

If they were like most people, the young couple wouldn't believe it. Neither would the middle-aged women with the rowdy boys. A mistake, they would say. Wrong identity. Because surely that sort of person wouldn't slither among them without their taking notice.

Living in the dark is a lot easier than facing the truth.

My gaze strayed back to the man in the corner—the man I'd come here for. Steve Simon sat alone. Facing the crowd, he casually tipped back his beer. Like me, his clothes were understated. He probably chose them as carefully as I did. For all I knew, he justified his behaviors. Perhaps he felt he was born this way, or that he was entitled. But I doubted he spent hours agonizing over his choices. That's not how his mind is geared. There is no cure for the sickness he harbors.

A group of laughing young women strode into Chetter's, and for a moment, I was painfully aware I was becoming invisible. At thirty-three, I still had my looks, but the sight of the young women in their prime reminded me how quickly time races forward. Tan and toned, every one of them still had the glorious firmness of their early twenties instead of the creeping softness of the thirties. The women commanded the attention of all the straight men in the bar. Except for Steve. He never noticed the hot women.

Why would he? He has a fetish for adolescent females. The younger the better. Anything over the age of fourteen is too old for his particular kind of sick.

His file was burned into my brain. Molested his kid sister when he was fifteen, released at eighteen. A bid for possessing child pornography a year later, and then our well-oiled system sent him back to the streets. That's when he got smart and started trolling online with the other cyber creeps. The Internet is the biggest double-edged sword in our technological history, but it's not going anywhere. The sickos get sicker and more numerous. The Internet gives them a hidden playground, and privacy laws actually protect them.

Behind the group of beautiful women and waiting to be seated were a mother and her pre-teen daughter. Her hair pulled back in a messy ponytail and clutching her daughter's hand, the woman had the slightly frazzled look I associated with motherhood. Working mom or stay-at-home mom, the results were the same: never enough time in the day accompanied by random bouts of sheer exhaustion.

The little girl was probably around ten, all legs and impatience. Shifting from foot to foot, her gaze never strayed from the pink phone clutched in her hand. She'd already taken off her coat and given it to her mom. The girl's almost-too-tight shirt revealed budding breasts and the smallest curve of the hips.

My Bettie Page server greeted the mother and daughter and began to escort them to their table. The nerves I'd managed to contain for the past twenty minutes rippled through me. The bottle hidden deep in my bag felt as heavy as a brick. They were going to walk right by Steve.

I knew his trick. I'd seen him do it repeatedly over the past two weeks.

Just as the mother and daughter passed, Steve started to cough. He quickly shoved his head into his right elbow, discreetly twisting so that he could watch the girl pass by. He didn't blink, didn't move. Just watched until the girl sat down. Then Slimy Steve returned to his beer.

The first time I saw him do it, I almost attacked him.

But all good things come to those who wait. My computer specialist—who is the main reason my turn as a private investigator paid the bills—spent the last few weeks trolling online to make sure Steve was still molesting girls. That's my number one rule. I wouldn't touch them unless I'd confirmed they were actively harming kids. That probably made me a hypocrite since I believed sex offenders couldn't be cured, but I figured I should have some sort of code in this operation. My girl found him in an online chat room recently soliciting a meeting with a twelve-year-old. Normally I took more time to act, but Steve's living with a girlfriend who's got a ten-year-old daughter, so he was escalated to Enemy Number One. His sentence came when I had a former colleague check the system at Child Protective Services and found out someone at the daughter's school had reported her sudden behavioral change. The revolting drawings from art class were what did the trick. While my CPS friend started her investigation, I began my own.

Family members of a pedophile pray for change. The truth is, it won't happen. The experts argue whether it's brought on by nature or nurture. I really don't care what they think. After a decade working at Child Protective Service, I'd learned an indisputable fact: pedophiles can't be cured.

So I've come for Steve.

Steve finished his drink. I needed to get ready. I liked a good routine, so I quickly ran through my mental checklist. Fifteen years ago when I was a nervous yet hopeful college freshman, I attended a seminar about success. The professor resembled the Gandalf of my imagination, and much of what he said was lost on me because I'd been busy dreaming about my freshman formal and of hopefully losing my virginity. But three sentences caught my attention.

"See yourself creating goals. Think of what you need to do to achieve those goals. And then, imagine the reward of hitting those goals."

I still lived by those words.

Time ticked by. I needed to act now, or I'd have to wait another night, and I was ready to be done with this filthy business. Every night like this drained a part of my spirit, and the recovery time got longer. But I believed in my decision. At this point in my life, nights like these were the only way I could make any kind of a difference in this world. I tipped my glass, making sure to drain it to the last drop. I stood and swayed just enough to look tipsy, like my night was just getting started. Making my way to the restroom, I made sure to keep my eyes hooded and my smile inviting. Several men smiled back. Steve ignored me.

The ladies' room had two stalls and both were empty, but a woman wearing too much makeup stood at the counter freshening up her lipstick.

I slipped into the first stall and waited. If the woman even noticed me, she probably thought I was either sick or doing what every woman does in a public restroom: waiting until the place was empty so I could relieve my bowels in peace.

Heels clicked across the floor. The bathroom door swung shut. I took a deep breath and steadied my hands. I didn't enjoy any of this process, but the next few minutes were the most dangerous. Since I'm not a livin' on the edge kind of girl, sometimes it was all I could do not to pee my pants when I started.

I checked to make sure the latex gloves hidden beneath the thin cloth ones were still in place and then put on the sweater I'd wrapped around my waist. Making sure my wrists were covered and all the buttons on the sweater fastened except for the top one—I didn't want to look like an uptight drunk—I pulled the clean martini glass and the black vial from my purse.

I carefully poured the contents of the vial into the glass and then put the empty container in a Ziploc bag and into my purse. My pulse beat at my temples, and the sweater felt hot. Or maybe that was just the adrenaline. I took a moment to collect my spinning thoughts. Steve sat two tables to the right of the restroom, against the wall. He'd been sitting hunched over his beer just like he does every other night. Almost recoiled, as if he were ready to run from a beating. Probably a habit picked up in prison.

Now was the time for the inevitable doubts. *What if I miss my mark? What if the reaction starts before I'm out of here? What if I get caught this time?* I simply couldn't allow them to creep in. Too many children hurt, too many kids lost, my own sister, gone. Because of men like Steve.

I left the stall, took a deep breath, and sauntered out of the restroom. My gait was again tipsy, head down far enough not to make eye contact while still allowing me to see the room.

Steve's table was empty.

Experience was the only thing that kept me from stopping in my tracks. Getting bumped into wouldn't be good for my health.

Damnit. He always finished his beers, and he'd just ordered another. Why had he left?

I couldn't stand there looking confused. A cough, a slight stumble to the left, and I quickly hurried to the bathroom. The place remained blessedly empty. I slowly poured the glass's contents down the toilet, making sure the liquid only trickled and left no splash on the seat. Just in case, I wiped it off with a cleansing wipe. I ran the martini glass under the hot water and then stuck it back into the plastic zipper bag in my purse.

So much for wrapping up this case tonight.

The crowd seemed to have doubled in the last few minutes. Steve's table was already taken. I chalked up my bitter defeat and headed for the door. The waitress would probably remember me after tonight, which meant I needed a new approach to Steve.

"Excuse me, miss." The man now sitting at Steve's table spoke to me. "Can I buy you a drink?"

I sized him up. Nice clothes, the casually preppy type, with strong cheekbones matching his full lips. An attractive man looking for a bar hookup. "No, thanks. I've got to call it a night."

He grinned, his smile listing somewhere between charming and arrogant. He stood to his full height—at least six feet, with broad shoulders and lean muscles beneath his long-sleeved shirt. Certainly easy on the eye, and apparently not willing to take no for an answer. I was in no mood for a hookup, but my skin warmed with egocentric pride. It felt good to be noticed.

I moved toward the crowd, but he was faster, closing the small distance between us. Standing less than an inch away from him, I smelled the pleasant scent of his cologne and caught a glimpse of bright blue eyes.

"Please." He stood close enough he didn't have to shout. "I'd really love to talk to you about something."

Anxiety licked at my veins. I plastered a sweet smile on my face and twisted to meet his eyes. They were really blue. And calculating. "About what?"

He leaned down until I thought he might try to kiss me. "About that cyanide you just got rid of."

TWO

My mouth tasted like someone had stuffed cotton balls into my cheeks. I didn't move, didn't break eye contact with the man. My pulse slammed in my temples. He might be bluffing. *Oh bullshit. He wouldn't have randomly guessed something as obscure as cyanide. He knew.*

He'd called me out in a way I couldn't ignore. What else did he know? How much of a threat was he? I'd never killed an innocent person, never even considered it to be an option. But I wasn't exactly ready to start thinking of decorating ideas for my cell on death row. Not yet.

"All right," I said. "I'm pretty sure you're delusional, but since you're cute, I'll have a drink with you."

He pulled out a chair. I sat. I honestly never imagined this moment happening. Not under these circumstances. Arrested, hauled in for questioning, accidentally spilling the cyanide on myself—those thoughts crossed my mind every day. But never a random, good-looking stranger in a bar who may or may not be a cop flat out calling me on the act.

I took a deep breath, inhaling the smell of greasy bar food

and warm bodies. Anxiety rippled in my chest, but I buried it. "What's your name?"

"I'm not a cop." His face was still friendly, but his gaze keen. I've never seen eyes so blue—or so perceptive. I instantly disliked them. He gauged my every move, no doubt measuring my body language just as I was his. He was probably counting my pulse considering the vein in my neck throbbed big enough half the bar could see.

"Good for you. So what should I call you?"

"My name's Chris, and you can call me an interested party." The response bordered on arrogance. My temper flared. I didn't like being backed into a corner. I nearly laughed, but his raised eyebrow sucked any mirth right out of my spirit. I tried to play it cool. He already had enough of an upper hand. But how did he know? Had Conner, the chemist who provided the cyanide, said something? Had my tech specialist, Kelly, charmed the wrong online predator?

"What are you interested in?" Thankfully the drone of the bar noise hid the shakiness in my voice.

"You. It's not often I find someone who's like me."

"Like you?"

"In the same line of work."

I said nothing.

"I don't like to use the popular name for it." He leaned over the table, into my space. His eyes burned even brighter up close. In another scenario, I would have matched his body language, flirted a little. A woman should always seize the opportunity to get up close and personal with a face like his. Unless he's a stalker with the power to send her to the lethal injection chamber. "You know, serial killer. The term is so... trendy. I like to call myself the garbage man. Just taking out the trash."

Of all the presumptuous, stupid things to say. I wasn't a serial killer, and I had no interest in aiding this man's sick fantasies. "I don't know who you are—"

"Name's Chris Hale. I'm a paramedic and an Aries. I love Indian food. Italian, too. And Mexican. Pretty much all food. I've got a major sweet tooth. Never done drugs, I'm an only child. I'll spare you the sob story. Anything else?" He smiled again, the lines around his eyes crinkling in a ruggedly attractive way that probably made plenty of women act foolish.

"Good for you. But you're way off about me. I'd guess it's delusion talking. And if you're thinking this game will get me into bed, I'm sorry, but I don't go home with guys I meet at the bar."

He laughed, throaty and packed with self-assurance. "Please, life's too short to dance around the truth. Let's be real. You were going to play drunk, dump that demon on the guy, and walk out of the bar. He's gone thirty minutes later. Not original, but very good methodology."

The walls closed in like a trash compactor. I felt trapped like a rat. I gritted my teeth and volleyed back. "You might want to seek a psych evaluation. There's a good free clinic not too far from here."

"The Iceman." Chris ignored the bait. "That's your inspiration, right? The mob hitman who lost count at two hundred murders. His method was easy and anonymous. He spilled the bad stuff, his mark got angry about it but didn't do anything about the wet shirt or pants. The goods seeped through the mark's skin and, twenty to thirty minutes later, into the bloodstream, and the Iceman was long gone. It's brilliant, really. Great choice, for cold weather anyway, considering the health hazards. I just hope you're more than a hitman. Woman, excuse me."

My chest tightened into an iron cast, and my jaw ached from the hard set. If this guy knew the routine, he no doubt had proof. "Seriously, have you ever thought about seeking professional help?"

He ignored me and kept rambling. "Like I said, I'm a paramedic. And I'm observant. I saw you at a scene a few months back. You were standing to the side, in the middle of the onlookers. But something on your face gave you away—to me, at least. Guess I'm good at spotting my own kind." He rested his chin on his hand and gazed at me with obvious admiration. To anyone else, we probably looked like we were on a first date and still stuck in the awkward getting-to-know-you stage.

"I'm not your kind." He was nothing like me. I was just sick and tired of seeing a broken justice system routinely fail children who've already been treated like disposable playthings. So I did everything I could to balance the creaking scales of justice —the same scales many people want to believe are designed to protect the vulnerable in society. But those scales don't shield anyone, even our most innocent victims. Their function is to balance the lines of bureaucracy.

Sometimes I have to fill the void.

He probably picked his victims at random and took them somewhere to torture them before finally killing them. If he was actually a serial killer.

"Your marks aren't good people," he continued as though I hadn't denied him. "I know because I've been tailing you for a while. And I watch the news, managed to put two and two together. Kiddie diddlers, which is another nice choice, by the way. Scum of the earth for sure. Me, I'm not that selective. Long as they've maimed or killed, I'm willing to get rid of the trash." He smiled again, and I was alarmed at how genuine he seemed. And his good looks were becoming an annoyance. "I gotta ask, though. The cyanide, that's tricky stuff. Not the easiest way to kill someone. Untraceable unless a medical examiner is looking for it, yeah. But aren't you afraid of spilling it on yourself? Or is sudden death not an issue for you?"

My throat constricted; my scalp felt clammy and hot. I was terrified of death, and the irony that I'd given myself the right to administer it without question hasn't escaped me. Death was a finality I could only fully comprehend in the dark of my bedroom, when I was on the cusp of sleep. Like an electric shock, it hit me with the force of a thousand watts. It's *the end*. There's no blackness, no tunnel, no sinking into oblivion. It's literally nothing. And it's the nothingness, the utter finality of ceasing to exist that scared me to the point of sitting up in my bed, gasping for air and covering my ears as if somehow that would stop my brain from dredging up the horrific reality.

I couldn't think about that right now. I focused on Chris's smirking face.

"Why are you bothering me?" How did I miss this man following me? He was the kind who drew attention everywhere he went.

"I admire your work. Thought maybe we could talk shop."

"There's no shop to discuss." *And we don't do the same kind of work.* I did it because it needed to be done. I wasn't a killer. Not in the real sense of the word. I filled a much-needed void in the most efficient way possible. I had to believe that, especially now. Even if he did claim to understand the need to get rid of pedophiles, his brazenness was repulsive.

He shrugged. "I'm a sociopath."

"Well, good for you, Chris Hale." Apparently this was the sort of man I attracted now. I reached for my purse. "I truly hope we don't meet again. Good looks don't cover your brand of crazy."

"Come on." His grin was part hypnotic, part dangerous. "I'm not the only one who knows your secret. You've got help."

Fresh panic set in. Did he know about Kelly and Conner? No way could he have found their identities just by following me. I had to draw a line in the bar dust right now. He wasn't going to bring them down too. "Excuse me? Are there more people out there suffering from your delusion?"

His twisted smirk made it clear he enjoyed my seeping panic. "There's no way you're doing this on your own. Maybe you're computer savvy, but I'd bet you have help getting the information. Not to mention the poison. You can't just buy that stuff at the pharmacy. So you don't work alone, and I do. But I'm willing to make an exception for you." He finally took a sip of the club soda he'd been fondling. Dingy bar lights reflected off the sliding ice as he drank, his Adam's apple bobbing and his eyes always on me.

"I'm leaving now."

He set the glass down. "Suit yourself. I think we could learn a lot from each other."

"No offense, but I really don't want to know any more about you," I said. "I just want to pretend this never happened."

Chris dug his wallet out of his pocket and tossed it across the table. "There. Look through it. Take my driver's license information. Look me up."

Now I was certain he needed the psychiatric evaluation. "Are you crazy? Besides, this could be fake."

"Except it's not. And you can easily confirm that."

I stood up and slipped on my coat. My insides burned with panic, and my brain felt sluggish. I needed to get away from Chris, into the fresh air. Figure out what to do next.

Chris scribbled something down on his napkin and then slid it over to me. A phone number. I put it in my purse. I'd throw it out later.

He stood and stretched. His shirt hiked up enough for me to see the muscles of his abdomen. I looked away only to see the women at the next table trying to check him out without being noticeable. "It was nice meeting you, Lucy."

"You know my name."

"I'm observant. I'll be looking forward to your phone call." He flashed me one last annoyingly captivating smile and then disappeared into the crowd.

My phone call? I wasn't about to get into any sort of partnership with some guy who'd crawled out of Chetter's woodwork, even if he turned out to be exactly what he said he was. *Especially if he turned out that way*. With him out of sight, some of the tension in my muscles evaporated. I leaned against the wall, trying not to throw up. Life had tossed me curveballs for as long as I could remember, and I was good at lobbing them out of the way with ease. Cops I could deal with. Angry family members, parents who feel they've failed their child because they didn't realize the kid was being molested—those situations I could handle. I knew when to fight and when to walk away and save the battle for next time. When I finally accepted our justice system wasn't black and white and decided to strike out on my own, I prepared myself for the inevitable day I was caught for my decisions.

But Chris Hale was an entirely different monster, and I had no idea what to do with him.

THREE

Sleep eluded me most of the night. Instead of dreams of falling into the black void of death, every time I closed my eyes, Chris Hale's face danced in my memory. He was unpredictable, and that sort of person is always the most dangerous. How long had he been following me? And why? More importantly, how did I miss him? *So much for being self-aware.*

Dawn cracked through my blinds, and I imagined Philadelphia beginning to wake up. Windows glowed with life, hopefully with happy families starting their day, and furnaces vented out tufts of white smoke that looked like swelled clouds. The thought made me feel peaceful. A rare emotion.

Since my first eradication of a sex offender eighteen months ago, I'd accepted that one day I'd likely be caught. With every scumbag I silenced—five in all, as of now—a dozen new scenarios of my own judgment day raced through my head, dramatic and filled with chaos. None of them included being approached by a man like Chris Hale.

A warm, chubby body pressed against my shoulders, flicking its tail in my face. Mousecop, the fat tiger cat I'd rescued a few months ago, needed sustenance. Meaning he could see a spot on the bottom of his food bowl, which somehow translated to starving in cat-speak.

I rolled out of bed, and Mousecop immediately rubbed against my side, purring loudly. I scratched between his ears, and his green eyes glowed with appreciation.

"Somebody knows our secret, Mousey," I said. "What am I going to do?"

He blinked and then rubbed his head against my hand, demanding more skritches.

"I wish my problems were solved with food and scratches."

I spent the morning catching up on paperwork and cleaning my small apartment. I'd only been working as a private investigator for a year, but because of my background in social work, I'd built up a solid network and already had a nice client base. I wasn't making big bucks, but I paid the bills.

By late afternoon, my eyes were glazed over from dealing with emails and billing. I rubbed my temples, contemplating taking a nap. My phone buzzed, and Kelly, the hacker who made my business run, popped up on the screen. Hopefully she had some information about Chris Hale.

If he'd been telling the truth about his motive, he was going to be a lot tougher to deal with than an old-fashioned blackmail. Not to mention lying about being a sociopath. I didn't believe that for a minute, and I was pretty sure it wasn't because I couldn't believe someone so attractive could be terrible. I'd been around enough to know looks mean exactly squat. My instinct about Chris went beyond common misconception and into the realm of something I couldn't explain yet.

I swiped the screen, expecting to see Kelly's information on Chris, but instead her words sent a cold rush of paralyzing fear through me. My body turned liquid, sagging down the chair as if it were ready to turn into a pool of shuddering mush. I'd been expecting this for months, resolved to it the same way a person accepts the diagnosis of a loved one's terminal cancer, but this was worse than I'd envisioned. Every parent's nightmare.

8 yr old girl missing in Beckett's area. Stop by asap. —K

Kelly lived on 18th Street, near Rittenhouse Square, in a tiny studio that was never warm enough. Parking down here sucked, and I ended up five blocks away and jetting through the open-air park. Rittenhouse is one of my favorite places in Philadelphia. While high rises are scattered throughout the area, the side streets boast historical brownstones, and during the summer, there's no better place for outside seating than at one of the many cafés. Usually when I come to visit Kelly, I make a stop at Di Bruno Bros., home of the best gourmet cheese in the city. Tonight I didn't have the stomach for it.

Even at night on a brisk October evening, minglers were scattered in the park. A couple walking a purebred dog that probably cost more than my high-tech mattress glared at me as I rushed by. A group of teenagers had taken up residence on the corner and were holding some sort of impromptu break-dancing contest, their music beating out the sound of traffic. I rushed past their party and into Kelly's building, using the code she'd entrusted me with. She answered after my first knock.

"You must have run half a dozen red lights to get here this fast." Kelly locked the door behind me.

I admired her new haircut, very short, which showed off the angular planes of her face and accentuated her doe-like eyes. "When did you get your hair done?"

"Friday." She smiled, both of us acknowledging the small victory. Seven years ago, she sat shaking and terrified in my office, resistant to any kind of unfamiliar contact. It took me three weeks to break through her walls, and I started the process with very small cracks.

"I almost didn't go through with it," Kelly said. "The last time I tried going that far from my apartment, I had a panic attack and almost passed out. But I made it."

"I'm proud of you." She'd come so damned far over the past couple of years. "Are the new anxiety meds working?"

"I think so. I slept for three hours straight last night. That's an improvement."

"I'm glad." I couldn't delay the dirty business of our meeting any longer. "When did the little girl go missing?"

"About six hours ago," Kelly said. "I heard it on the scanner." Most consultants were required to work in a secured area of the station, but Kelly was given an exception due to her skills and PTSD. Her visits to the precincts were sporadic, but her connections were my inside ticket.

"School released early today for a teacher workday. She was supposed to walk home with a group of kids, but she never showed up," Kelly said. "They didn't realize it until they were halfway home. One kid told her mom, and she called the police. Luce, she lives in the apartments across the street from Justin Beckett's duplex."

Justin Beckett. My legs weakened, and I grabbed Kelly's arm before remembering the girl was still sensitive about touching. "Sorry."

"It's okay. Come sit down."

I followed Kelly to her office. Two large monitors were hooked up to a powerful desktop, and a partially built computer occupied most of the extra desk. Her gait was light, her lithe hips swaying as though she were dancing to her own soundtrack.

Kelly's emotional growth had been so stunted, sometimes she still seemed like a confused adolescent. I longed for the day when she felt secure enough to engage in a normal activity, like dating or even going to the movie theater with me. I supposed that was too much exposure, considering the way her stepfather had treated her.

"So, Justin Beckett," Kelly said. "What don't I know about him?"

I really didn't want to go back to these painful memories, but Kelly needed to know the whole story in order to do her job. I took a deep breath. "Not much. Ten years ago, Justin Beckett was one of my first cases as a newly minted social worker. Back then, I still believed I could change the world and that no amount of horrors would be too much for me to bear. Then I met the Becketts." I hesitated, afraid this might hurt Kelly, but she nodded for me to continue.

"A neighbor called CPS after hearing fighting from the house on numerous occasions. I was sent to investigate and found eleven-year-old Justin and his seventeen-year-old brother, Todd, who was in charge while the parents worked." I still remembered the stale smell of the house, the way Justin's small form shrank away whenever my attention turned to him. I stood up and walked to the small window. Below, the breakdancers were still going strong.

"The brothers had been fighting, and what at first seemed like normal sibling issues, especially with latchkey kids, quickly turned suspicious. Justin was withdrawn and secretive, but he was prone to outbursts. He also had bruises he wouldn't account for." I should have pushed the issue. I was young and naïve, and my instincts weren't enough to get him removed from his home. Irrationally focused on being new and shiny and full of determination to change lives, I'd ignored my base instincts—instincts honed from years of watching my sister's strange behavior and never knowing what it all meant. Until it was much too late.

I pushed on. "I suggested follow-up visits and interviewing the parents more thoroughly, but my superior nixed it. Not enough evidence and a backload of cases. Two weeks later, Justin Beckett molested and beat a ten-year-old girl to death."

"I remember reading because he was far too young to be tried as an adult," Kelly said, "Justin was remanded to a youth psychiatric facility to serve his sentence."

I nodded. "He was given extensive treatment. I visited him several times in those first couple of years. Since the DSM-5 requires a person to be sixteen years old and at least five years older than their victim, he was never classified as a pedophile. Still, every time I visited I saw the same darkness smoldering in his eyes." I gnawed at a hangnail and looked away from Kelly's sad eyes. "And then the state released him last year, without making him register as a sex offender. The family and I petitioned the court to keep him in the psychiatric facility, but no one listened. You know the decisions I made after that happened." I rubbed my temples. "What's the chatter?"

"There's a neighborhood-wide search in progress." Kelly chewed her fingernails, which were already down to the nub. "Police are questioning all the parents and teachers, plus bus drivers and anyone else with access to the kids. And it gets better. You mentioned his half-brother Todd? He went on to become a cop."

I last saw Todd when our petition went before the judge. He wore his dress uniform and refused to look at me. He'd been seventeen when Justin committed his crime, an angry teenager who couldn't stand his stepmother and hated me on sight. "So?"

"He's the detective in charge. Kailey Richardson's disappearance is in his jurisdiction."

"You're kidding me. Why hasn't he recused himself for conflict of interest?"

Kelly raised her eyebrow. "No idea yet. I'm trying to find out how he's handling his brother because he's got to consider him a suspect. From everything I've been able to find out about

Detective Todd Beckett, he's by the book. We'll see how it goes when little brother is back on the seat."

"Nothing on the scanner?"

"No. But I've got a call in to a friend at the Philly PD about it. Hopefully I'll hear something soon."

I tried to think my way around this. "What do we know about Justin's current life?"

"He works at Jiffy Lube within walking distance of his place. I've been doing the pedo-crawl on the various creep chat rooms, and so far I can't find any illicit online activity. He does have a driver's license." Kelly tucked her legs beneath her and sat cross-legged in a position that made my back ache from just looking.

"So I need to get into his car and his apartment."

"Not yet," Kelly said. "Police are all over the area, so you'd be busted. And unless Todd's completely blind to what his brother is capable of, he'll do that. Or see to it that someone else does."

She was right. "What about other registered offenders in the area? You know, since Justin gets to go without that label."

"Two in an eight-block radius," Kelly said. "One for statutory of his consenting girlfriend, and the other exposed himself to a group of teens."

"And Justin." My chin dropped to my chest, my shoulders sagging until the muscles ached. I hated being right about this. There were no special cases when it came to pedophiles. The state of Pennsylvania had failed Kailey Richardson. Guess I had, too.

"I need to find out if Justin's been skulking around Kailey," I said. "You said the older kids realized she wasn't with them about halfway home? So it's likely the police are focusing their search around the school right now. Hopefully that's where Todd is. I'll head over to Kailey's apartment, see what I can find out. See what Justin's up to."

"Your best bet is to talk to the mother," Kelly said. "You're a private investigator. See if you can get her to accept your help."

The breakdancers were still going strong when I left Kelly's, the rhythm of their heavily synthesized music bleating into my skull and providing me with inappropriate exit music. I didn't understand the song they were playing, but its spirit was positive and upbeat—a far cry from the dark pit my mind was in.

A chilly, late-October wind nipped at my skin, and I hastily buttoned up my coat. Kelly's place was a decent walk from my parking spot, and I wished I'd worn long sleeves. My stomach grumbled, the lunch from hours earlier threatening to reappear. Was Todd running interference for his brother?

FOUR

Philadelphia's ever-changing neighborhoods whipped by as I drove. Irish pubs and Italian eateries blended with sports bars and blue-collar businesses until I reached the Richardsons' apartment building in Poplar, a working-class suburb.

Three police cars lined up in front of the three-story complex. Several uniformed officers milled around the sidewalks and at the intersections. Neighbors peeked from their windows, home from work and probably wondering what the police were doing hanging around in the darkness of the evening.

I went back over the information Kelly gave me. The mother's name was Jenna, a single mom and a nurse. Came off a shift at two. Kailey should have been home due to an early dismissal, but there was no sign of her. Mom called the older neighborhood kids Kailey walked home with, and they said she wasn't with them. She hadn't even left school with them—a fact they didn't notice until they were halfway home.

This is why I couldn't be a parent: I'd seen too much, and I didn't trust anyone. Not even older kids. Especially not older kids. Even if they had the best intentions, they were too easily

distracted, their maturity not fully developed enough to understand the consequences of taking their eyes off the younger
child. Kids are self-centered by nature. It's a biological trait
some never grow out of.

I hopped out of the car and headed up the sidewalk. The
cherries of one of the police cars rhythmically flashed, the red
light piercing the night sky like a frantic pulse. Keeping my
head down, I pulled my private investigator's license out of my
purse and steadied my nerves. This wouldn't be the first case I'd
barged in on without permission, but the personal stakes were
definitely higher.

The uniform guarding the door looked like he'd just walked
out of the academy. He shuffled nervously as I approached,
glancing everywhere but directly into my eyes. Good to know I
could still turn heads. Thirty-three had been a tough birthday,
with fresh wrinkles and gray hairs popping up almost overnight.
Add that to my mother's constant digs about my malfunctioning
biological clock, and I sometimes felt like I should be applying
for assisted living. If I didn't genuinely care for my stepfather,
I'd stop speaking to the woman.

"You live here, ma'am?" The officer rolled his shoulders
back and stuck out his chin, but his cracking voice betrayed him.

"No, I'm here to speak with Jenna Richardson." I held up
my license. "A friend of the family called me."

The rookie's hand fluttered to his shoulder mic. "I didn't
know you were coming, and I'm not supposed to let non-resi-
dents in. I'd better—"

I didn't let him finish. "You're wasting time. I'm a trained
counselor with ten years' experience in CPS. I can help find
that little girl before her abductor does something terrible."

"It's only been a few hours. We don't yet know she's been
abducted. She may have wandered off."

I sidled up to the nervous uniform and lowered my voice to
a conspiratorial tone. "Your superiors are no doubt busy as hell.

Are you really going to bother them over a visit from a private investigator who was called in to help, just because I'm not on your list?"

"Let me see your license again."

I obeyed and waited in silence. Rookie finally nodded. "Ten minutes is all I can give you."

The Richardsons lived on the second floor in a corner two-bedroom apartment. Another uniform answered my knock, and I assured him the officer downstairs had cleared me. "I've only got ten minutes." I brushed past him.

Jenna Richardson sat alone in what appeared to be the main living space. I made my way over to the small woman who reminded me of a china doll I once had. Pale remnants of a summer tan lingered on her skin. I knelt next to her curled form in the recliner.

"Jenna, my name is Lucy Kendall. I'm a private investigator."

She gazed at me with vacant eyes, clutching a cellphone to her chest so tightly I saw white knuckles against the pink of her scrubs.

"Have you found my daughter?" Her voice cracked.

I held out my license. "No, not yet, I'm sorry. I used to work with CPS, and I'm a private investigator now. I heard about Kailey's disappearance, and I want to help."

Her eyes were bloodshot, like she'd just gone a round with a prize fighter. "I can't afford a private investigator."

"Don't worry about that. I'm taking the case pro bono, if you'll have me."

Jenna's pale lips pinched together. "And then you'll saddle me with a bill?"

"Absolutely not." I took her hand in the hopes she'd under-stand how much I wanted to help. "I just want to find Kailey."

Jenna gazed back at me. Fine lines dotted the corners of her eyes. She liked to laugh, probably spent a lot of time doing just that with her little girl. "People keep asking me if Kailey was angry with me, if we got along, if I think she'd run away." Tears bubbled in Jenna's eyes. "The answer is no! She's a happy little girl. I have to work a lot, but she loves her babysitter. And we get along!"

"I'm sure you do." I sat down next to Jenna, giving her plenty of space. "That's why I'm here. I'd like to know your thoughts on who might have done this. Where is Kailey's babysitter?"

"She lives on the first floor." Jenna wiped her red eyes. "Kailey usually stays with her after school until I get home. She's retired, misses her grandkids. We've never had an issue."

"What's her name?"

"Ellen Troyer. She's wonderful."

I made a note to have Kelly get as much information on the babysitter as possible. "That's good to hear. Tell me about Kailey's friends—the ones she walked home with. How old are they?"

"Eleven. Fifth graders."

"And they treat her well?"

"As well as older kids treat the little ones. I know they some-times got irritated with her tagging along, but Kailey never mentioned them being mean. The oldest girl, Bridget, lives in the next apartment building. I've known her mother for a couple of years. They're good people too." Jenna nodded her head as if she were trying to convince herself.

The worst humans often come from the best people. "What about other neighbors? Has Kailey mentioned anyone new in her life lately?"

"The police asked me all this." Jenna hugged her small waist. Her gaze flickered past me to the clutch of pictures on the wall. They all looked to be of Kailey in various stages of her young life. Jenna stared at them as if she hoped one of the

pictures would flash to life and Kailey would magically appear.
"I don't understand why you're asking me again."

"I'm just getting a feel for her life," I said, keeping my tone
calm and soothing.

"We know everyone in the building." Jenna continued to
stare at the pictures. "Kailey's never complained about anyone.
And no, she hasn't mentioned anyone new."

"What about people outside the building?"

"The kids she walks with live down the block and in the
other building in the complex, like I said. Other than that, we
don't know anyone else in the area."

I kept my voice soft. "What about online friends? Does
Kailey have any social networking accounts?"

Jenna shook her head. "We just have my laptop, and she
isn't allowed to go online unless I'm supervising."

"Does Kailey have an email address she uses for anything?"

A tired smile broke through Jenna's tears. "Littlebug05. It's
a generic account at Google. She just uses it for the educational
games I approve."

I smiled back. "Good to know. Would you be willing to
share her password so I can have my technical gal check things
out?"

Shadows overrode her smile. "Why? There's nothing to
find."

I nodded. "It's just to double-check any communications
she might have had. Sometimes kids don't realize they're
being tracked by people who can hurt them. I'm sure the
police will ask for your laptop and exhaust their resources,
but I'd like to do my own checking, if you'll allow it." I
showed her my license again and handed her my card.
"Here's my information so you can do any checking you'd like
about me."

Jenna clutched the card, running a neatly manicured nail
over the plain, black lettering. "The password is 'pinkydo.' She

loves pink. She wore her new pink shoes this morning." Jenna choked back a cry.

I opened the Internet browser on my phone, noting Jenna's wireless connection for Kelly, and the picture I'd already cued up popped onto the screen. "Do you know this man?"

Jenna took the phone and peered at it through her watery eyes. "That's the kid who lives across the street. Is he a suspect?"

"Everyone in the area will be checked out." I chewed on my lower lip, wondering if the shitstorm I was about to unleash was worth the additional pain to Jenna Richardson. My gaze landed on a picture of a bespectacled little girl with two front teeth missing and a big ponytail. Somewhere, that little girl who loved pink was trapped, already subjected to immense horror even if her captor hadn't assaulted her.

"This boy," I said, "is Justin Beckett. Do you recognize the name?"

The hovering uniform sucked in a breath and left the room. My minutes were numbered.

"It sounds familiar," Jenna said.

"A long time ago, he did some not very nice things. And I want to make sure he's not bothered Kailey. Has she ever mentioned the man across the street?" I tapped the picture on the phone. "He's a handsome kid. Black hair, green eyes, lanky. Kind of reminds me of one of the kids from the latest boy band. Did Kailey ever mention that?"

"No. Not that I can remember. She didn't really talk about boys much. She likes drawing. And Barbies." Jenna's shaking hands went to her mouth, and a raw-sounding sob shook her entire body. "My baby girl. This morning she was so excited for school. I bought her new shoes last night. Pink, sparkly shoes. Did I already say that? She loved them so much. She wore them for the first time today."

Jenna sobbed harder. I swallowed the guilt brewing and

leaned forward, tasting my own salty tears. I laid my hand on Jenna's knee. The woman jerked as if the touch stung her. I quickly pulled away. "I swear to you, I will find your daughter. I won't stop looking until I do."

"That's not your job, Lucy Kendall." Detective Todd Beckett's voice pierced the room. I stood up to face the detective.

I quickly did the math; Todd was around twenty-seven now. Likely a rookie detective. Physically, he hadn't changed much. He'd been a gawky, angry teenager then, and now was an awkward and apparently crabby adult. His acne was gone, but a few pockmarks were scattered over one cheek. He wasn't unattractive, just decidedly plain. The only thing unique about him was his mustache. It made him look like an aging adult film star, and I longed to offer to shave it off for him. Now, instead of being mad at the world like he'd been as a teenager, he exuded the weary ambivalence caused from witnessing too much of the dark side of human nature.

I felt his pain.

"It's been a long time." I offered him a reserved smile. "Last time, I believe you spit on me."

"I was a snot-nosed teenager." His voice was deeper than I expected. It had a sultry quality that really didn't belong with his average face. "And you'd helped lock up my little brother."

"We both know what he did, Todd."

"Is it true?" Jenna stood, arms crossed as if they could keep her from falling apart. "Is there a sex offender living across the street that we didn't know about? Are you related to him? I want another detective!"

Todd sighed. "Because his crimes occurred when he was a child, he was released without status. But I promise you, we are doing our due diligence and making sure he isn't involved, and my partner is handling speaking with my brother. Kailey is our first priority, and there will be no conflict of interest." His gaze landed on me. I expected seething hate. Instead I saw worry and resignation.

"Lucy, can I speak with you privately?"

I nodded, my gaze on Jenna. "Call me anytime. I promise you I won't stop looking until we find out what happened."

I followed Todd's stiff shoulders into the hallway. He marched ahead and didn't speak until we descended to the first floor.

He whirled on me. "I should call your boss and have your ass for this. And throw you into jail for interfering."

"If I were still with CPS, I'd say you should. But I'm a private investigator now."

"That's right." His sneer reeked of satisfaction. "You had some sort of breakdown and left the department."

"Sorry to rain on your parade, but no breakdown." *At least not at work. In the confines of my apartment, yes. Your brother's release was the last straw.* "I just got sick of the system failing kids one after another and decided I could do more as a PI. Which is why I'm here."

"Uninvited and unnecessary. You had no right to come in here and mention my brother."

"Please," I said. "Registered or not, he's living right across the street, and Kailey's nearly the same age as Justin's first known victim."

"His *only* victim. He was an eleven-year-old kid, and now he's got a second chance." Todd pushed his glasses on top of his head and rubbed his eyes. He sighed, the sound belonging to a man much older. Empathy soothed my righteous attitude. None of this was Todd's fault, and like so many family members of offenders, he bore the brunt of the dirty looks and mudslinging.

"This isn't a personal vendetta against Justin. It's about saving a child."

"The hell it's not! You specifically mentioned my brother to her." His veins throbbed against his reddened skin. "You know what she's going to do now? You think that will help us find the kid?"

"Probably not, but she has a right to know. Especially since you're responsible for finding her daughter. Can you honestly say you're unbiased? Why on earth haven't you recused yourself?" I really did feel like a heel for asking him this. Todd didn't ask to be in this position any more than Kailey Richardson asked to be taken away.

"Because we're damned shorthanded right now. One detective is on maternity leave and another's in the hospital after a heart attack. We need every available SVU detective, and that's why I've got my partner and a uniform handling all interviews with Justin. He's been told he's a suspect because of his past."

"Is he in custody?"

"No," Todd said. "He's being questioned in his home."

"Across the street," I reminded him. "Is he cooperating?"

The angry twitch of Todd's mouth made it clear Justin wasn't playing along. "Justin's dealings with the police aren't your concern. But you know what I find interesting?" The pace of his words matched the pulse of the angry, blue vein in his forehead. "Someone's been following my brother. Someone with a dark, four-door vehicle. My officer said you exited out of a car matching that description. You been keeping tabs on Justin?"

I hadn't expected that. Fortunately, I didn't have to lie. "No, but since I'm a private investigator, I know where he lives. When I heard about Kailey, there was no way I wasn't coming over here."

"Don't lie to me." He smacked his hand against the wall. "When he was released last year, you vowed to make sure he didn't hurt more kids. Now a dark, four-door compact car has popped up at his work. And his house. And here you are."

"Did he get a license plate number?" I challenged. "And my Prius isn't that dark. It's blue."

"No. He just said it was a shade of black or dark blue."

I wanted to tell Todd he had to be a better detective than that, but I knew that would only put me in deeper water. "But he didn't say it was a Prius, did he? Because I'm not following your brother. You can't honestly tell me you're surprised I think he may have taken Kailey?"

"Goddamnit," Todd said. "I know you mean well, but you're pushy, and you're not a trained law enforcement officer. And you're just as biased as me. Despite two registered offenders in the area, Justin is your first suspect."

"I didn't expect you to allow anyone else to talk to Justin," I admitted. "But if he's not cooperating, you're going to need a warrant. Is your partner digging deep enough for that?"

"Listen to me." Todd's eyes flashed. "My partner is a good cop. If he thinks Justin's done something that justifies a warrant, he'll push for it. We're going to do whatever it takes to find this child. And unlike you, we aren't honing in on one suspect and turning blinders to the rest."

"I would hope not. But your brother is clearly—"

"Clearly a person of interest. Nothing more at this point. And frankly, I'm starting to think the same about you."

My fingernails dug into my purse strap deeply enough to leave marks. "Excuse me?"

"You fought against Justin's release. Fought against his not having an offender status. You've been trolling the neighborhood, and you've obviously got plenty of informational resources. Now Kailey's disappeared. Makes me wonder."

I didn't say anything. I hadn't been trolling the neighborhood, but Todd wasn't hearing any of that. Keeping my mouth shut was probably my best strategy right now.

"You're good with kids. And green police officers," he said dryly. "How do I know you didn't take the child so you could pin it on my brother?"

I started laughing and then quickly snapped my mouth

shut. I didn't need him snooping around my life, and Kailey certainly didn't need him running down the wrong path. "Yeah, because I'm a criminal mastermind."

"I'm going to assume you're joking. For now. But I'm serious, Lucy. You're way too involved, and that's a red flag for me."

"Noted. But I'm not going to back off."

"Obviously." He ran a hand through his thinning hair. "I know you want to help. That's the only reason I'm not arresting you."

Todd suddenly looked drained. I felt sorry for the man, truly. But I also saw an opening. "And I appreciate it. What can I do to help?"

"That doesn't involve railroading my brother?"

I didn't argue the specifics. "That involves finding Kailey. I'm going to be searching whether you want me to or not. Jenna Richardson gave me permission. But things would go a lot smoother if we worked together."

He crossed his arms, debating. I gave him the time. Finally, he sighed.

"Why don't you join the search team tomorrow? We're expanding the perimeter. If she's not found tonight, we're starting at 6 a.m. Now you need to leave before I really lose my temper."

I headed for the door.

"I'm still keeping an eye out for you."

I braced myself against the door handle. "Understood. Can you do me one favor, though?"

Todd stared. "You're kidding."

"It's not really for me. The rookie outside. I sort of bullied my way past him. Give the kid a break, will ya?"

Todd grunted and bounded up the steps. Shivering and suddenly exhausted, I headed outside into the cold night air.

FIVE

I was in no mood to cook, and I didn't have much food at my place anyway, so I stopped at The Coffee Bar, a semi-upscale café with good coffee and sandwiches. I'd found it while following Slimy Steve. Fortunately, the food made up for my means of discovery.

The gourmet grilled cheese I'd ordered looked delicious, but I'd barely touched my favorite comfort food. When we were little, grilled cheese was the only thing my sister and I knew how to make, and it was our Saturday morning staple when our mother was too lazy to get out of bed. This late in the evening, I was one of the few customers in the café. Steve usually came to eat around lunchtime, and I was grateful he didn't change up his schedule and show up tonight. With the mood I was in, I might have thrown my plans out the window and stabbed him with the steak knife the waitress gave me to cut my sandwich.

A few college kids with laptops, headphones, and espresso were scattered around, but I'd snagged a corner booth with plenty of privacy. Still unable to eat, I took out a notebook and started writing down everything I knew about Kailey's disappearance so far.

"Mind if I join you?" The voice sparked a confusing mixture of dread and anticipation. I sat rooted to the spot as Chris Hale slid into the booth across from me. With a buttoned navy pea coat and a matching scarf draped casually around his neck, he looked even more arrogantly preppy than he had last night. Five o'clock shadow accentuated his strong jawline, and his dark jeans fit his legs nicely in all the right places.

"What are you doing here? Are you following me?"

He shrugged as if the accusation were an everyday occurrence. "I was going to keep my distance, but you looked upset, so I thought I'd stop over and see if you wanted to talk."

I gripped my pen so tightly I heard it crack. "I don't have time for your bullshit right now. There's a little girl missing."

"Do you have any idea who might have taken her?"

I didn't want to share a damned thing with him, but the urge to hash over the information beat out the boiling suspicion. "Do you know who Justin Beckett is?"

Scratching his scruffy chin, Chris nodded. "I think so. He killed a kid, right?"

"After he raped her. Released as an adult last year without sex offender status. A little girl who lives across the street from Justin disappeared on the way home from school today. She's around the same age as the one he attacked."

Chris blinked. His smile drooped into a twisting scowl, and the brightness in his eyes evaporated. "You're joking."

"I wish."

"So you're going to find the little girl and take care of Beckett?"

What the hell was I thinking? This crazy possible sociopath didn't need to know my business. "Leave me alone, please."

"I'd like to help."

"Despite your stalking, you don't know anything about me.

And I know even less about you, so beat it. I don't have the time to humor your twisted fantasies."

He settled into the booth. "Told you, I'm a paramedic for the Philly Fire Department, Field Unit 35, off Broad. My name is Christopher Alan Hale. I'm thirty-three. I live on 63rd Street—"

"63rd Street? You live there on a paramedic's salary?"

"Family money. You can probably verify that too. Grandpa was a doctor, uncle's a lawyer, aunt's an engineer. You get the picture."

Lucky for him. I supposed money gave him more time to indulge his killing habits. "And you're the average Joe with the supplemental income?"

"Trust fund, thank you." He winked.

I said nothing more but internally flagged the information for Kelly to check. "Good for you. Now leave before I call the manager and have him throw you out."

He laughed, his broad shoulders shaking with the movement. Tucked in the back, we probably looked like a couple trying to make up after their first real argument. He struck me as the sort of person to adapt to any situation, like the chameleon I had in college. My roommate named her Mystique. I shook my head to banish the distracting memory. In the meantime, Chris showed no signs of believing my threat.

At least I had more information on him. "What do you want with me?"

"Exactly this. An open line of communication."

I rolled my eyes. "Why?"

"I'm intrigued. And bored. More that than anything, really." He slung his arm across the back of the booth. "Confirm my information. Then maybe you won't be afraid of me."

I snorted. "I'm not afraid of you. I just don't have time for you."

"You're afraid of what I might do to your operation." *He*

makes it sound like I'm running some covert killing ring. "But I think you'll find I'm telling the truth, and then you won't be able to resist talking to me."

"Why?" I shouldn't challenge him. Even if I had yet to catch him in a lie, he owned the upper hand—at least for now. But I couldn't help pushing. My pride was wounded, and I felt completely off-kilter, bombarded with new information I didn't know how to process. Chris wasn't something I could categorize in black or white, and that left me with a hopeless feeling I abhorred.

"Because I'm a product of the monsters you hate so much."

Adrenaline slashed through my veins, and I forced myself to sit still. "What are you going on about now?"

"Do you know who John Weston is?" A raw tone accompanied the words.

I thought for a moment, his question tugging at the hazy corners of my memory. "The name sounds familiar, but I can't place it."

"He lived in Lancaster and murdered at least three teenaged girls in the mid-eighties. His son and wife found the fourth one barely alive."

Sickness boiled in my stomach. "I've read about the case. The authorities believed there were more victims. But I didn't know the son found the survivor."

Chris leaned across the table, invading my space and making my heart thunder. "The boy kept hearing strange noises from the barn. Crying. He was told it was a sick horse. He was only five and believed his parents."

My blood felt slushy and slow in my veins, and Chris's voice sounded like an echo in a cave. I was about to hear something bad. Very bad. "So how did he manage to find them?"

"He couldn't stand the sounds any longer. The crying kept him awake at night, gave him nightmares." A darkness flickered through Chris's eyes. He stared at me so intently I could barely keep from turning away. "One day he made a run to the barn, and his mother couldn't stop him. She was afraid of his father too. They were forbidden from entering the barn, and she'd had enough beatings to know what might happen if they opened the doors." Chris's skin paled, his eyes jarringly still.

"Thank God he had the courage." My heart rammed against my ribs until they ached, as if it sensed the boom was about to be lowered.

Chris leaned forward, closing the space between us. I wanted to lean back, but I couldn't move. "The father was arrested, the mother too damaged to raise her son. The little boy was adopted by his aunt and uncle, who changed his name from Weston to Hale. He never stopped having the nightmares. And now he's pretty sure what he saw as a kid made him a sociopath, and he's desperate to find some sliver of humanity inside him."

Ice rushed down my spine, invading my bones like poison. The chattering background of the other restaurant patrons faded to white noise. "Are you telling me you're the Weston kid?" I whispered through lips that felt like tissue paper.

Chris leaned back in his chair, his eyes never leaving mine. "I was born Christopher Alan Weston in Lancaster on April 7, 1986. I thought you'd want to get to know me."

I could have sworn I heard *The Twilight Zone* music playing. Maybe I'd actually spilled the cyanide on myself last night, and this was my purgatory. Stuck with a good-looking, traumatized maybe-sociopath wanting to play serial killer house with me.

"I have no idea why you would think—"

"Don't you see?" Chris's low voice seemed to boom in my ears. "My father was a pedophile, a rapist, and a killer. I witnessed at least part of it. Some days I feel nothing at all. Other days I'm so angry I can barely function."

My head felt as if I'd been smacked with a mallet, and I

didn't know what to think at this point. "I'm sorry for what happened to you, if you're even telling the truth, but—"

"I'm sure with your connections, you can verify it."

"Why would I want to do that?" I couldn't grasp what he wanted from me. I wasn't a psychologist, couldn't diagnose his problems, and didn't know how to help him. I couldn't even help myself.

"Don't you see? I attack because of what I saw. I know *exactly* what kind of scum lives on this earth." He gave me a sad smile. "Lucy, I get why you do the things you do. I know the anger you carry around inside, because I've got it too. Is there anyone else you can say that about?"

"You know nothing about me." I instantly regretted the words. They were too close to an admission of guilt.

He leaned forward across the table, undeterred. "I think you're curious about me, or you will be, once everything sinks in. And I think you're lonely. Whatever your associates do to help out, they don't know what it's like to spill the cup. You're the one who looks the person in the eye and reconciles ending their life. That's got to take its toll on you, especially when you don't believe you're a real killer. Your head must be a very loud place."

Stripping me naked in front of the rest of the diners would have felt less violating. It wasn't the words, but the tone, the inflection, the depth of empathy in his voice. The understanding. Sociopaths don't have any of that. They might fake it when it is necessary, but when Chris spoke, his sincerity went beyond his words. It flooded his eyes, making his gaze beseeching and understanding and laden with pity. Either he was kidding himself about being a sociopath, or he was a dangerously good one.

God, I wanted him to go away. Stop making me think so hard. Let me get back to my life and whatever meaning I could eke out.

Could he really be telling the truth? Was it possible he understood?

He waited, and when he finally realized I wasn't going to say anything, he stood to leave. "I'll leave you alone from now on. But if you need help with Justin Beckett or ever want to talk shop, give me a call."

I never wanted to see him again.

SIX

I pulled my tattered, blue scarf tighter around my neck. The end of October brought an early morning frost, and I wished I'd worn something other than fingerless gloves. The chill matched the mood of the searchers; Kailey was still missing, and the police had few leads. After a short briefing, a small crowd of volunteers dispersed to search for Kailey, and Todd informed me I'd be with him. He waved me over, his scalp looking pink and cold beneath his thinning hair. Circles lined his eyes. He smelled strongly of coffee.

"I'm guessing you probably didn't sleep much last night." I fell into step beside him.

"Not even two hours. And those were spent at the station house."

At the briefing, eager volunteers received a hundred fliers with Kailey's picture. Now they fanned out, canvassing the designated area. A forensic team would search the vacant lot just two blocks away from Kipling Elementary.

"Her mother isn't here." I stated the obvious.

"She didn't want to leave the house in case Kailey came home." Todd walked briskly toward North 7th Street. "There's an empty building up here. Used to be a paper factory, and it's known to house vagrants. I want to go through and see if anyone's seen Kailey or knows of anyone suspicious."

"Shouldn't I be with the other civilians?"

"I'd rather you were with me."

No surprise there. Not that I could blame him. "You have any leads?"

"Besides my brother?"

"Yes. By the way, have you gotten a search warrant for his vehicle and house?"

"I've already discussed this with you, and I'm not doing it again." Todd's lips thinned beneath his mustache. "My partner is a ten-year veteran detective, and he's handling anything related to Justin. If you've got questions, talk to him."

"Fair enough. I'm sure you're checking out the locally registered scum. What about Mom's friends or significant other?"

"No significant other. Been single for quite a while. Yes, we're talking to friends, canvassing the neighborhood. You know, our job." I couldn't miss the sarcasm. "We have searched for missing kids a time or two."

I didn't press my luck further. Jamming my hands into my pockets, I worked to keep pace with Todd's quick strides. Between the cold and the silence and the nervous energy rippling through me, I couldn't keep quiet. "So, how long have you been a detective?"

Todd gave me the side-eye. "I made detective a few weeks before Justin's release."

"What made you decide to become a cop?"

"Isn't it obvious? I work in special victims."

"You were seventeen when it happened, right?"

"Yeah."

"Do you feel guilty?"

Todd came to an abrupt halt. "What?"

I really had no idea where that came from. I guess the word

had been on my mind since Chris shot off his mouth. I mirrored his defensive stance, shading my eyes as I looked up at his angry glare. "About not knowing what Justin was. Or what was happening to him. Feeling guilty about that would be pretty normal."

"I was a senior in high school trying to get out of the house because I hated my stepmother and resented my father. Justin was an afterthought. Of course I feel guilty." He squared his shoulders and forged ahead, but his face was drawn, his lips pinched.

"Who hurt him?" I asked the question that haunted me for the past decade. I'd known from the moment I became Justin's CPS worker he'd been abused. I'd just never been able to get him to admit it—or been able to prove it.

Todd flinched and started walking again. "Don't know. And if I did, I wouldn't tell you. That's his business."

The paper factory loomed ahead. Weathered gray and sporting multiple jagged cracks, the exterior made me think of the pottery I'd never been able to master. I took it up as a stress reliever a few years ago, but everything I tried to make ended up limp and sad-looking. I tried not to think of that as a metaphor for my life.

The building did resemble a giant, clay square that had cracked in the oven. Several of the windows were busted out while others had been repaired with dark plastic. Its double front doors were closed, but a broken windowpane ruled out any chance of the place being closed off. *What a sad place to endure.*

"We've usually got five to ten homeless in this place, and we don't mess with them unless they cause trouble," Todd said. "A couple of them have been here since last summer, and I've talked to them a few times. They're good people, just down on their luck."

I stared up at the dilapidated building. "You want me to search other rooms while you—"

"God, no. We don't know who's in here. I may not like you, but I don't want you getting hurt."

I almost smiled. Todd really was a decent guy.

The inside of the building smelled like rotting wood, body odor, and Porta Potties at an outdoor music festival. Most of the downstairs was empty save for various piles of rubble. Footsteps above told a different story.

"Stay behind me."

I followed orders as we ascended the stairs. A man with a scraggly beard and weary eyes rested against the wall at the top. He might have been thirty or fifty; life had clearly been hard for him.

"Hank." Todd waved his hand in greeting. "How are you?"

"All right. What brings you to these parts, Detective?"

Todd eased the duffle bag he'd been carrying off his shoulder and unzipped it to reveal a loaf of bread, two packs of bologna, and several bottles of water. He gave them to Hank. "I know you'll share these with whoever else is around."

Hank's sunken-in eyes glittered. "Thank you."

Todd nodded and then glanced at me, his cheeks flushed with something more than the cold. I was struck with the urge to sincerely pat him on the back. He wasn't giving Hank the food because he wanted information—he did it because it was right. Every once in a while, people surprised me.

"We've got a missing little girl." Todd motioned for me to give Hank a flier. The man nodded at me and focused on the paper. "Nine years old." Todd explained what we knew of Kailey's disappearance. "You know of any creeps who've moved in? Anyone in the area too interested in little kids or mentioned a little girl who might fit Kailey's description?"

"Not really." Hank rubbed his beard. "Only four of us here now, and we pretty much keep to ourselves. Most of us round here aren't into drugs or bad shit. We just can't get back on our feet."

"I know." Todd spoke without any judgment.

"What about other kids?" I piped up. "I assume you probably know the area pretty well. Do you see any of the older kids being cruel? Threatening the younger ones? Or any adults hanging out who don't belong?" I wanted to add Justin's description, but judging by the way his eyeballs were popping out of his head, another word and Todd might throw me down the stairs.

"Course I see kids being cruel," Hank said. "Most of them are little assholes who don't know how easy they've got it. But never anything that stood out as unusual. Just typical brats."

"No one new in the neighborhood?" Todd prompted.

"Not that I've seen, but I'm not usually out and about when the kids are milling round after school, you know? Figure they don't need to see the lousy side of life just yet." The man's voice lost its edge. "Ain't my job to tell them how rough it is as an adult." Hank's eyes brightened. "Hey, hey, wait a minute. There is one thing."

I held my breath.

"Yeah, Sly Lyle, he sometimes squats here." Hank opened one of the bottles of water and took a long drink. "We call him Sly because he fancies himself a ladies' man. Don't ask me why —man looks like a bearded troll. Anyway, couple of weeks ago, he was going on about seeing some dude messing with a kid. Grade-school girl, he said."

"What did the girl look like?" I asked, as Todd barked, "Did he get a description of the man?"

"Naw. You gotta understand, Sly sees something crazy every other week. I think he makes up stories just to talk shit." Hank dived into the bologna like it was a filet mignon. "This time, he bragged about running the guy off. But Sly's about as big as a puppy and even more awkward. Afraid of his own shadow."

"I still need to check the story," Todd said. "Where does Sly usually hang out?"

"When he's here, he's downstairs," Hank said. "Afraid of the floor falling in, you know. He's short and stick-thin, wears a trench coat that looks like it's got mothballs in permanent residence. You can't miss him, but I haven't seen him in several days."

"If you do, see what you can get out of him. You still got minutes on that prepaid cell I gave you?" Todd asked.

"Yep. Will keep my ears open. I hear anything, I'll call you right away."

They shook hands, and Hank headed to what I assumed was his room. "You gave him a phone?"

"How else is he supposed to get ahold of me if he needs to?"

"Good point." I was starting to like Todd, which couldn't be a good thing considering he was a cop, and I had a dark secret.

"By the way, good job on staying quiet."

"Sorry."

"No you aren't."

Two other men called the building home, and neither were Sly. Both had heard the same story, however, and neither believed him. We exited, and I was surprised by how much warmth the battered shelter provided. I pulled my coat closer as Todd checked his phone.

"Nothing so far," he said. "Not a damned sign."

"There's not going to be. Whoever took her had time to watch and plan. He's got a good hiding spot. If she's still alive."

"And my brother had the most time to watch and plan, right?" He'd lost all the kindness he'd shown the homeless men. I wanted to bristle, but I couldn't blame him for his anger.

"He did," I said. "But to be fair, I'm sure plenty of others did, too."

He ground his teeth, his glare fierce.

"I'm sorry about this whole mess." Emotion welled in my throat so that I nearly choked, and my voice warbled, carrying over the frigid air. "Sorry for you and Justin and Kailey. And believe me, I would love to be wrong about Justin. I would love for you to be right about him—you *deserve* to be right. I just can't muster the hope that you are."

The deep creases around his eyes softened. "I know. And as much as I don't like to admit it, I understand your position. You're speaking from experience. Shitty experience."

"So we're at a crossroads."

"That's up to you." A cold gust of wind swept in from the north, and Todd pulled his coat more tightly around him. "I can't change your opinion on Justin any more than you can change mine. And I won't stop you from searching for Kailey, because I'm not a petty bastard. But I won't let you railroad my brother into something he's innocent of."

"I'd never do that."

An uneasy and confused tension hung between us for a moment before the ring of Todd's cellphone shattered it. I stepped aside while he took his call. I meant what I said. I'd never send an innocent man to jail. That was an unforgivable sin in my book. But seeing Justin as innocent wasn't something I was prepared to do.

Todd ended his call and shoved the phone back into his coat pocket. The creases on his forehead were crater-deep again. "Searchers are having an issue with one of the neighbors. I've got to go sort it out."

"I'll head into the church." I glanced down the road at Our Lady of Immaculate Conception, which looked forlorn and foreboding against the bright morning sun. "See if anyone there recognizes her."

"I'll try to catch back up with you, but once you're done there, can you work your way back up the street?"

"I'll talk to everyone I see."

Todd didn't move. "It's kind of a rough neighborhood. I hate to leave you."

I'd rather he'd act brusque. Liking Todd didn't make my job any easier. "I've got my pepper spray, as always."

"Text me when you're finished with the church." He turned and hurried back up the street, his long coat waving in the wind.

Todd's presence now a memory, I trod toward the church, the soaring tower reminding me what it was like to be shunned. My devout Catholic mother still attended mass, despite all the shunning and whispering that had gone on when my sister died. I was forced to attend, but I never saw the church as a refuge again. So many of the parishioners judged my sister for taking her own life and chose to forget the reasons behind the suicide. My mother, the woman who should have seen the truth and protected her daughter, relished the role of victim. I often thought the woman believed she needed to make up for her daughter killing herself to preserve her own space in heaven.

The familiar hurts of my past licked at my conscience as I loitered on the church steps, and then I immediately felt selfish. Kailey needed help. I bounded up the cracked concrete and tried the heavy door. It opened easily into a cavernous entryway. The ceiling was dome shaped, with faded murals decorating the walls. The heavy silence seemed like an admonishment. I carefully shut the door so as not to disturb the quiet.

Despite its aged appearance, the church smelled clean, with the faintest scent of flowers. A door to my right opened. A middle-aged nun smiled at me.

"I thought I heard the door close. We don't have service today, and the priest is conducting a meeting. I'm Sister Abigail. Can I help you?"

Her friendly and open attitude surprised me; the nuns in Catholic school hadn't been cruel, but they were the stereotypical stern-faced, serious women. Then again, they had a bunch of hormonal, cocky teenagers to deal with on a daily basis, so I couldn't exactly blame them.

"I hope so." I offered the nun a flier. "I'm looking for this little girl. You wouldn't have seen her?"

Sister Abigail's smile evaporated. She took the picture and studied it carefully. "No, I haven't."

"It was a long shot. She goes to Kipling Elementary, and I doubted she'd have come by the church on her walk home. But I wanted to check. Would you pass the flier around?"

"Absolutely." Sister Abigail looked at the flier again. "She's only eight years old, and she walks home alone, in the city?"

"No, she actually walks with two older girls. But they somehow got separated yesterday."

Sister Abigail's eyes narrowed. "These girls, how old are they and what do they look like?"

I quickly checked the information Todd had briefed me on this morning. Josie and Bridget walked Kailey to and from school for the past year. "They're ten and eleven. Both brown-haired. One's got long hair and the other short. Typical little girls, I think. Why?"

"If one of them has a backpack with a boy band on it—I can't remember the name, something about a direction—then I do know those two girls. In fact, I ran them out of the vacant lot behind the church yesterday after lunch." The nun clucked her tongue, shaking her head. "I thought they should have been in school, but they said they had an early dismissal. I let them know the lot was no place for them to be playing. We have our share of hooligans around here. But your little one"—she gestured to the flier—"wasn't with them."

My pulse kick-started. "When you say after lunch, do you

remember what time exactly?" The police were right. The two girls lied.

"It was before one o'clock," Sister Abigail said. "I'm diabetic, so I have to keep to my schedule. And I'd just finished my lunch and washed the dishes. The window over the sink overlooks the lot, you see. That's when I noticed them."

Josie and Bridget had told everyone they'd taken their normal route. The church was not on that route or anywhere near it. The girls' lie meant the police didn't have the correct information about Kailey's disappearance.

My jaw ached from the force of my clenched teeth. "Thank you so much, Sister Abigail. I don't think we have the full story from those two. I need to call the police right away. If you remember any more or come across anyone who's seen Kailey, please call the number on the flier."

Sister Abigail promised she would, and I hurried out of the church, barely able to think straight. What were those girls thinking? The answer was obvious: they'd disobeyed their parents about the route they were to take home from school and were covering their butts. Typical children who couldn't fathom problems beyond their own.

I punched in Todd's number and hoped he'd let me go with him to talk to the girls. Probably not, but I'd ask anyway.

"Find anything?" He wasted no time.

"Josie and Bridget lied about the route they took home. A nun ran them out of the church's vacant lot yesterday. Before one o'clock."

"Goddamnit. So our timeline and location of her disappearance is off. I'm going to have those girls' heads."

I felt the same, but I had enough experience dealing with kids to know that was the wrong approach. "You can't be a bull in a china shop. They're scared and probably feel guilty. Let them know this is about helping Kailey. Be nice, not a bully."

"Kailey doesn't have time for me to be nice."

"Why don't you let me go with you to talk to them? I've worked with a lot of kids and—"

"Nope. This is as close to the investigation as you get. Thanks for the tip, and please keep searching if you have the time."

He ended the call.

I hoped Josie and Bridget were still in school when I arrived this afternoon.

SEVEN

I searched for another hour before heading back to my apartment in Northern Liberties. None of the volunteers found any more information on Kailey. A dull ache had taken up residence in my head. I kept thinking of Kailey's mother, of her vacant eyes, of the shock freezing her expression into a mask of disbelief. As much as I hurt, what about Jenna Richardson?

The sight of my building brought a sliver of solace from the storm I'd ventured into. As a historical junkie, modern apartments with cheap building materials don't impress me. I needed some character in my home, something to distract me from the muck I usually swam in.

Unfortunately, many of the older homes in Philadelphia are in neighborhoods still deep in the process of gentrification and surrounded by industry and crime.

Two years ago, I lucked out and snagged an apartment in the Northern Liberties Historic District. The building is a Federal-style home and dates back to 1809. Some innovative restoration expert saw life in the old house, and the apartments were salvaged while still keeping their historical bones. I lived on the top floor, on the western side, which means I was blessed with some amazing sunsets.

My apartment wasn't much bigger than the dorm suite I'd shared in college. The bedroom fit my double bed with about a foot to spare, and the living room and kitchen all blended into an open concept that kept the space from looking too much like the inside of a tin can. But the walk-in closet complete with very useful cubby holes and a killer shoe rack made living in miniature worth it.

A demanding yowl greeted me. Mousecop wrapped himself around my ankles, purring loudly. I scooped him up and snuggled him, listening to the sound of his motor. "Hi, fat one."

He twisted in my arms, his tail slipping around my neck. I knew his game. I carried him to my small kitchen, cradling him like the spoiled baby he was. His food bowl wasn't empty, but I could see the bottom, and that was a no-no in Mousecop's world. I poured him some expensive food and left him purring and chowing.

My eyes drooped from the early morning, and I checked my messages yet again, hoping to have something from Kelly. She'd managed to log into Kailey's email address and was painstakingly going through every contact. The police would do the same, but I wanted the information for my own investigation. She also found Slimy Steve on yet another disgusting website, with a new screen name and trying to meet up with a young girl. I needed to take care of him.

The phone pulsed, rattling on my miniscule end table. I slouched in the chair when I saw my mother's name pop up on the caller ID. If I didn't answer and deal with her now, she'd keep calling.

"Hello?" I'm sure I didn't sound pleased to hear from her.

"You were supposed to call me three days ago."

My chin dropped to my chest. I didn't need this right now. "Sorry. I've been busy."

My mother heaved a sigh, and I pictured her sitting in the kitchen, sipping her iced tea. Once a raven-haired beauty, age and bad choices had marked her face with deep wrinkles. Her makeup only made the lines more visible. No longer lustrous, her hair hung limp to her shoulders. "You're always too busy for me."

"I've got a backload of cases, Mom." Not true, but I certainly had plenty of crap to muddle through.

"I know. But you've only got one mother. And who knows how long I'll be around?"

"You're only sixty-seven."

My mother sighed with the imagined weight of the world. "I've had a hard life, Lucy."

"I remember. How's Mac?" Asking about my stepfather was the only way to keep from hanging up on her. The three of us had dinner together the other night, and Mac wound up with chest pains. I spent hours stuck with my mother in the emergency room, half-wishing she was the one in peril. Thankfully Mac was all right, but I still worried about him. He worked too hard and refused to retire.

"He's fine," my mother said. "But I have to force him to take it easy. It's so hard when he won't listen to me, Lucy."

Never mind how tough it is for an aging construction worker and lifelong outdoorsman to admit he needed to slow down. It was always about Mother. "Tell him I'll stop by to see him as soon as I can. I've picked up a case, and it's pretty urgent."

"Your job is so sad," my mother said. "I'll never understand why you chose to work with these kinds of people when you could have been anything."

"These kinds of people, Mom? As if they're any different from us?" Hypocrisy was one of my mother's star attributes.

"That isn't fair."

"Fair? Do you actually think life is fair?"

My mother sighed. "I didn't say that."

"You just said it." I tried not to snap. It would only cause an argument I couldn't win. "And I do important work. I help families, and every once in a while I help put a piece of trash behind bars. I'm sorry my work puts me in contact with 'those kinds of people.'"

"You're twisting my words. I never said there was anything wrong with the type of people you help."

A familiar ache pulsed in the back of my neck. I knew better than to get sucked into this game. "Fine. So what did you call for?"

"Because you never call me. Here I am, with only Mac and my daughter as family, and you choose to ignore me." My mother sniffled. I imagined her dabbing her nose with a scratchy tissue. She never bought the name brand. "What if something happened to me? How terrible would you feel then? Would I finally get some attention?"

My tired body sagged into the chair. I hated that after all she'd done—and all the things she didn't do—my mother still had the ability to make me feel like the bad child.

"I'm sorry. I'll try to do better."

Another sniffle. "I hope so."

My throat knotted. The blades of a thousand knives dug into the back of my neck. Life would be so much easier if I didn't love my mother. If some part of me still didn't long for her approval. For her affection.

She cleared her throat and sighed—a signal the conversation was taking a turn. "Are you seeing anyone?"

I groaned. My mother fit the passive-aggressive, yet excessively nosy cliché mother mold perfectly. And we'd had this conversation the last time we saw each other. Did she really think I'd met some Casanova in a few days' time? "Not seriously, no."

"What happened to the doctor?"

He wasn't a doctor. He was the chemist who provided me the cyanide. But my mother couldn't know that, so I said he was a pediatrician. Wasn't a total lie, as he did have a doctorate.

"I see him occasionally. We're both busy."

"You're thirty-three years old," my mother said. "A couple more years, and pregnancy will be a bigger risk for you."

"Women in their forties have babies all the time, Mom. Besides, I'm not sure I want kids."

Vigilante killer of pedophiles and mother. Somehow those two ideas didn't gel.

"Lucy, I'd like to have grandkids, and you're my only hope." The self-indulgent, whiney tone made my teeth grind.

"And why is that, Mother?"

"Please don't bring up your sister's death now."

"I didn't. You did." Twenty-two years ago, my sister had taken her own life because of our mother's sick boyfriend. Anger burned inside the usually hollow pit of my heart. I tasted it in my mouth, felt it in my pounding head. The same anger that fueled my extracurricular activity threatened to overwhelm me.

"You know, I lost a child." Now Mother sounded petulant. She probably looked like she was sucking on a lemon. "I suffered more than you can imagine."

"I think you forget it was Lily who suffered the most."

"You know I did the best I could."

The best she could was turning a blind eye to all the obvious signs her live-in boyfriend was abusing her oldest daughter. Even when I insisted something wasn't right, Joan ignored me. And then my sister was gone. As I got older, I could have forgiven my mother's ignorance. I couldn't forgive the way she used my sister's suicide to evoke sympathy and manipulate everyone around her. She excelled in an argument, never failing to make herself the victim regardless of the barbs she dished out. Debating with her was a waste of energy.

I sighed. "I'm sorry. I'm just really stressed out right now. A little girl went missing after school yesterday, and I'm afraid one of my former cases might have taken her."

"The little girl from Poplar?" Joan sucked in a whistling breath. "I saw that on the news this morning."

"Remember Justin Beckett?"

"Yes. You were obsessed with that kid. I didn't hear from you for nearly a month after he was arrested."

"Right. Well, he lives across the street from the missing girl."

"What do the police think?"

I wasn't about to get into an ethics discussion with my mother. "They're looking at everyone."

"Well, I hope they find her. What her mother must be going through."

"She's a mess."

"I've no doubt," she said. "You know I've been having those heart palpitations again, ever since Mac's incident the other night."

Typical. No one could direct a conversation back to the topic of herself better than Mother. "Have you gone to the doctor?"

"I don't want to. You know I'm afraid they'll find something serious."

"Better they find it than to just hope nothing's wrong. What does Mac think?" I'd yet to figure out how my stepfather put up with my mother's emotional manipulation. He was a decent, hardworking guy, perpetually optimistic. He deserved more than melancholy, damaged Joan.

"He thinks I should go to the doctor." Her tone cheered up the way it always did when Mother talked about herself. "I suppose I should. But I don't know what I'll do if they find something serious."

"You'll let them treat it." I checked my watch. Almost time

to head to school. "I've got to get going, Mom. I have an appointment. I'll call you."

"No, you won't."

I forced myself to smile in hopes I'd sound semi-pleasant. "Of course I will."

EIGHT

My fingers dug into the steering wheel as I answered Kelly's
call. I sat a few blocks down from Kipling Elementary, ready to
head into the school when she called with a double whammy.

Kelly didn't bother to say hello. "Kailey's Internet access has
definitely been restricted because a lot of the stuff in her email
is from game sites and whatnot. But, if you look in her trash
folder, there are five emails from a RRangerFan1, and every
single one of Kailey's replies came when she was at the babysitter's, within a half an hour after school."

"Did you trace the email back to anyone?"

"It took me a while because I had to trace the email back to
an online forum for *Mighty Morphin Power Rangers* fans."

"Say what? Didn't that show end a long time ago?" I was
never much of a cartoon kid, but my oldest friend Kenny loved
the Power Rangers. He still had a bunch of toys he insisted were
valuable memorabilia.

"Yeah, but there are still people who love it and do role-
playing stuff. Anyway, I found our guy. And guess who it is?"

Stinging air rushed up my esophagus. I didn't want to be
right about this. "Justin Beckett."

"Yep. He's not very smart because he registered that email to the message board under his real name. From what I can tell, he and Kailey have been emailing for a few weeks."

"What do the messages say?" Part of me didn't want to know. As much as I was driven to stomp out the filth of this world, I constantly fought the urge to stick my head in the sand and pretend humanity was wonderful.

"Here's the weirdest part. He's not hiding who he is," Kelly said. "He signs it Jay, but he's not trying to talk to her like he's a kid. He clearly talks like an adult trying to cheer up a lonely little girl."

"Of course he does."

"Sounds like Kailey had been bullied at one point, and Justin may have stuck up for her," Kelly continued. "I can't get the whole story from emails, but it's definitely enough for the police to get a warrant."

"If you found this, so will they. As long as Todd Beckett plays it straight." That could be a big *if*. Stalwart cop or not, Todd was also human and fell into the messy tangle of loyalty versus responsibility. He wouldn't be the first cop to choose loyalty.

"I thought his partner was handling Justin."

"Yeah, but Todd doesn't want his little brother to go back to prison. You don't think he might try to cover up evidence? What if he thinks he needs to convince Justin to let her go and take off or something? Anything would be better than another round of prison."

"I don't know, Lucy. Todd's been pretty decent to you so far, and he's got a really good reputation."

"Which is on the line because he vouched for his brother and promised to keep an eye on him. Did you find out anything else?"

Kelly cleared her throat. "Yeah. One other thing, and it's worst of all."

I braced myself, pushing my feet into the car's floorboards. "Hit me."

"Justin Beckett started working at A&M Sanitation three weeks ago."

I swallowed back the shock. Justin had access to dumpsters all over the city. The perfect place to drop little Kailey's used body.

My head bounced against the back of the seat. "God Almighty."

With ten minutes until dismissal, parents were already lining up to pick up kids. A whiteboard at the main entrance—the only one unlocked—announced a strict sign-in policy. I didn't expect to get past the office, but I just needed an excuse to be milling around when the kids came out. If I were lucky, I'd manage to talk to some parents.

Although one of the older buildings in the district, Kipling Elementary had the standard security cameras on all the doors, with a second set of alarmed interior doors acting as a barrier for unwanted visitors. The inside of the school showed its wear, scuff marks decorating the tile in long streaks. Yellow, textured walls boasted scratches, and I envisioned kids trying to claw their way out of their imagined prisons.

Inside the office, a grim-faced secretary greeted me. "May I help you?"

I plastered a smile on my face and hoped I didn't look like a hyena.

I leaned against the tall counter, which was cluttered with various signup forms and pens with ugly flowers taped to the ends. "I'm Lucy Kendall, and my husband and I are looking at a house in the area. I'd like to check out the school."

The secretary, whose nametag announced her as Mrs.

Harris, was unfazed. "We don't give random tours. It's a matter of student safety, which I'm sure you can understand."

"Of course. I just thought I could maybe talk to the principal, get a feel for the place."

"He doesn't take walk-ins unless your children actually attend Kipling," Mrs. Harris said. "And he's in a meeting right now. But I can certainly schedule you an appointment."

I cleared my throat and checked my watch. "I'm not sure I can schedule that right now. I took today off work to check out the area. I'll have to look at our calendars and call for an appointment. Sorry to have bothered you."

Turning up the collar of my coat, I headed out of the office and into the hall. Outside, uniforms milled around, watching for someone suspicious. With Jenna's permission to look for Kailey, I had every right to be here. But I knew Todd wouldn't appreciate it.

Near the entrance, a janitor with a jingling key ring fiddled with the latch on a worn-looking display case. I gave him a wide berth, not wanting to disrupt his work.

"Ouch." He cursed under his breath and dropped his screwdriver. The tip of his index finger was red from being pinched in the uncooperative latch.

I quickly bent down and grabbed the screwdriver. "Here you go."

"Thanks." He shot me a cursory glance, and then he froze, the tool clutched in his hands. His face was cherubic, although his expression distinctly hostile. Beneath a shock of blond hair was fair skin that looked like it hadn't seen the sun for a while. "Sallow" came to mind, ravaged with the dark shadows of either drug use or insomnia. Darkness flashed through his eyes, and his fist clenched. I swear he started to step toward me.

I stepped out of the stranger's reach. "Excuse me."

The janitor said nothing, looking at me with such hate I

wanted to run. I hurried outside, my skin burning from nerves and the heavy sensation of being watched.

My throat felt swollen, caked with anxiety. Students began to trickle out, and their voices were muted, as if I'd thrown a thick towel over them. I didn't know the janitor. I'd remember that face. But he thought he knew me.

More students burst happily out of the doors as the bell rang. I took a deep breath and tried to focus. After Kelly heard about the older girls fibbing, she'd scoured the school website in the hopes of finding a picture of one of them. Turned out Josie was quite the actress and had the lead in the fourth-grade play last year. Her picture was front and center on the fine arts page. Now I waited for her to exit.

She trailed out with the last group of students, looking tired and sad. She walked alone.

"Josie?"

The girl stopped and eyed me suspiciously. "Yeah."

I quickly showed her my badge. "I'm helping Jenna Richardson look for Kailey, and I have some questions."

Josie's eyes flooded with tears. "I already told the detective I was sorry. He yelled enough."

"I'm not here to scold you. We all make mistakes."

"I'm not supposed to go with anyone."

"Of course you aren't." I stepped out of the way of the milling kids and settled near the bushes adorning the school's front. "We can talk right here. I just have a few questions."

"Okay." Josie came close enough to hear but maintained a safe distance. Good girl. "I know I wasn't supposed to be in the lot."

"That's between you and your parents. Can you tell me about Kailey? Did she ever mention any adults or older kids who scared her?"

"No. And I told the cops that, you know."

"I know. What about anyone in your neighborhood? You ever notice any adults hanging around when they shouldn't be?"

Josie shrugged. "I don't pay that much attention. But no one's ever freaked me out."

"Good." I opened the browser on my smartphone to the picture of Justin. "Do you know him?"

Josie flushed. "Sure. That's the boy who lives across the street. He's really cute. My mom says he's out of high school, so I shouldn't be calling him a boy."

"Do you know his name?"

"Justin." She managed a small smile. "He's nice to us. Sometimes we see him when we're coming home after school. He likes to sit on his porch and draw. He's really good."

I nodded. "But if he lives across the street, you probably don't get to talk to him much."

Josie's cheeks flamed brighter. "Well, he's really cute. So... me and Bridget like to walk home on that side of the street in case he's out. When he is, we get to talk to him. But we don't stay long. Bridget always tries to get him to draw our picture, but he never will. She's good at drawing, too, and yesterday morning she stopped to give him a picture she'd drew for him. We were almost late to school."

I sucked in a hard breath and hoped Josie hadn't heard. "Do you know if Kailey ever hangs out with Justin?"

Josie nodded. "A few weeks ago, one of the boys in Kailey's class started pushing her around. He lives on our street, and he is always hanging out. He's mean and smelly and no one likes him."

"I bet they don't," I said. "What happened?"

"I told Isaac to back off, but he didn't listen to me. He's kind of big for his age, big as me. He started pushing Kailey, and she fell into a mud puddle. Justin ran across the street and told Isaac to get lost. He asked Kailey if she was okay and helped her get cleaned off."

"That was very nice of him." My cheeks hurt from pretending not to be disgusted. "Did he take Kailey to his house?"

"No, he just went over and got some towels and dried her off, and then he went back to his drawing." Josie's eyes narrowed. "Why are you asking about Justin?"

"I just want to know about Kailey's friends." I gave her yet another encouraging smile. "Do you girls see Justin a lot?"

"Sometimes after school, but we aren't supposed to talk to him." Josie pushed a lock of her brown hair out of her eyes.

"Why?"

"Our moms say he's too old and that we're bugging him. But that's not why we leave. Justin always tells us to go on home before our parents get worried."

"Where's Kailey when this happens? Is she with you, or does she go on to your building?"

"Until Justin got rid of Isaac, she just hung around. She's shy and little." Josie's tears returned. "Last week, she fell on the way home and ripped her jeans. Her knee was bleeding, and we didn't have anything to put on it. Justin saw her crying. He gave her some paper towels and a Band-Aid. He's so nice, isn't he?"

That's how these guys work. The smallest acts of kindness go a long way to earn a child's trust. My stomach rolled. "It's very nice. Do you know if Kailey ever saw Justin without you or Bridget around?"

Another shrug. "She never said anything. But she didn't really tell us stuff." Josie wiped her cheeks. "We sort of ignored her. And I never should have let Bridget talk me into going to the lot. She likes to go play just because she knows she isn't supposed to. But I think she just wants to keep from going home and helping out with her little brother. He's a brat." She shivered, drawing her arms around her. Her eyes clouded over. "I hate the vacant lot. If I hadn't gone there with Bridget, Kailey would have stayed with us and she'd be okay."

"It's not your fault." Her face pinched so that it resembled a pug as she tried not to cry. I wanted to give her a hug. "Bad things happen. Now we've just got to find Kailey."

A uniform on the fringe of the crowd glanced my way, and I knew it was time to go. I handed her my card. "Listen, if you ever need anything or you remember anything else, you call me anytime, okay?"

Josie shoved the card in her pocket and wiped her tears. I patted her on the head and slipped between chattering parents and kids. So Justin and Kailey must have started emailing after he'd gained her trust with Isaac. He didn't need to hide who he was in the email because she already thought of him as a good guy. No doubt Todd and his partner would find out this information, but I'd make damn sure it happened today.

I noticed a sleek, black Audi parked behind my car. Through the tinted windows, I saw Chris Hale behind the wheel. The car's black rims gave the stealthy appearance of a government official. Or a terrorist.

Chris exited the car looking cocky, his bright eyes dulled by black-rimmed glasses. "Hi."

"You seriously have to stop following me."

"I can't help it. And I didn't follow you this time. I had a hunch."

"Really?"

"Sure. I knew the little girl disappeared from Kipling, and I thought you might be snooping around. So I took a chance and came looking for your car." He glanced in the direction of the school, completely at ease, as though he wasn't the creepiest guy in the vicinity. "What did you find out?"

My adrenaline still pumped from Josie's information, and I was pounding with the urge to tell someone. I didn't get the chance.

"Excuse me." The throaty voice came from behind me. Instinctively, I reached into my pocket, my hand closing around the canister of pepper spray. I turned to find the janitor standing a foot away, the same seething question still glued to his face.

"Can I help you?"

He took a long step into my space, his action so quick he was within an inch of me before I realized it. "You killed my brother."

NINE

I'd like to say I was prepared for this moment, that I had a smooth response at the ready, but I froze like a confused deer in the headlights. Cold air whooshed into my chest; I was breathing too fast. My mouth opened, but the words didn't come. They didn't even generate in my brain. The only thing I could muster in my terrified, shocked mind was, "Oh shit."

Suddenly I stared at the back of an expensive wool coat. Chris had stepped in front of me. He and the janitor were about the same height, and the tension resonating between the two reminded me of the UFC fights Kelly liked to watch. Two prized fighters circling, each trying to outdo the other one with stony looks and rippling muscles.

"I don't know what game you're playing." Chris's voice was low, thick with anger. "But you need to turn around and walk away."

The janitor didn't move. "She knows what I'm talking about. She dated my brother, and she killed him."

What the hell did he mean? I never targeted any of my own cases. How did he know who I was?

"I think I'd better call the principal," Chris said. "You're not stable enough to be around children."

I snapped back to myself. "Good idea. And while you're doing that, I'll tell that uniformed officer this man is harassing me."

The janitor flinched. "The police said it was a heart attack brought on by drug use."

"I'm sorry for your loss, but you're crossing the line with this, mister." My own heart thrashed. It sounded like my mode of operation, but I didn't recognize this man. Then again, it wasn't my policy to get to know family members.

His pale skin was bright red with his anger. "They didn't listen to me because he had a bad history. But I knew a woman was involved, and when I saw you, I knew it. I've seen your picture."

Impossible. I never left a trail. I never got close enough. This man was reaching.

"You're mistaken." The steadiness of my voice amazed me.

He shook his head. "His name was Cody, and he had a heroin problem. I might not be able to prove it, but I know it was you. And now you won't be able to forget my face."

My brain stopped working again.

Cody Harrison had a brother named Brian.

"Get out of here," Chris said. "Walk away before I have your job and your ass in jail."

I could only see the side of his face, the hard set of his jaw and the curl of his lips, but he must have looked mean enough because the janitor nodded and stalked off, skimming his way through the last of the kids trailing out of school.

Sudden dizziness washed over me, and I braced my hand against Chris's back. The words clung to my throat.

"Let's get out of here," he said.

"I'm not going anywhere with you. And I have my car," I finished weakly.

"There's a diner two blocks west. Meet me there." His urgent tone seduced me. I remembered his admission that he was just like me and understood the choices I made.

I don't know if it was the shock or the desperate need to pretend someone could truly understand, but I said yes.

Fifteen minutes later, I found myself at a neighborhood diner boasting it had the best cheesesteaks in the city. What a crock. Any real Philadelphian knows Jim's Steaks on the northeast side has the best Philly cheesesteaks, period. Across from me, eyes glittering behind his glasses, Chris waited. And my mind raced.

I had lived my life in a strange mixture of carefully calculated moves and impulse decisions. Cracking the skull of the man who molested my sister and was coming for me was impulse. My teenage years were spent acting out, making impulsive—and often stupid—decisions in a hopeless effort to get my narcissistic mother to truly see me. And then I started to grow up. Acting on impulse became a nearly forgotten sensation. *Until today.*

A waitress appeared at our table. Chris ordered a cheeseburger. I passed. We continued to stare at each other.

"So..." Chris rubbed his scruffy chin with the back of his hand, his index finger trailing along the narrow scar on his jaw. "Did you kill his brother?"

The question hung between us like a grenade with its pin dangling, ready to blow everything into a million pieces. For some reason, I remembered one of the last conversations I'd had with my sister.

"Luce, I want to tell you something."

"Sure." I bit my tongue, trying to figure out a math problem. I hated math.

"People are selfish. Even if they don't want to be. They are.

They might think they're doing the right thing, might make some shitty excuse for themselves, but in the end, they're making the choice based on whatever's going to bring them gratification. Selfish. That includes you. Don't be afraid of self-preservation. You can't win in this world if you don't put yourself first. Don't forget that."

I'd promised her I wouldn't. Self-preservation. I'd worked hard at it, but it came with a steep price of loneliness. Before I fully agreed to the thought, the answer rolled out of my tense mouth. "Yes. Cody Harrison."

It's okay. He's not a cop. Kelly's checked him out. Everything he's told you so far has been true. He can't hurt you. If anything, you'll say he's crazy. But he's not going to go to the police.

A charged beat of silence passed between us, Chris's gaze as piercing and unreadable as it had been the first night he approached me. Finally, he exhaled. "Well shit, Lucy. You're supposed to be a professional. How does this janitor know who you are?"

His response felt surreal, but it ignited my temper. I leaned forward and pitched my voice low. "I'm not a hitman. I eradicate sex offenders. I make sure they've been given a lethal dose of whatever I'm using, and then I walk away. I don't see them die. I'm not a freaking killer. Killers do it for the thrill, or by compulsion. I fill a void the justice system has chosen to ignore."

I knew the semantics were stupid, but they mattered to me. I don't expect my soul to ascend from the vacuity of death into heaven's fluffy happy-ever-after, but I've got to have some sort of line. I can't be lumped in with *those people.*

"But this could send you to the lethal injection table."

"It won't. I never allowed Cody to take any pictures of me."

"Then how did this brother know about you?"

Good freaking question. "I played dealer to get to Cody. Let him think we were going to date. He probably described me to his brother."

"Come on. Don't be stupid. You're pretty enough, but you're not a unique face. Unless this dude's accosting every redhead in the city accusing them of killing his brother, he's seen your picture. He knew it was you."

The waitress appeared with his burger. The bacon smelled heavenly, and my mouth watered.

"But he doesn't have proof," I said after she'd gone. "This supposed picture doesn't exist. If it did, I would have been identified and be sitting in prison. So I'm safe."

"Except he's seen you in person now. You don't think his need for vengeance isn't renewed?" Chris took a huge bite and moaned in appreciation. My stomach growled.

He was right. I needed to find out exactly what I was dealing with. "Just... let me think. I'll make a phone call, see if a friend can find out something."

Chris shrugged and chowed down, studying me with such transfixed perception I longed to duck under the table. He stopped to take a drink and then wiped his mouth. "It's your freedom. Now, on to the missing kid. Why is she so important to you?"

I broke free of his stare to look out the window. Kids still walking home from school filled the sidewalks, and the candy store across the street was hopping. "Ten years ago, I was assigned as Justin's social worker. I couldn't get him removed from his home, and then he killed a child. One of the lead detectives on Kailey's case is Justin's brother, and I'm afraid he's not going to allow himself to see his brother for who he really is."

"I see." Chris took his glasses off and rubbed his eyes. "So it's a guilt thing. And you don't think the police can handle the case? I mean, there's no way they aren't going to find out the same information you've got. Probably already have."

"But Justin has a relationship with Kailey." I quickly briefed Chris on the information both Kelly and Josie had given me.

His mouth turned down, his bow-shaped upper lip curling like an angry dog's.

"So he's a damned good suspect. But the police likely already know this."

"Probably," I said. "But even if he's got someone else handling his brother, Todd's still the lead officer. It's his call to bring him in, to get a search warrant. That's a shitty position for anyone to be in, especially when Todd's reputation is partially at stake."

Chris pushed his plate away. "What if Justin didn't take the little girl? He's been out for eighteen months and flying under the radar. Pretty risky move to snatch a kid he lives so close to."

"Maybe he snapped." I couldn't help but snatch one of the few fries left on Chris's plate. "And he's got plenty of evidence stacked against him. Given his history, police will be able to get a warrant."

"Then why don't you let them do it?" he asked. "You don't think Todd could make his partner cover for Justin too?"

I scrunched up my nose and gave him my dirtiest look. "Of course not. I just... I need to do something. That's why I left Todd a voicemail on the way here. He needs to know that I know about Justin and Kailey. Hopefully he won't be too pissed off to call me back."

Chris downed the rest of his soda. He sat the glass down on the table and leaned forward, the corners of his mouth turning up deceptively. "I just worry you have your priorities twisted."

"Excuse me?"

"Finding the kid comes first. Justin Beckett second. You sound like you're more about a witch hunt than a rescue mission."

"I am trying to find her," I said. "I can't risk Justin Beckett not being thoroughly investigated. And if he really didn't take her, then I pray the cops will find the real pig, and fast." That was true. Wasn't it? No, it wasn't an absolute that Justin had taken her. But it was the logical conclusion, and even if Todd were able to be objective, there was no way I could hang around and wait to see what happened. I was too selfish.

Chris kept watching me, and I wanted to demand to know what he was thinking. Better yet, what was I thinking, enlisting his help? A stranger who claimed he was a serial killer, a sociopath with an unnecessary interest in my choices?

"Here's what I think." Chris wiped his mouth, crumpled the napkin, and then tossed it into his now empty plate. "You're a control freak with a guilty conscience who wants to help yourself as much as you do the kid. And that's fine. But you should be aware of it so it doesn't cloud your judgment. Because Kailey needs to be the first priority in all of this."

My insides steamed. "How dare you question my priorities? Whether or not I feel guilty has little to do with any of this."

"Fair enough. But you do feel guilty. That's a start."

I pushed my drink aside. I needed to reassess. "I appreciate your helping me with the janitor back there. But since I've turned stupid and bared my soul to you, I've got some questions I need answered before we go any further."

"Ask away." His smirk made it clear he knew exactly what I was going to ask.

"How exactly did you find out about me? In detail, please."

He leaned back, tipping the chair onto its hind legs. I thought about kicking it over. "Let's see. A while ago, I followed a fat dude with an ugly birthmark on his cheek. Noticed him watching the little kids in the park, found out he had a record. He had a dog too. A cocker spaniel he used to lure the kids."

"Mark Scott." I'd taken care of him when Kelly confirmed he'd been trying to set up dates with young girls. There'd been no reason for Mark to complete his third offense for the charm of a permanent prison sentence. That would mean one more child violated.

The little cocker spaniel had been so damned sweet. He'd

been with Mark when I made my move, and I'd scooped him up before he could run off. He'd ridden in the front seat of my car like he belonged, and I'd damned near kept him. I took the dog to a no-kill shelter and then convinced a co-worker he was the perfect rescue animal for her.

"I happened to be the paramedic on duty when Mark died. I'd seen you following him. When I saw you in the crowd, I figured you had something to do with his death and decided to keep an eye on you."

"I never noticed you following me."

Another Casanova grin. "I'm good."

"So even it out. You're a paramedic. And in the"—I glanced around—"garbage business like me, as you so eloquently put it the other night. What's your game?"

"Similar. Rig comes in handy. It's a good place to hide, good mode of transportation. People never do DNA tests in there." He looked at me through impossibly thick eyelashes. "As for method, it varies. But I have to get rid of the bodies. That's a job in itself. That's why I admire you so much. You've got a great system."

I closed my eyes, breaking his hypnotizing stare, and sipped my water. Without the pervasive influence of his eyes and his accompanying charm, I could think clearly enough to listen to my instincts. Killing another human being was the dirtiest of filthy deeds. My way offered a sense of detachment—the reprieve of never having to see the life drain from my victim's eyes as he becomes nothing—and it was the only way I could do it.

But Chris insinuated personal physical involvement of the worst kind, disposing of the corpse. Ruthless and utterly messy. He might have been an excellent actor, but Chris also had a life-style that shot a giant hole in his story. Fancy car, nice clothes that made him stand out. Too opulent.

I decided to call him on it. "I don't think so."

"I'm sorry?"

"You're not a garbage man. I'm not sure you've ever taken out the garbage." I watched for a tell in his expression, but he remained stoic. "You want to—or at least you think you want to —but you haven't. Maybe you've got a lot of pent-up rage and think that's the best way to release it." I tilted my head, narrowing my eyes. "But you're also materialistic. You like dressing nice, you like being the center of attention. You won't like the garbage man's punishment if you get caught. So that's why you don't act, not yet. You probably followed Mark Scott around, thinking he'd be the perfect first-time dump. You stumble on me and think you've found some sort of mentor. Am I right?"

Chris licked his smirking lips again. "You can go with that if you want. Point is, I know what you are, and I like that you believe you're in the right. Takes balls, if you'll excuse the language."

I matched his challenging tone. "Excused. As for who's in the right, that's funny since you claim you're just like me."

"Told you, I'm a sociopath." He spread his hands as if to say, *What can I do?*, still smiling. He seemed very proud of the idea of being a sociopath. I wondered if he realized that was his biggest tell. "A highly functioning one, thank you very much. I don't need a moral compass."

"But you have one, according to what you said the other night," I said. Not to mention his compassion for the war he believed was going on in my head. "You choose the bad guys too."

"I figure that'll give me a little leniency if the book gets thrown at me."

"So I'm just for your entertainment, since you're a sociopath and all." I resisted the urge to make air quotes. Sociopathy cast a pretty wide net, but Chris didn't strike me as the sort of person who didn't give a damn about anyone else, or chose to do things only for his own benefit. I saw the disgust on his face when I told him about Justin's relationship with Kailey.

"Something like that." His eyes wrinkled when he smiled. *Let him cling to sociopathy. But I still don't think he is any sort of killer.* "Maybe I just want to get to know you."

I snorted. "Sociopaths don't care about getting to know someone. They only care about what's in it for them."

"Right. And what's in it for me is talking to someone who truly fascinates me. I can't say that about anyone else I've met. Most people bore the shit out of me. And I'm a pretty affable guy." He leaned back in his chair and smiled.

I couldn't resist the dig. "Or maybe you're not a sociopath and just a really lonely, needy man."

"Do I look like the kind of guy who'd be lonely?"

He spoke with the feigned confidence of the insecure. "There's a huge difference between emotionally lonely and physically lonely. Emotional loneliness makes people do crazy things."

For the first time, I saw a fleeting glimpse of defeat on his face. "Agreed. But I'm not lonely. Or maybe I am. Either way, you hang out with me long enough and you'll find out."

I drained the last of my water. "Time to go."

He insisted on walking me to my car. I would have called it gentlemanly except he'd parked behind it. While we walked, I left a message for Kenny, who I hoped would be able to use his street connections to dig up some information on the Harrison brothers.

"So thanks." I stopped at my driver's door.

"For what?"

"For stepping between the janitor and me and handling things when I froze."

"You're welcome."

I felt like I should say more, but what else was there to talk about? Chris now knew more of me than any man who'd ever seen me naked.

"So what are you going to do now?" Chris broke the silence.

"Go home. Make some calls and try to find out what I can about the Harrison brothers. Hope Todd calls me back. If he doesn't, I've got other ways of getting inside the investigation."

Chris leaned against my car. "And then what?"

"What do you mean?"

"What are you going to do after Detective Beckett chews you a new ass and tells you to back off?"

"Keep looking."

He raised his eyebrows. "For Kailey, or for Justin, or for this janitor?"

"All three." I didn't like the way his accusatory tone made me feel coated in guilt.

"You've got someone with serious computer skills," Chris said. "You have them looking beyond Justin? Checking out other creeps in the neighborhood? What about the kid's social networking stuff? They're all online nowadays."

"Yes, and so do the police. At this point, my time is better spent on the streets."

A cold wind gusted between us. Chris zipped up his jacket. "If I were you, I'd be worried about janitor dude first. Justin second. No matter what you tell yourself, the police are more equipped to find the kid than you."

"You're right. But I have to try." I unlocked my door and quickly slipped into the car.

Chris leaned over the open door. "I want to help you."

"Why? You're a sociopath, remember?"

"Maybe this is my chance to avenge my own wrongs. And I think you're in over your head." He looked pointedly away and then glanced down at his shifting feet. For the first time, I realized he wasn't telling me the whole story.

Part of me wanted to call Chris on his evasiveness, but I didn't have the time. And I figured I owed him the decency of butting out since he'd stepped up for me. Instinct told me getting any more involved with him would be a mistake. I should drive away and forget his phone number. But right now, his expression made him look so vulnerable, I had a hard time considering him as anything but a lonely soul. But people wore many masks, and sociopaths were adept at disguising their true colors. Chris might be nothing more than a very skilled chameleon.

"Tomorrow?" he asked.

"We'll see."

He stood up. "Listen, Luce. Don't let guilt blind you on this." He headed for his car and drove away.

The nickname needed to go. He didn't know me well enough for that.

TEN

I'd just about fallen asleep on the couch with Mousecop in my lap when my buzzer sounded. I jumped, and the cat rolled off onto the cushion, staring lazily up at me.

"Who the hell?" I crossed my small living area and punched the intercom. "Yes?"

"It's Todd Beckett." The detective's sharp voice told me I was in for it. "We need to talk."

I hit the buzzer to allow Todd into the building and did my best to prepare myself. I'd done nothing wrong. Jenna, while she hadn't signed a contract, had given me verbal permission to investigate. And I'd turned all my information over to the police immediately instead of confronting Justin myself.

He banged on the door, and I quickly pulled it open, gesturing for him to come inside. Dark, slightly tattered trench coat trailing behind him, he marched inside. Mousecop bolted into the bedroom.

"I got your voicemail from this afternoon. You've heard about Justin's contact with Kailey. By snooping around at the school."

"You knew I would." I folded my arms across my chest,

planting my feet shoulder-width apart. Hell if I'd be submissive.
"I assumed you already knew, but I thought I should call you
anyway."

"You knew we already had the information. You just can't
stay out of the case."

"A child's life is at stake," I said. "I wasn't going to take the
risk. But I guess you've got your number one suspect, don't
you?"

His curled lips sent his mustache into his nostrils. "You'd
love that, wouldn't you?"

"I don't love any of this, Todd."

"Yeah, right." He snorted. "But just to make sure you're in
the loop and not gloating on the sidelines, we executed a search
warrant for Justin's an hour ago. No sign of Kailey. That
includes his vehicle."

"What about his job?" I didn't miss a beat.

"Ongoing search, but I don't think we'll find her."

I failed at keeping my expression neutral. "So what's his
story?"

"Some brat named Isaac was beating up on Kailey. Justin
stepped in, she latched on to him." Todd gave a sharp jerk of his
head. "Dumbass. He felt sorry for her. She doesn't have a dad,
needed a father figure. She wanted to come over and hang out,
he said no. But he agreed to email."

"And you believe that?"

"It checks out," Todd said. "Her mother confirmed the issue
with the kid, and so did Josie. As you know. And there's nothing
in her email or on her computer to indicate any wrongdoing on
Justin's part."

"Because he didn't have to register and his sentence is
considered complete, I suppose his contact with a minor won't
be further investigated?"

Todd sucked in his cheeks. "He served his time and is free

like anyone else. Unless he's done something wrong, his contact with a minor isn't an issue."

I threw my hands up. "You're telling me he's going to be able to walk away again? No responsibility for his contact with Kailey?"

"Not unless we get any real evidence that says he took her. Right now, every correspondence between them is benign."

Unbelievable. Tension rippled through my shoulders. I rolled my neck and forced myself to take deep breaths. "So what now?"

"I keep looking. You do whatever it is you do. I just wanted to make sure you understood Justin's situation is being handled."

"And you came here to personally tell me?"

Todd glanced around my little home, and I suddenly became aware of the two bottles of cyanide hidden deep in the walk-in closet.

"I don't know why I came here," he said. "Maybe I thought talking to you in person would help me get through to you."

The day's events weighed me down with the force of a piledriver, and I dropped onto the arm of my couch. "You're not going to convince me there's no chance Justin hasn't done this. And I'm not going to convince you he's still a threat to society. And neither one of us has the energy to argue."

The corner of his thin mouth lifted into a weary half-smile. "That's the truth. I'm exhausted."

"How's Jenna holding up?"

"Better than most people," he said. "She's by herself, though. No family's come to be with her. A couple of friends from work have been in and out, but as far as I know, no one else."

"I'm sorry she's alone." Jenna was lucky, in my opinion. Most friends and family who come to help in times of crisis never know what to say, and the person suffering ends up trying to make everyone else feel like they matter. *Unless you've got a mother who demands the attention be solely on her. Never mind the girl who's just found her sister dead in the bathroom.*

"Do you have any leads?" I asked, deciding to omit the obvious one.

"A couple of creeps in the neighborhood we're following up, but so far, there's nothing. No one saw her get into a vehicle with anyone. She just disappeared."

My throat tightened, and I asked the question I'd been thinking since I heard Kailey was missing. "Do you think she's still alive?"

Shadows passed through Todd's eyes, his tall frame seeming to wilt in front of me. "We have no reason to believe otherwise."

His tone said differently. I knew the statistics and so did Todd. After the first twenty-four hours, chances of finding a missing child alive plummet. I thought of Kailey's smiling face in her school picture, of the innocence shining in her eyes. I hadn't prayed in years, but I would pray for Kailey tonight.

Todd's stomach growled. "I need to get going. Get something to eat and sleep a few hours."

"I'd offer you something," I said as I got to my tired feet, "but there isn't much here. I forgot to go to the grocery store."

"I'm a bachelor. I'm used to fending for myself."

An awkward silence simmered. I noticed Todd's coat was buttoned up wrong, leaving a goofy-looking gap. "Let me just fix that for you."

He stiffened as I reached for his coat and fumbled with the button. "There." I patted his coat. "Now you look slightly less harried."

"Thanks." The planes of his face relaxed. His eyes misted over. "You did that once for me before, remember?"

I shook my head. "No, I don't."

"When Justin was arrested, you showed up at the house. You looked pale as a ghost. I remember your hair looking extra red against your skin, almost like you'd colored it. Your eyes looked like they were stuck wide open."

"I couldn't believe it." The words made my throat raw. "I never thought something like that would happen."

"I was sitting at the kitchen table. My dad and stepmom were with the police. You tried to talk to me."

The spark of memory flickered to life. I remembered Todd, slouched and glaring at me, acne spattered across his chin. He was too thin as a teenager, his metabolism barely able to keep up with his height. "You told me to go to hell, that this was all my fault. I should have saved Justin before he did something like this." I felt the tears welling in my eyes and quickly rubbed them before they fell.

"I'm sorry for that," Todd said. "I was an angry kid and looking for someone to blame."

"Do you know who hurt him?"

He looked at the floor, the lines in his forehead deepening. "Both of them did—my dad and stepmother. Verbally and physically. But I never saw them do anything sexual. I never thought..." His voice caught.

"You couldn't have," I said. "It's nature and nurture, and it's a shitty mess."

He grunted and then cleared his throat. "I told you to get lost that day, and you didn't push me. But you did fix my coat."

Laughter bubbled in my throat and escaped before I could stop it. "That's right. It was one of those fake leather things that buttoned up. You were so skinny you were swimming in it."

"Yeah, I was pretty nerdy." He raised his shoulders and then let them fall with a deep sigh. "So I'm sorry."

"Me too. I'm sorry I didn't see it."

"Like you said, no one could have." He turned for the door, clearing his throat. "You did do the right thing by reporting your information. Thanks for that. If you find out anything else—no matter what it is—call me right away. Kailey's got to be our priority."

"I will, and for what it's worth, I hope you're right about Justin."

He smiled. "Goodnight, Lucy."

Some time after midnight, the shrill ring of my phone dragged me out of a troubled sleep. Sharp fear pierced my pounding heart; middle of the night calls only brought bad news. I didn't recognize the number.

"Hello?"

A moment of quiet, accompanied by quick, hushed breathing. "Um. Hi." The whisper belonged to a child. "Is this Lucy?"

I sat up. "Yes. Who is this?"

"It's Josie. Do you remember me? You gave me your card at my school."

Scrubbing the sleep out of my eyes, I stifled a yawn. "Yes, of course. Are you okay?"

"I'm not supposed to be on the phone."

"It's awfully late," I said. "You should be sleeping."

Josie sniffed. "Do you think they'll find Kailey?"

This poor child. She'd carry the guilt of Kailey's disappearance her entire life. "I hope so." I paused, wondering if I should push her. "Did you have any more information? Something you just thought of?"

"I never should've let Bridget talk me into going to the lot. That place is horrible." Josie sucked in a shaky breath. "I hate it."

"We all make bad decisions," I said. "What happened to Kailey isn't your fault."

"I didn't want to go." Josie's whisper splintered into a hushed sob. "I never want to go back there."

"You don't have to," I said.

"I don't want to go to school, either. But my mom is making me."

This is the part of CPS I missed: comforting the kids, letting them know that no matter what terrible things are in their lives, I'll be there for them. "Why don't you want to go to school? Are the other kids mad at you? If anyone's giving you a hard time about Kailey, go to the principal. That's not okay."

"They're not. It's just... I can't get away from it."

"You can't, but you can't run away," I said. "The best thing you can do is think positive thoughts for Kailey."

Josie hiccupped. "You know what he's doing to her. If she's still alive, I bet she wishes she was dead."

The sudden flatness in her voice sent an icy dagger of fear down my spine. "Josie, you can't think like that. We can't give up."

"It's how I would feel."

"Josie, have you talked to your parents about this? I bet they could find someone for you to help sort out your feelings—"

"I have to go."

The beep of my phone told me she'd ended the call. I sat it on the nightstand and lay back down, the hopelessness in Josie's voice embedding into my spirit. I knew it would accompany my dreams, providing the soundtrack for the fear that chased me at night.

I rolled over and grabbed my e-reader. Sleep isn't for the wicked.

Kenny called me at the crack of dawn. I managed to peel myself out of bed and meet him in Chestnut Hill, on the northwest side of the city. I grumbled at the drive, but Kenny was protective of his lucrative clientele and had no interest in being seen with a private investigator.

Although he's a small-time drug dealer specializing in marijuana and wary of anything resembling authority, Kenny's one of the best people I've ever known. He's the one link from my past I cherish.

By the time I arrived at Pastorius Park, the sun was truly breaking over the eastern sky, making the fall colors of the trees shimmer in reds and golds like some beautifully mixed-up rainbow. A few early risers had already brought their canine buddies out to play, and I watched a fat beagle chase a poodle in circles until Kenny knocked on my window.

I unlocked the door, and he jumped into the passenger seat, bringing with him the delicious, honey-sweet smell of hot donuts. I licked my lips.

"Goose!" He leaned over and pecked me on the cheek. "Old-fashioned chocolate donuts just for you." Kenny still called me by the same stupid nickname he gave me during our short months of dating in high school. The romance fizzled, but the friendship never wavered.

"Kenny G." I snagged a donut, moaning when the sugary goodness melted in my mouth.

He laughed at the old joke, and I noticed the laugh lines around his face had deepened. With his short, wavy hair gelled into an artful swirl, he looked more like a college kid than a drug dealer.

"So what's new?"

"Same old, same old," he said. Kenny was one of those rare people who never let anything get him down and managed to see life through magic glasses. "Working the day job, staying careful in my side business like I promised. I started volunteering at a shelter in Spring Garden, trying to help out some of the kids."

"Good for you," I said between mouthfuls of donut.

Kenny was an enigma. He made a living as a mechanic, but selling pot was too lucrative for him to give up. He insisted he'd retire early and move somewhere warm.

"So, you said you were searching for that little girl who disappeared out of Poplar?"

"Kailey Richardson."

"No news on her?"

A wave of tiredness rushed over me. "We know the older girls ditched her, and she walked home alone. Beyond that, nothing. She's vanished."

Kenny scowled. He had a soft spot for kids. His own father was a mean drunk, and he often said he wouldn't have made it through high school without me. "Doesn't that mean she probably knew the person who took her? Trusted them?"

"Maybe. It's hard to say."

"You said Justin Beckett might be involved. You think he took her?"

"I think he's a damned good suspect. But his brother's involved in the investigation. Claims to be unbiased but..." I spread my hands wide.

"Right." Kenny nodded. "What a shitty position to be in."

"Police did get a warrant after seeing the emails, and they came up empty. Have you heard anything?"

Kenny had amassed a pretty wide network as a dealer, his contacts stretching beyond Poplar and into the north and west sides of the city. He was the type of guy people wanted to confide all their secrets in. "None of my connections know him. I mean, some of them remember the coverage, but I asked all around, and no one remembered him."

It was a stretch. I couldn't hide my disappointment. "What about the other thing I asked you to check on? The Harrison brothers?"

Kenny started in on his second donut. "I told you about Cody a few months ago. He lived near one of my main clients, and he'd been released for molesting a girlfriend's kid. Soon as he got out, he found a new girl, with a kid the same age, of course. I called you about him, and you said you were going to send someone over." Kenny knew I still had contact with Child Protective Services, and he was good about giving me leads. He just didn't realize what I sometimes used them for.

"That's right." I played dumb. "I'd have to check with my old boss to see—"

"Don't bother. He overdosed a couple of months ago, not long after I called you. Good riddance, 'cause you know he was probably messing with that other kid."

Yes, he was. Cody Harrison fell into the dumb class of pedophiles, using his own IP address to post on a forum dedicated to the love between men and special little girls. His overdose had been a carefully administered dose of the newest synthetic heroin. Cody was already a user, although he'd been clean since his arrest. Selling him the drug had been risky, and I'd had to play along long enough to see him inject himself. I didn't wait around to see the overdose. Thankfully, my chemist had access to the good stuff, and I didn't have to make a return visit.

"So where does Cody Harrison fit?"

Kenny smiled grimly. "Heard his brother, Brian, is nearly as bad as Cody. And guess what? He moved into your little girl's section of Poplar just after Cody died. While back, got his ass beat by a neighbor who claimed Brian hassled the neighbor's thirteen-year-old daughter for sex. And get this, word has it he's a janitor at some elementary school. Apparently he's never had an offense, least not one that's on record. You'd think the school would be more careful."

I wanted to beat my head against the table, but I took a drink of hot coffee instead. It burned my throat. "Why didn't the neighbor go to the police?"

Kenny gave me a dubious look. "Same reason I don't, except he deals with harder stuff. Anyway, couple of weeks ago, Brian got smashed and bragged that he'd had some fun with a sweet, young thing at the vacant lot next to that big, old Catholic church on 7th. Immaculate something."

My heart skidded. "Our Lady of Immaculate Conception?"

Sly Lyle really had seen something. I'd have to swing by the lot to see if I could find him or Hank before I went home tonight.

My adrenaline bottomed out, leaving me hollow as Josie's words from last night echoed in my head. She didn't want to go to the vacant lot. Or school. If she were Kailey, she'd wish she were dead. She sounded like a jaded grown-up—which was how a victim of sexual abuse usually sounded.

Could Josie be the little girl Brian Harrison attacked in the vacant lot?

Familiar rage thrashed through my already racing blood. If I could prove Harrison's guilt, I'd add him to my list of cyanide suckers.

"That's it. His neighbor—the one who beat his ass—said he was acting all weird the other morning, same one your kid disappeared. I talked to his neighbor this morning before I came over. He and I run in the same circles, you could say. Harrison's car was in the driveway, but he never answered."

Kenny knew where Brian lived.

"What kind of car?" Kailey lived across the street from Justin. What if he wasn't the one being watched? What if someone was actually watching Kailey's routine?

"Blue Neon," Kenny laughed. "Girls' car."

So much for that idea. This was risky territory. Telling Todd meant answering questions about where I got my information. I could handle those, but if he interviewed Brian the janitor, he'd no doubt mention me and his brother. Todd had already voiced his suspicions of me. I couldn't take the risk of letting him talk to Brian. Not until I had better information.

I really am a piece of shit work. Brian might have Kailey—he certainly knew her from school. And I was thinking about my own hide. But Todd would need a search warrant, and that takes time. I had other means.

"Something else," Kenny said. "Word on the street is that Brian's been pretty volatile since his brother died. Shook him up pretty bad."

Something in Kenny's normally relaxed expression had changed—the faintest tightening around the eyes and mouth, a tighter set to his jaw. He was the only person who ever came close to understanding the anger I carried around, and if he ever found out my dark secret, he might understand. But I couldn't risk involving him. He deserved better.

My guard inched up. "That's tough to go through."

"He says his brother was clean. Only smoking pot since he got out. And he was afraid of anything but old-fashioned heroin, so he wouldn't have tried the synthetic stuff that killed him."

"Addicts do what they have to for the high."

"He also claims his brother bragged about meeting some hot redhead just days before he died." Kenny's words came a little slower, as if he were measuring them. His eyes stayed with mine. "Brian says his brother had a date the night he overdosed. He thinks the redhead gave him the bad shit. Maybe even intentionally."

I scrubbed my hands with the cheap paper napkins Kenny had brought. "Did he talk to the police?"

"Oh yeah. Told them about the redhead. But nothing was ever found. And by the time Brian made the accusation, Cody's house had already been cleaned, so any forensic evidence was gone. But he still says Red killed his brother. Says he'd know her if he saw her."

"Why?" I hoped my hands weren't shaking.

"Guess his brother took a picture with his cellphone and showed Brian. Picture was blurry and from the side—guess she didn't know he took it—but Brian thinks he could recognize her. That's another thing. Cody's cell was never recovered."

Jesus Christ. No, the cell was in the landfill under several tons of trash. Brian didn't have a copy of that picture or he would have gone to the police. But I needed to make sure, and I needed to find out if he had Kailey. And I sure as hell couldn't tell Todd about any of this right now.

"How far from Kailey does Brian Harrison live?"

"Other side of Poplar. Ten-minute walk, probably."

That meant Todd's canvassing would eventually get to Brian's neighbor, who would then tell Todd about the jerk who lived next door to him. Todd would talk to Brian, who would then rant about his brother's murder. But Kailey could be trapped in Harrison's house enduring unspeakable things.

"You think he could have taken her?" Kenny studied me with those eyes that always seemed to notice everything.

"It's definitely possible. Thanks so much for your help, Kenny G."

He didn't smile. "What are you going to do with the information this time?"

I didn't miss the emphasis Kenny put on the last two words, but I played it off. "I've got to let the investigating officer know, of course."

"Of course."

What I planned to do was hit the vacant lot and see if Sly Lyle was around. Maybe if I described Harrison, Lyle could confirm he was the one messing around with the little girl, or maybe he'd talked to Hank since Todd and I had been there. Hank hadn't put any stock in Sly's story, so he may not have called Todd.

"You didn't find out anything else about Brian Harrison, did you?"

Kenny shrugged. "Besides the janitor gig, he works part time at a garage. Need his address?"

"That would be great," I said. "Thanks again, Kenny. I can always count on you."

"You and me, Goose," he reminded me. "I probably would have killed the old man if you hadn't kept talking me down."

"You turned out all right," I said. "Just be careful out there, will you?"

He nodded. "You too. Whatever you do. And don't make hasty decisions you'll regret, Lucy." That same knowing look flashed through his eyes and then disappeared.

He rarely called me by my first name, and I knew, without a doubt, he guessed my secret.

ELEVEN

I preferred to work at night. Most of my extracurricular activities were done under the cover of darkness, and I was at home slinking around in the shadows. But for once, I was happy to be in broad daylight, even if it was cloudy as smoke and the wind chapped my face. Poplar wasn't exactly the hood, but any place where transients live and drug deals go down isn't safe for a woman at night.

Patrol cars drove up and down streets, still canvassing and still searching. I parked my car near the church and hoofed it down to the empty building Hank called home. My pepper spray was tucked into the coat sleeve of my dominant hand, and the weight of the cool plastic put my nerves on edge. I'd never had to use it, but the ominous silence in the chilly air made me feel like today might change that.

Up close, the vacant factory reminded me of Vlad's castle, its turret-like stacks reaching high into the cloudy sky. The broken windows were less eerie than the empty ones: great, gaping holes, the eyes of the beast waiting to consume me as another hopeless victim.

No more Gothic novels for me.

My chilled hands shook as I opened the doors. They announced my entrance with a groaning creak and a scraping of metal against the wood floors. So much for subterfuge. The stink I'd noticed yesterday was stronger, emboldened by the crisp, cold air. Clutching my flashlight, I edged forward.

"Who's there?" a gravelly voice called from the gray chasm.

"I'm looking for Sly Lyle." My voice came out garbled, as though I'd just eaten something. I cleared my throat. "Have you seen him?"

"You police?"

"No. I just need to ask him a question."

"Police ask questions."

"Well, I'm not the police."

The man grunted and went silent. To the right, a scuffle of paper and a heavy object sent my blood pounding. I slid the pepper spray canister out of my sleeve and into my tense hand.

"I just need to ask a few questions."

"I'll answer any question you got." The smoker's voice came from my left. I twisted around to see a tall, heavyset man emerging from the shadowy corner. He was dressed for warmth, wearing at least two layers and a wool cap. His beard was well maintained and his teeth in decent condition. He either hadn't been homeless long or was able to take care of himself. Another step closer, and I caught a whiff of bourbon.

I wished I had my flashlight. "Are you Lyle?"

"No. But you have questions. I've got answers."

"You don't even know what my questions are about."

"I still got answers." He came closer, his dark eyes sparkling like coals.

I held up the spray and steadied my voice. "I will burn your eyeballs."

"You got some pretty red hair. And skin. I bet you're a really clean lady. Shaved real nice. You shave down there, Red?"

I've dealt with enough angry and lewd drunken men to not

get rattled. "I'm not here to discuss hygiene, but thanks for the compliment. Have you seen Lyle around?"

"Lyle's a crazy schizo," my new suitor said. "And he's about as big as a junior high schooler. What do you want with him when you've got me?"

"Did you witness a man molesting a little girl two weeks ago?"

He stopped short, a look of shocked disgust on his face. "What the hell's wrong with you, lady?"

"I'm a private investigator, and I have questions for Lyle."

"Knew she was a cop!" the first man who'd blown me off yelled from the corner.

"He's not here." Hank's voice sent a spasm of relief down my spine. "Jimbo, leave her alone. She was here yesterday with the detective."

Hank came down the stairs, looking wobbly. "What are you doing back here, miss?" Hank said. "And alone too."

"I'm desperate," I said. "Remember what you said about Lyle's story? About the man and the little girl?"

"Yeah, but I told you—"

"A man who lives near here—and near the girl who's missing—bragged about something similar, around the same time Lyle claims he saw it. Do you remember anything he said or have any idea where I could find him?"

"He could be anywhere." Hank scratched his beard vigorously, and I callously wondered if he had fleas.

"Tell me exactly what he said."

"Shit, I don't know. I tried not to listen. I don't want to hear about that sort of thing."

"Please try."

"All right, all right. Let's see, it was around suppertime and on a Wednesday. I know because I was heading to the soup kitchen at the church. Lyle came in, looking green and gibbering. Said he saw a guy messing with a younger girl at the end of the lot, over in the weeds where there's a bunch of old iron and millwork. Same place where those kids go messing around. Guess they can get in there and hide." Hank coughed, harder than he had yesterday, and made his way to sit on the bottom stair.

"I said big deal, and he says, no, she weren't no of-age girl. Little girl. No more than twelve, maybe younger. Said she looked scared as hell, like she was frozen. Lyle claimed he ran the man off."

"What did the man look like, other than tall?" Brian Harrison was tall, but so were countless men. But he had very short, very blond hair, and fair skin that got patchy red when he was excited. Just like his brother. Swedish or Norwegian descent, apparently. "What color hair?"

"He didn't say."

"Is there anything—"

Hank waved me off. "He went on about how big the guy was. Looked like a construction worker type, but he was wearing a uniform. Dark, I think Sly said. He couldn't get the name on it—although it had red lettering, he said. Guy was too busy running from Sly like a bitch, face red as a tomato, for Sly to get the name."

My breath caught. Red face. His janitor's uniform was dark with red lettering. And Brian was a big man. "What about the girl? Did she have blonde hair? Brown? What color were her shoes?"

"I don't know. Sly just said she looked like a little girl."

That was good enough for me. Brian Harrison could have Kailey, and I needed to find out as soon as possible. If he didn't have Kailey, he might have attacked Josie, although I had little proof of that. Just instinct. Not to mention he could possibly identify me as his brother's killer.

I thanked Hank for his information, gave him a ten-dollar bill, the only cash I had, promised to stay away from the bad neighborhood, and hurried toward my car. Conflicting emotions raced through me. I couldn't put myself entirely first. I'd go straight to Brian Harrison's and find out for myself if he had Kailey. If I didn't turn anything up, I'd have to tell Todd we might have another suspect and pray I didn't pay the price.

But what if he did have Kailey, and I caught him in the act? My brand of justice was black and white, an eye for an eye. I'd have to stop at home and get the cyanide.

I'd almost made it back to my car when I saw Todd Beckett hoofing toward me like a wayward steam engine.

"What are you doing back here?"

I pushed the hair out of my face and dropped the pepper spray back into my pocket. "Thought I might find Sly Lyle. See if there's any truth to his story."

"Is your ego really that big? You think I can't do my job? That we're all a bunch of flailing idiots?"

"Of course not," I said. "I just wanted to help. I was at home, I couldn't settle down. I thought maybe if Lyle were here, I could convince him to talk. That's all. I know you're overloaded and doing everything you can."

He half-extended his arms, looking like he wanted to shake me.

"Look, I'm an overbearing pain in the ass, and I'm sorry."

He shook his head, gritting his teeth. "You have got to stop interfering. You're going to get yourself in trouble."

"You know I just want to help."

"Because you think I can't be impartial with Justin."

Right now, Justin wasn't my only issue. "We've already discussed that. I'm sorry I couldn't help him." A gust of wind rushed over both of us, and I shivered. "Because of that, I couldn't help his victim either. So if Kailey was taken—"

"I don't care."

"Excuse me?"

"This isn't about you, Lucy. Or my brother. It's about a

missing kid, and I don't get to have tunnel vision. I have to be objective, even if one of the persons of interest is my brother. I don't think he'd do it, but I can't risk a child's life and look the other way. So I've got to suck it up and do my job, and I can deal with that." Todd squared his shoulders and looked down at me with cold eyes. "What I *won't* deal with is a guilt-stricken, miserable former CPS worker-turned-private investigator trying to make a difference by sticking her nose into things she isn't qualified for."

Anger coursed through me, in part because he was right, but mostly because I didn't dare argue. "I'm not here because of your brother."

Todd sighed like I was the dimmest light bulb in the box. "No, but you're bumbling around here, leaving more physical evidence that might have to be sifted through. And what if you'd been attacked? Then I would have to stretch my resources thin and away from the Richardson girl while we dealt with your assault or God knows what else. You see how selfish your help is?"

"I'm sorry," was all I could muster. He was right. Here I was, risking my own life, not just to find Kailey but to cover my own ass. I didn't see any other course of action. I couldn't help anyone from prison. *And I'll be damned if I'd go to jail over the likes of the Harrisons.* "I just want Kailey to be found."

"Then let the police do our job." He closed his eyes. "I still think you're way too close to this. There sure as hell is something you aren't telling me."

I tried not to grimace at the swarm of nerves in my stomach. "What are you getting at?"

He opened his eyes, lips pressed into a line so tight they disappeared beneath his mustache. "The whole neighborhood knows my brother's got a record. Now he can't go back to his home."

Good. "You don't expect me to feel sorry for him, do you? Where's he staying? Do you know where he is?"

He flinched, looking over my head at the old factory. "That's none of your business."

So he was out roaming the streets, possibly having taken Kailey, and Todd didn't know where he was?

"I know what you're thinking, and it's not like that. I know where he's at. I'm just not telling you."

I didn't believe him, but I didn't have time to debate. "I hope so." I stepped to move around him, and he caught my arm.

"How do I know you didn't plan all this? Steal Kailey, expose Justin, and then she suddenly turns back up?"

No, no, no. He couldn't go down that rabbit hole. "You've got to be a better cop than that."

"I am a good cop. That's why I know you're up to more than just finding Kailey." He came nose to nose with me. "What if I searched your apartment? What would I find?"

Hopefully not my cubbyholes. "You were there last night. You saw my life is pathetically boring. Feel free."

"Keep this shit up, and I might."

I wanted to point out how that would detract resources from Kailey, but I didn't dare. "I'm sorry for interfering." I pulled free of him and headed for my car.

"I don't want to see you around the neighborhood again. You get me?"

"Absolutely." I slid into the car, started the engine, and drove out of the lot.

I'd been lying, of course.

I was headed for Brian Harrison's, and I decided I needed help.

TWELVE

Chris wanted to drive, but I refused. I needed the control. In my economical Prius, his knees were nearly at eye level with his chin, but he didn't complain. I parked across the street from Harrison's duplex. I hoped Chris would come in handy during my search, and if Harrison did have Kailey, I had no idea if he worked alone. Cyanide was a fast-acting weapon, but not faster than a bullet. Plus, I figured this was a good test for Chris.

"So you really think Harrison could be the guy instead of Justin?" He peered over my shoulder at the plain duplex.

"I don't know, but I've got to find out." Truth was, I wasn't sure Harrison had Kailey. It didn't feel right. Sly Lyle had described the girl as twelve, maybe younger. There's a large physical difference between a nine- and a twelve-year-old girl, especially if the latter's hit puberty. And Kailey was small for her age. The neighbor girl Harrison had been accused of bothering was thirteen. If I had to make an armchair guess, he was into pubescent girls like Josie, and Kailey wasn't his type. But I couldn't take the risk. And I was too selfish not to check things out for myself. If I could save my own hide in this, so be it.

"And you can find out what kind of information Brian Harrison has on you," Chris said.

"That too. But Kailey's first priority."

"If he does have her, what are you going to say to Todd? You just happened to have a key and stumbled on her?"

"I'll worry about that if it happens."

He flopped back into his seat. "So who's your informant?"

"Can't tell you that."

"Does he know you kill people?"

His putting it out there so bluntly made it sound harsh, as though I were of the same ilk as a serial killer. "He's never mentioned it."

"Good. Plausible deniability."

I rolled my eyes. "Spoken like a lawyer's relative."

"Comes in handy sometimes."

"What, does your uncle keep your nose clean? Have the cops looking the other way while you clean up the garbage, as you put it?" I didn't believe he'd killed anyone in his life, but he was a paramedic with an exorbitant lifestyle, so I had to believe his wealthy family gave him a second income. Guessing his uncle put the pressure on local police to keep his nephew out of trouble wasn't that much of a stretch.

"Never needed to." He flashed me a grin. "I don't get caught."

He had the kind of cockiness brought on by one of two things: not getting caught, just as he'd said, or never taking any risks and pretending his deep thoughts and plans accounted for something. I was pretty sure it was the latter.

My phone beeped with a text from Kenny. He'd just confirmed Harrison's car was in the Kipling Elementary parking lot. "Let's move."

I led the way across the street, head up, confident but not drawing attention. People in this neighborhood usually didn't bother with anyone else's business. None of them wanted additional trouble. A baseball cap he'd retrieved from his car pulled low, Chris followed behind, hands in his pockets. If he was nervous, he didn't act like it. The duplex was standard with tan siding that needed washing and brown shutters. Nothing on the shared concrete slab of a porch evoked a homey feeling. The neighbor hadn't picked up his paper.

I knocked, waited a full thirty seconds, and then got down to business. Lock picking is an art, but once you've got the hang of it and with the right tools, it's easy work. I had the cheap standard lock open in seconds. Behind me, Chris tensed. The only safety precaution I'd brought was pepper spray; I didn't plan on killing anyone unless it was self-defense. Easing the door open, my heartbeat thrummed in my ears. I'd been told Harrison lived alone and didn't have a pet, but I never knew. A roommate I could handle. A snarling Doberman, not so much.

Only stale silence greeted us. We slipped into the place and locked the door. I checked my watch. Twelve minutes. The flickering street light seeped in around Harrison's cheap, plastic blinds revealing a lonely looking living room. Worn, neutral-colored carpet, a very tattered and stained blue sofa, and a well-loved faux-leather recliner. A large flat-screen television and several gaming consoles dominated the room.

I motioned for Chris to check upstairs. Nerves mottled his skin in pink dots, and a thin sheen of sweat on his forehead gave his virginity away. *He's never done an illegal thing in his life.* Quietly and systematically, I checked the small downstairs. Closet, nothing. Kitchen, a sink full of dishes, but nothing. Refrigerator full of beer. No milk. No snacks for a child. No sign of a child, no telltale scent of fear, no whimpering. Bathroom, extremely dirty and nothing of consequence.

I went back to the television. Harrison had a stack of DVDs, several of them standard pornography. All of the discs matched their covers, but none looked very used. Probably for show. No sign of his computer downstairs, so I hurried to the second floor.

Chris was already in the second bedroom, which looked more like a storage shed. My stomach clenched as I recognized items from Cody Harrison's apartment: a lewd poster of a naked woman on a motorcycle, legs spread; a creepy-looking bong in the shape of a caterpillar; and—my heart stopped—the Dell laptop that had sat in Cody's living room. I picked it up. I'd gotten rid of the phone, but it was possible Cody had the picture on this laptop. It would be days if not weeks before his brother missed it.

"I don't think that's his computer," Chris said. "It's in the bedroom."

"It's not. But I need it. Did you try Brian's computer?"

He nodded. "Password protected."

Figures. Kelly hadn't been able to find an email for Brian Harrison, but the laptop I had might solve that problem. Surely the brothers had emailed.

"Why do you need that?"

"This is his brother's computer. It might have Brian Harrison's email, and my hacker can use it to send a picture embedded with a program that will give us remote access to his desktop. If he'd been stalking Kailey or any other girls, we might find evidence there."

"And your picture might be on there."

I brushed past Chris, quickly eyed the other bedroom. No sign a child—or a woman or a cleaning person, for that matter— had ever been here, just as I suspected.

"There's nothing here. We need to go."

A text from Kenny. "Harrison just drove away."

I stuffed the laptop inside my coat, grateful I'd thought to bring it, and hurried down the stairs. Chris had the sense not to question me. We slipped quietly out of the house, locked the door, and then ran across the street to the car. Inside. Laptop in the backseat. Driving away. Passed a blue Neon, nerves in my throat.

I didn't breathe until we were several blocks away with no sign of the Neon on us.

Chris finally broke his silence. "So Brian's a pedophile, too? Like his brother?"

"Sometimes it runs in families, especially if they're indoctrinated young." That's the story the dead Harrison brother had given to the police when he was first arrested. That his uncle molested him and ruined him for life. I didn't know if it was true, and while the cycle of abuse is very real, it's also something pedophiles like to lie about. Only a very small percentage of people who are sexually abused go on to repeat the pattern. Most pedophiles are just born with something horribly out of whack inside their heads.

"It doesn't look like he's got Kailey. At least not at his place."

Chris glanced at the laptop now sitting safely in the backseat. Hopefully Kelly had a charger, and hopefully the damned thing's hard drive wasn't shot. I knew Kelly had near magical ways of salvaging information, but I didn't understand the process and didn't like waiting for it. But if she found evidence of Brian molesting girls, I'd be able to get rid of him without any additional guilt about saving my own ass.

"Do you consider it noble?" he finally asked when I parked next to his Audi.

"I'm sorry?"

He faced me, eyebrows knitted together, his nose crinkled. "What you do, do you consider it noble? Don't get me wrong, I get it. I support it. These perverts aren't going to stop hurting kids and should be put down. If the system won't do it, then might as well be you. But do you ever think about your own fate?"

"I don't plan on going to jail."

"I don't mean that. I'm not trying to get all existential on you." He talked with his hands, waving them in front of his face in a circular motion. "I don't sit around pondering the meaning of life and why humans are the way we are. But I do think about cause and effect, action and reaction."

I wished he'd stop making me think so hard. Focusing on only the task at hand was so much easier. "I'm not following you. Are you asking about my soul?"

He laughed. "Nah. I'm not sure I really believe in that stuff. I just... something like this, your calling, if that's what it is, you know it won't end well, right? People who go down your road don't get to step off, at least not without major consequences." He leaned on the center console as if he were spilling a dark secret. "Maybe you'll get arrested someday. Or maybe some pissed-off family member will catch you. Or you'll screw up and dump cyanide on yourself. Whatever it is, there's no happy ending for you, is there?" He paused, glancing down at his hands and then back at me, a sad, resigned smile on his face. "You don't get to just walk away."

A stinging rawness, like I'd breathed in bleach, built in my chest and left me struggling for a response. After every eradication, I'd take a scalding hot shower as if that would somehow cleanse my sins, followed by single shot of bourbon, making sure my stomach matched the heat of my flesh. Those nights, I never remembered my dreams, and I never wanted to, because they all ended the same way: being consumed by nothingness with no meaning left behind.

"I'm aware," I finally addressed Chris. "Nothing you're saying is anything I haven't thought a thousand times." Speaking helped my head to clear. "And of course, I assume you go through the same thing?"

"What?"

"Being like me, as you say. I assume you've asked yourself the very same questions." The malignant tone I used made me feel powerful and only slightly ashamed.

Chris's smile was forced. "Right."

He opened the door, and I took a deep breath for the first

time in what seemed like hours. "Let me know if you get anything off the laptop. Or if you need any more help searching for Kailey."

He shut the door without waiting for my response, and I wondered if I'd ever hear from him again.

Stupidly, I hoped I did.

THIRTEEN

My sister's lifeless body lay on the bathroom floor, arms and legs stretched out as if she'd started to make a snow angel. Her glassy, vacant eyes faced the tub. Blood pooled beneath her body, trickling down the uneven tile and sitting in the grout like tiny crimson streams. I screamed her name again and again, but she never stirred. Never took a breath. How could she? Long, vertical gashes on both wrists had drained her life away.

Death was real. It wasn't some terrible thing that happened to other people, to be discussed in whispers. My sister didn't live forever, and neither would I. All the vibrancy of her life—both good and bad—now stained my mother's white tiles. As I stared at my sister's corpse, the brightness of the blood dimmed. I no longer saw the bluish tinge on her slack mouth. I saw only her eyes. And they saw nothing. One day, I would see nothing too. How would I look in death?

I'd never know. I'd never see myself again. Never talk to anyone again. As terrible as if the corpse itself reached for me, I suddenly grasped the true meaning of death. I understood its harsh reality, understood that I would simply end as if I'd never been here. Buried in the ground, cold and stiff and nothing.

I woke up screaming. Mousecop flew off the bed and skittered across the floor. Heart throbbing in my head until I thought my skull would explode, I gasped for air. The nightmare wasn't new, and it wasn't even a nightmare. More of a memory with high definition to enhance the viewing experience.

You're not dead now. You've got a long life to live. You're making a difference. I chanted the words that had become my refuge over the years. Taking deep breaths, I searched for the positive things in my life, for the happy place to help me stop shaking.

As my heart rate slowed and the protective layer of my brain dimmed the real truth of death, hypocrisy took fear's place. Five times now, I'd served as judge, jury, and executioner of the thing I feared most. I didn't watch my marks die because I couldn't. I couldn't stand the idea of watching their eyes slip into the void.

Enough. I needed to sleep, and this was an old battle I'd never win. So I'd die someday. In the meantime, I'd do everything I could to make a difference in this world.

Kelly didn't have a charger for the old Dell, but she did know how to take it apart and get the information from the hard drive. With some luck, she'd find out if Cody Harrison had the photo of me and, more importantly, what his email address was. Not that I expected to find any evidence of Kailey. But I might be able to figure out who he'd molested, if the story were true, and how to get the girl some help.

Saturday dawned bright and cool, with the last vestiges of leaves shivering their way to the ground. Todd refused to answer his phone, likely screening his calls, and the only information I had on the search for Kailey were the snippets Kelly gleaned from her sources. I needed to check in with Jenna Richardson, so I drove into Poplar where every inch of the neighborhood had been searched by police, but volunteers were still meeting, going door to door, combing through the thicket of woods thin enough to see through on a sunny day. Fliers of a smiling, gap-toothed Kailey now decorated every light pole and fluttered in most windows. In the business district, a group of women stood in front of the nail salon, handing out fliers to everyone who passed.

From what I could see, Jenna Richardson wasn't taking part in the search. I supposed she was home, manning the phones. Not all that unusual, but with no ransom by now and Jenna being on the high side of lower class, this wasn't about money. And Kailey wasn't going to suddenly call with directions to her location.

My eyes strayed to Justin Beckett's house, and I realized why Todd wasn't taking my calls.

Some ballsy artist had spray-painted the words "CHILD KILLER" across the peeling paint in an ugly, neon green shade that stuck out like a clown at a funeral. A window had been broken, presumably by a rock, and hastily covered with what looked like a black trash bag. Justin's car wasn't in the driveway. I hoped Todd really did know where he was.

A tiny prick of guilt needled at me. If Justin hadn't taken the girl... but it didn't matter. These people deserved to know who lived among them.

I'd been right about the lack of uniforms. Jenna's building was unguarded, but I still needed her to buzz me in. It took her a moment to remember who I was.

"I can't pay you," she said.

"It's pro bono, I promise."

"Do you think Justin Beckett took my daughter?" The desperation in her voice was heartbreaking.

I debated, wondering how much information Todd had

shared with her. "I think he's a valid suspect, and I and the police are looking at every possible scenario."

"He emailed her." Her shrill voice coming through the intercom reminded me of a dying rabbit I'd heard as a child after a neighbor's dog attacked it.

"I know he did," I said. "Search warrants were issued, and to my understanding, no more evidence has been found."

"Detective Beckett said his brother stepped in when Kailey was being bullied and became a friend. I looked at the emails." She stopped for a sharp breath. "He sounded nice. And she sounded so lonely. Why didn't she tell me?"

"Kids are perceptive," I said. "Maybe Kailey knew you had enough on your plate as a single mom and didn't want to stress you out."

This time, instead of the screech, her voice came out as a baby's whimper. "I would have helped her."

I choked back the urge to cry. "I know you would have. Could I come up for a few minutes?"

The buzzer signaled permission for me to enter.

Jenna didn't bother with a greeting or the standard, superfluous beverage offer. She looked at me through tired eyes. "What do you want to know? And what could you possibly do that the police can't?"

Break the law to find out if Justin Beckett's taken your daughter. "As I said, I have a lot of contacts in the city. I still keep in touch with some of the children I've worked with and their families. It gives me a network to reach out to. I don't know if it will do any good, but it can't possibly hurt, can it?"

She ran her hands through her hair, hanging limp around her heart-shaped face. Her tanned skin had turned the color of the almond milk my mother loved to drink. The neatly trimmed nails had been ferociously chewed to jagged edges and pink fingertips that looked as fragile as a newborn's. She sat cross-legged on the couch, clutching a soft and well-loved-looking teddy bear. I assumed it was Kailey's.

"Tell me about her," I said.

Jenna's lips pursed with the effort of holding back tears, making her look as though she'd had a sudden Botox injection. "She's a good little girl. Smart. Easy. We're close." The lips wobbled, and she sucked in air hard enough it whistled. For some reason, that noise cut through me deeper than a tear could have. I clenched my own jaw. "She always said I was her best friend."

"Josie and Bridget," I started.

"I trusted those girls." Jenna's grief switched to powerful anger faster than I could register. "If they hadn't left Kailey to walk home alone, this wouldn't have happened. How could they be so stupid and selfish?"

"They're children," I said. "And they don't think about the consequences. No matter how much we drill into their brains that there are bad people out there, kids have this weird sort of shield that convinces them we're overprotective and that nothing like this could happen to them."

"They let her walk by herself." She spit the words as though they were laced with burned coffee.

"They did. And I'm sure both of them feel terrible, but do you realize that statistically, Kailey was probably taken by someone she knew? If not, then someone in a position of authority?"

Jenna's jaw set hard, and she looked past me, eyes half-glazed over, like she was caught in a memory. "Sometimes statistics are wrong."

"Still," I continued, "I'm not sure you can put the blame on Josie and Bridget. If Kailey's abductor falls into either of those categories, they would have found a way, sooner or later."

"Detective Beckett said it could have been random." She seemed desperate to believe that.

"And it could have been," I said. "There's no way to know right now, and blaming the girls is only going to make you feel worse."

"I can't possibly feel worse." Her washed-out face twisted to ugly, tear-stained rage. "My child is gone. I don't know if she's alive or dead. I'd rather hear she was dead than sit in this limbo every day, waiting. And if she's alive, being tortured... I can't bear to know she went through that." She buried her head in her hands and sobbed.

I probably should have gone to her, but she struck me as defensive. Not in the sense that she was guilty, but that she had a personal space issue. Reaching out would probably make her feel worse. "Jenna, is there anyone I can call?"

"No. My parents are gone. No close family."

"Is Richardson your maiden name?"

She jerked as if I'd stung her. "Excuse me?"

"Sorry, I just meant, what about Kailey's father? Were you married at one time? Is he in the picture at all?"

"No, he's not. My name is Richardson." Clearly, that subject was taboo and closed to me. I'm sure Todd was looking into the father, but the father's swooping in and taking the kid didn't feel right, either.

"You haven't seen anyone odd in the neighborhood? No one doing anything that made you feel uneasy?"

She started gnawing on what was left of her thumbnail. "A few of us have noticed a black car driving down this street. Its windows are tinted, so we can't make out the driver. But it usually happens at night. When the kids are in bed. So no one knew what to think. It does slow down in front of this building, though. At least according to my babysitter. Of course, now that she knows about the child killer across the street, she's sure someone was checking on him."

I thought back to Todd's accusation that I was following Justin. I'd figured the kid's guilt made him paranoid, but now I wondered who else knew about his past. Why else would they be checking on him? Or perhaps they were looking for Kailey all along, scoping out Jenna's schedule, but the late drive-bys didn't add much credence to that idea.

"When did this happen?"

"In the last few weeks, I think."

"Was Kailey a leader or a follower?"

Jenna attempted something that resembled a smile. "She liked for everyone to get along. She used to come home with stories about how she mediated arguments between classmates. They're already forming little cliques at this age."

"I know, believe me." My best friend in kindergarten had been as shy and awkward as I. I thought we'd be buddies forever, but the next year, we were put into a different class, and one of her new friends didn't like me. That was the end of that.

My eyes drifted to the pictures on the side table. Several showed Kailey at an indoor pool, hair dripping wet and smiling wide. "Is Kailey a swimmer?"

"She loves it. Took lessons over the summer and did really well. I was thinking about putting her on a local team, but it's really expensive. Still, she wanted to. And it would be good for her. Less expensive than dance." Jenna reverted back to fighting tears. "She wanted pink ballet shoes."

I thought of the bright pink shoes Kailey wore when she disappeared, and a vision of my sister Lily attacked, razor-sharp in its clarity. Lily had a pair of pink jelly shoes, and I always hated them. But Lily was just the opposite, and she wore those shoes that whole summer. The strap broke the day before school started, and she cried for an hour. My mother teased her.

"My sister was the same way about pink."

"Was?" Jenna asked.

"She died when I was eleven."

"Was she... taken?"

"No. But she was molested, and that led her to a very bad choice." I assumed from Jenna's sad nod she got the message.

"I'm sorry."

"Thank you." Taking condolences from a woman whose child was missing made me feel like I'd bathed in garbage. "So there's no boyfriend for you? No circle of adults Kailey might trust?"

"No. Her babysitter and parents of friends. I work a lot of hours, and my work friends stay at work. I don't really socialize. Kailey's my social life."

All of which Todd would check out, just like he'd turn Kailey's routine inside out. I was starting to wonder what I was really doing here. Any names Jenna gave me would go through the system with Todd. He probably had more access to records than I did, especially if he got the FBI involved. Had I just been nosing around, trying to test Jenna Richardson? I didn't believe for a moment she had anything to do with her daughter's disappearance. Nothing about her pain seemed manufactured. And yet, as I watched her, I was hit with the distinct feeling there was more to her story. Not the lack of socializing—she was a single mom who worked a lot.

Did she really have no family? Literally no relative or close friend to come sit with her? That in itself seemed odd. Not suspect-odd, but just... odd.

Jenna's eyes had gone glassy again, as if she were caught in some haze of memory that wouldn't release her. She drew her knees to her chin, the friction of the couch pulling her right sock down. I saw a distinct scar made by something tight and likely metal, perhaps a handcuff or wire. Judging from its color, it wasn't recent. She rubbed it absentmindedly. All at once, I knew there was something very dark in Jenna's past, and I felt like an intruder trying to break through her protective walls.

She didn't seem bothered that I didn't ask for names to check or details about Kailey's routine life. She'd almost gone catatonic, still rubbing the scar. Her goodbye was barely audible.

Outside, my shivers had little to do with the temperature.

I called Todd without pausing to think of his reaction.

"What?" His caller ID apparently worked.

"Are you checking into Jenna Richardson's past?"

A beat of silence. Then the outburst. "Are you kidding me?"

"I stopped by and saw something on her ankle. I'm not questioning your investigation. I just want you to know. It looks like a scar, almost as though it were from some sort of bondage. It's not a recent scar, and maybe it's from when she was younger, but it bugged me. She sat there, half out of it and rubbing that scar, and I'm telling you, Todd, something happened to that woman. I don't know if Kailey's disappearance is related, but I had to tell you."

I braced myself for the lecture about going behind his back and being in the neighborhood. He sighed. "Thanks for the information. I'll check into it. Have you seen my brother's place?"

"I have."

"Good. Now leave." He ended the call.

I texted Kelly and asked her to dig into Jenna Richardson's background to see if she could find anything useful. I couldn't put my finger on it, but instinct demanded that Jenna's past was important.

An idea ghosting around the recesses of my mind finally took shape. What if Todd had it partially right, and someone else with a grudge against Justin re-conned the area and then took Kailey to set Justin up? I wasn't the only one with a grudge against him. And the family I was thinking of drove a black car.

FOURTEEN

Jonelle and Frank Smith lived in Havertown, a nice residential area about twenty minutes west of Greater Philadelphia. They'd moved to Havertown after Justin murdered their daughter, determined to protect their younger children—fraternal twins—from the perils of the city. The twins didn't remember their older sister Layla very well.

I hadn't seen the Smiths since Justin's release a year and a half ago, although we'd spoken on the phone a few times. Both had been crushed, but resolute. Frank was more prone to forgiveness, while Jonelle would have locked Justin in solitary for the rest of his life.

On this sunny and cold fall afternoon, the Smiths' son—Braydon, I think his name was—played basketball in the driveway with friends. He was sixteen and all gangly limbs, with spotty acne on his cheeks and features that seemed too out of place: sharp jaw; a long, equine nose; and wide, Grecian eyes. Another ten years, and he'd probably be gorgeous. An equally long-limbed girl sat on the edge of a black, four-door sedan, watching the boys play. Brandie fared only slightly better in the looks department than her twin brother, and she'd probably never be a beauty.

She watched me park in front of the house, sliding off the black car I thought might be following Justin. With the gait of a lazy horse, she strode into the house. The four boys in the driveway eyed my approach, their shuffling stance and shifting eyes and chin-rubbing and chest-jutting reeking of teenage hormones. I smiled, and the boy next to Braydon grinned back. Another one waved shyly; the third looked at his shoes. Braydon's dark scowl reminded me the twins lived in the shadow of their dead sister, and I'd just doubled its size.

Jonelle greeted me at the door as Brandie brushed past in a cloud of heavy perfume. I wondered which boy she had her eye on.

Part Italian and self-professed foodie, Jonelle was round in her middle age, doughy in the center and plump in the face. Her children had inherited her angular features, but they looked better on her, most likely because of the extra flesh to soften them. I'd always wondered what Jonelle was like before her oldest daughter's murder. Ever since I'd known her, she was edgy, controlled, but always on the verge of some sort of emotional outburst. She'd probably been boisterous and funny before her daughter's murder.

"Lucy, it's good to see you, although your call did surprise me."

"Sorry about that, but it's important."

She sat down at the dining-room table. As always, Jonelle's house was as clean as a doctor's office. My gaze crept to the fireplace. Layla's last school picture was placed prominently with current ones of the twins. A chill slithered down my spine.

"You said it had something to do with that boy." She never said Justin's name.

"Yes. Is Frank here?"

"Out of town on business."

"Is the black car outside his?"

Jonelle's thin, black eyebrows knitted together. "What? No. It's my old vehicle, but the twins share it now."

"Sorry." I'd practiced my questions on the drive, but every one of them seemed to have evaporated. I took a deep breath. "An eight-year-old girl living across from Justin Beckett disappeared yesterday morning."

Jonelle went still.

"Now, police have nothing solid on him. But he's a person of interest as far as I'm concerned."

Jonelle looked like she'd eaten something rotten. "Do the girl's parents know who he is? What about the rest of the neighborhood?"

"They do now, yes."

"I'm going to the newspapers. This is outrageous."

"You can't, please. Not yet." Was I telling her this to protect my own ass from Todd or because I really wasn't sure of Justin's involvement?

"Why?"

"Because the police are trying to keep it out of the newspapers, and right now, that's best for Kailey," I said. "If the word gets out where he lives, people will be all over, and that could destroy potential evidence."

"We knew this would happen." Jonelle's anger boomed through the house. She began to pace, shoving a dining-room chair out of the way. "Didn't I say it? Didn't you? Maybe now this liberal city will listen, letting a baby killer out on the streets to do it again."

I snatched back control of the conversation. "A black car has been seen on Justin's street for the past three weeks. It slows down, as if the driver is watching or looking for someone. This happens well after the kids go to bed, so the assumption is an adult is the target. Some think that target is Justin."

Jonelle narrowed her eye—yes, just one. I never quite knew

how she did that, but the effect was startling. Her entire face was thrown off balance. "Is that why you asked about my car?"

"Look, Jonelle. You know how I feel about Justin. I was sick when he was released. I understand the need for revenge, for wanting to make an example."

"An example?"

"Of Justin. And the system. To show them exactly how bad their decision was."

"What are you accusing me of?" Her lowered voice somehow managed to carry more force than her shouts.

"I don't know. The lead investigator thinks I might have been following Justin, going so far as to suggest I'd snatch the little girl—Kailey—to get revenge, and to get Justin off the streets."

"Did you?"

"No." I paused a beat. "Did you?"

I'd taken a risk, but Jonelle once scolded me for beating around the bush like a manic rabbit. Her words, not mine. She glared at me, both eyes now narrowed, her thin lips drawn tightly over her teeth and jaw sticking out. She looked briefly like she wanted to leap across the table at me, and then she exhaled.

"No. I wouldn't put a child through that."

Relief rushed through me. "I didn't think so, but I knew you guys had a black vehicle, and I had to ask." I slouched in the chair, a torn piece of wicker poking me in the shoulder. "She's just... gone."

"Did she know that boy?"

"She'd spoken to him, yeah."

Jonelle's chin stuck out. "He's done it, you know he has."

I asked the question that had been tumbling around in my head. "Do you remember him, before all of this happened?"

"Why?"

"I don't know, honestly. But I just feel like it's important."

Probably because I always felt I must have missed something about Justin, some warning sign that he was violent. A thought niggled at me, whispering in Chris's voice.

You're being selfish. This is about you as much as it is Kailey.

"He and Layla were classmates. And friends. You know that. She always wanted him to come over."

"Did he?"

"Every once in a while, but I got the impression his mother didn't like it." Jonelle flopped into the chair, her vigor giving way to exhaustion. "Layla wasn't supposed to be in their house because his father was a drunk. I don't think she was welcome. Martha Beckett wasn't very hospitable. Never socialized, really. Rarely said hello. Layla didn't like her. No one did."

"She was a strange woman," I said. "And she certainly didn't want me talking to her son. Then again, no parent wants CPS coming in. But what about Justin? Were there any signs of violence from him?"

"You know there weren't. He was quiet, observant. He used to watch Layla with us and look almost confused. I always wondered if he ever saw any real sort of affection." Her face went slack, her skin suddenly looking weathered. "You think that's why he did it? Because he was jealous of her relationship with us? He sexually assaulted her. Why? I never understood that. Or any of it. Why didn't he ever tell anyone why he killed my daughter?"

"I don't know." We'd had this conversation so many times. The answer resided in Justin's impenetrable head. I found myself again wondering what the hell I was doing here. "I'm not sure he even knows."

"I can't believe he's living over there in Poplar, no one knowing what he's done." The corner of her mouth twisted in a vengeful sort of smile. "I guess they know now, though."

A quick jolt of energy flicked through me. "I never told you he lived in Poplar. How did you know that?"

"I..."

"Jonelle, is it you?"

"I didn't take that girl!"

"I don't think you did." She wasn't that good of a liar. "But are you the one driving around Poplar, checking up on Justin?"

"No. If I went near him, I wouldn't be able to keep my hands off his neck."

"Then how did you know where he lived?"

"I heard about the girl on the news, Lucy." Jonelle ducked her head, messing with the hem of her shirt. "Kailey Richardson, missing from Poplar since yesterday afternoon. When you called her Kailey a few minutes ago, I put two and two together."

That sounded like a load of bull. "What about Frank?"

She actually laughed, but the sound was rough, a pseudo-smoker's cough. Anger coated her lungs, not nicotine. "That man wouldn't have the cajones to do anything like this. He thinks we should forgive that boy and consider what must have happened to him to make him do such a terrible thing. As if I could forgive him!" She slammed a meaty fist on the table, fat tears welling in her eyes.

Fatigue washed over me. This woman's pain, Jenna's pain, my own memories. I was sick of wallowing in death and despair. "Can I use your bathroom?"

"Down the hall." She pointed. "Last door on the right."

"Thanks." On my way, I glanced into the open bedrooms. Both belonged to the twins, and both were typical. I didn't have to go to the bathroom. I hadn't had anything to eat or drink in hours. Perhaps that was why my head was spinning, and my equilibrium issues had nothing to do with the increasing sense that I was chasing my tail while the answer danced just outside of my vision, laughing and pointing at the dummy.

I splashed water on my face, rubbed my temples. Coming

here had been a long shot, but not checking Jonelle out would have driven me crazy.

So I was back to square one. Still waiting on Kelly to get into Harrison's computer, and still wondering if Justin had anything to do with Kailey's disappearance.

FIFTEEN

Stuck in traffic on the way back to the city, I obsessed over Justin's whereabouts. I didn't believe Todd knew where his brother was, and despite the police's lack of evidence to hold him, the idea that Justin roamed free while Kailey was still missing made me extremely anxious.

I called Kelly and asked her to go over the information we'd gathered on Justin since his release last year. "Is there anything that might give me a hint of where he could be hiding?"

"You called his job, right?" Kelly's voice crackled over the speaker.

"Twice. He's taking some personal days. And Jenna says he hasn't been at home since someone spray-painted his duplex."

"Convenient." Kelly hummed as she searched, the snappy click of her computer keys echoing over the line. "We don't have much on the details of his release since it was kept out of the media. God forbid the state explain why they chose not to register him as an offender."

"I know, but I did tail him for a few days, and there were a few places he frequented. They should be in his file."

"Let me look." More clicking noises from the other end. "I

lost Slimy Steve on the forum, by the way. Looks like he's using a different IP. I don't know if he moved or what. I'm going to have to dig him up all over again."

"Awesome." Guys like Steve knew how to roam online without being seen. Kelly would find him again, but in the meantime, who knows how many girls he would solicit.

"Okay, here we go," she said. "For the first sixty days after his release, he had a pretty solid routine. Ate way too much McDonald's and took the bus to his work every day, plus three days a week he spent time at a homeless shelter in Spring Garden. West Garden Shelter on Noble Street."

My heart rate kicked into high gear. "That's right. We thought he might be volunteering as part of his release."

"Check it out," Kelly said. "But be careful. Whether he's innocent or not, he's going to be pissed off at you."

"Believe me, I'm used to it by now."

Spring Garden is a mostly residential area of the city loaded with brownstones and cultural attractions, namely the Philadelphia Museum of Art. I've visited several times, spending hours with the paintings, gazing at the portraits that have such brilliance and depth it is as if the subject were staring at me through a window. Kenny, of course, stood on the "Rocky Steps" of the museum, where the movies were filmed, and had his picture taken. But not all of the neighborhood is bright and shiny.

The words *colossal mistake* dominated my thoughts as I pulled up to the shelter on Noble Street. Less than a mile away from Northern Liberties, this section of the city was vastly different. Instead of the smells of the bakery down the street or the wafting scents of a food truck, Noble Street had an industrial feel. A tire factory was just a few blocks away, and the exhaust from the factory's enormous stacks made the area smell like cooked rubber. Two blocks north was the abandoned Spring Garden subway station, a place loved by urban explorers and anyone looking to hide out from the cops. I hoped I found Justin at the shelter and didn't have to venture into the station.

I locked my car and headed into the shelter, head down against the wind and hands in my pockets. To my complete irritation, I found my mind wandering to Chris.

Had our escapade at Harrison's house scared some sense into him?

I hoped so. I didn't want to see him again. Except I had questions. Did he really consider himself a sociopath? I've dealt with my fair share of mental illness and personality types. Sociopaths are more terrifying than schizophrenics because of their ability to act like a well-adjusted person. The best ones wear humanity like a perfectly tailored suit, a second skin. Either Chris wore the best-fitting suit I'd ever encountered or he was lying to himself, or me, or maybe both.

West Garden Shelter housed men only and stood two stories tall. It reminded me of my old elementary school, right down to the blue shades. A couple of men sat on the concrete stoop, both nodding to me as I approached. I wondered if offering them cash would be considered an insult.

Unlike a lot of homeless shelters I've been in, West Garden was warm and smelled relatively clean. Still, the atmosphere weighed heavily. I was immediately struck with the instinct to be silent and respectful, not unlike the smothering nervous energy I felt every time I walked into a church.

"Can I help you?" A short man with ill-fitting clothes, a pastor's collar, and weary eyes stood in the doorway of a small office.

"I hope so. I'm looking for a young man named Justin Beckett."

The pastor smiled. "A lot of the guys here don't give us their names. At least not their real ones. Can you describe him to me?"

"He's tall and lanky," I said. "Shaggy, dark-brown hair and a baby-face and tends to slouch. He's a nice-looking kid. I think he volunteered here a year and a half ago."

"You must be talking about Jay," the man said. "Nice, quiet kid. He's one of our best volunteers. Does a wonderful job rounding up supplies and food. And he's a heck of an artist. His drawings decorate our main room. I think he's there now, actually, working on something new." The pastor's voice lowered as he glanced down the hall. "He's stayed with us the past few nights. I'm not sure what's happened, but he knows he's always welcome."

I thanked the pastor for his help and found my way into the main area. Shaped like a giant rectangle, the room was full of neatly made cots. Men were scattered throughout, talking quietly. Justin sat in a plastic chair against the wall with a sketch pad balanced on his legs.

He'd lost weight. His slender hands moved quickly as he worked, sketching and erasing. Several pencil drawings, mostly of different places in the city, hung on the wall to his right. He was a talented kid.

As if he sensed someone staring at him, Justin's head slowly raised, and our gazes locked. The angular planes of his face twisted into anger. His bright blue eyes were cold as ice.

"My brother told you to leave me alone and stop following me."

"I haven't been following you," I said evenly, quickly crossing the room. I stopped a foot in front of him, out of arm's reach. "This is my first time."

"Bullshit." Up close, his face didn't look as youthful as I remembered. Baggy shadows layered his eyes; a day's worth of scruff made his face look dirty. "A black car has been tailing me for weeks."

"Like I told your brother, you know how many black cars are in this city?"

"I'm not a car guy."

"No." I looked at the sketches. "You're an artist. You like to draw outside. Landscape portraits, or have you moved on to living models?"

He winced. "I didn't take that little kid, and I don't have to answer to you."

"No, you don't. But why didn't you tell the police right away you and Kailey were buddies?" Part of me wanted to believe whatever he told me. Maybe this boy could be the exception to the rule. He'd been a victim too. He deserved to be the exception. But I was too much of a realist to believe he actually had a chance.

"Because I was scared, and I hadn't done anything wrong." His knuckles whitened as he gripped the pencil hard enough to snap it. "She needed a friend, and I felt sorry for her. Stupid on my part."

"I know the search of your place turned up empty," I said. "Police haven't found any evidence you took her. And yet you've run off."

"I haven't run off," he snapped. "People in my neighborhood are mad. Someone sprayed my place and then later tossed a brick through my window, telling me if I stepped outside, I'd get my ass kicked. My brother had to come and get me." His cheeks heated. "I couldn't stay with him. Not right now."

"So here you are. And Kailey is still missing."

He finally broke the pencil. "And you'd love to railroad me into admitting I took her. But I didn't."

"Is that what you think happened when you were a kid?"

He took a sharp breath, closed his eyes, nodding his head like he was counting. "I haven't done anything to break the terms of my release. I go to counseling like I'm supposed to. I stay away from areas with kids."

"Why did you communicate with Kailey, then?"

He scrunched up his nose, stuck out his trembling jaw. I realized he was trying not to cry. "Like I said, I'm stupid. But I know what it's like to feel you don't have anyone. It was all email. I was never alone with her. And I don't have to tell you anything. Wait until my brother knows you're still harassing me."

Any reaction from Todd was worth it if I could find something that would lead me to the missing little girl. "I'm just trying to find Kailey."

"I didn't take her!" Justin's voice cracked. "Why do you assume I'm going to hurt someone? Yeah, I did something really freaking terrible when I was a kid. I'll never forgive myself, but I won't do it again. I'm not like the others." Moisture invaded his eyes, his shaking chin jutting out the way a toddler's does when he's in trouble but can't admit he's done wrong.

A tiny part of my dark heart cracked for him. He really believed that. And he'd been a victim himself. "I'm sorry I can't accept that. Every one of you says the same thing."

"Of who?"

"Pedophiles. It's in your genes. You can't stop. Maybe you can go dormant, but the urge can't be squashed."

"I am not a pedophile." Anger turned his face puce, his fists clenching. I held tightly to the pepper spray, making sure he could see it.

I glanced around, lowering my voice. "You raped a ten—"

The broken pieces of pencil clattered to the floor. "There are things you don't know." Justin grabbed his head with both hands and pulled at his thick hair until it stuck out in crazed-looking tufts. "I didn't want to... there's so much more... you don't understand."

He gasped and put his fist to his mouth as if to shut himself up.

"Justin." I used the same tone I would with a scared child

because in so many ways, that's exactly what Justin was. His emotional growth had been stunted long before he made the decision to attack another kid. I wanted to kneel in front of him, but I'd likely end up with a swift kick in the face.

"Why didn't you ever tell me who hurt you?" I didn't want to betray Todd's trust and admit I knew it had been his parents. "I tried to get you out of that house." I had no idea why I was telling him this now, but I owed him, didn't I? "Remember when I saw that jagged scar on your arm? I knew that wasn't from an accident. But I was young and new to the job. More worried about security than doing what was right. My boss said I didn't have enough evidence, that my gut couldn't be filed as evidence. And I backed off. For that, I am very sorry. If I'd tried harder, maybe your life would have been different." My voice cracked. I swiped a tear from my cheek.

He blinked and stared. "You... are you being honest? You're not just feeding me a line of manipulative crap? 'Cause in my experience, your kind is pretty damned good at that."

"Social workers? I know, the system is pretty screwy. Although it worked out better for you than it does a lot of people. But don't worry, I'm not a social worker anymore."

"Not social workers." His angry eyes roamed my face and then looked me up and down. "You're all good at fooling a guy. Mindbanging us until we're so twisted up, we don't know what the hell is going on. Especially ones with power and authority."

He meant women. I flashed cold at the realization. It was my turn to stare, and as I gaped at the man I'd spent so many years feeling alternately guilty and hateful toward, I realized I could be looking in a mirror. I didn't know if Justin's mother was the one who'd physically hurt him, but she'd done a nasty number on his mind. Maybe his mother had ignored his pain the same way my own had neglected my sister.

A bone-numbing sadness seeped through my body.

He had mommy issues. *Just like me. Just like my dead sister.*

I stepped back. Felt wetness on my cheeks. Justin watched in silence, but as we stood face to face, truly seeing each other for the first time, confusion stole my breath.

More to the story, he'd said. Things I didn't understand.

"Make me understand. Why did you hurt your friend?"

"You won't believe me if I told you."

"Give me a chance. Please." I fought for control, trying to remind myself of the other people in the room. "I swear on my sister's grave, I'm being completely honest with you. I have always felt I failed you. I blame myself, and so if you took Kailey, that's on me. It makes me personally invested, and I need to know why you lashed out. I always thought I misread signs. That your problems in school were worse than I realized. That your parents had downplayed your temper tantrums. But there was never any indication you would hurt someone else! Why did you do it? Please tell me why. What I missed, what I could have done."

"Nothing." Justin had gone pale. "I remember you, you know. From when I was a kid. Your hair was longer then, and you smelled like cherries. Made me think of the girl in *The Outsiders*. I liked the way you talked. Your voice was soft. Concerned. Like you actually gave a damn. I never said thanks."

"I did care." I couldn't stop my voice from cracking or more tears from stinging my eyes. "I still do."

"You should stop." He rubbed his eyes and then reached to pick up the pencil pieces. "What happened wasn't your fault, and I absolve you of any guilt. Things were over for me the day I was born." He stood and headed into another area labeled "Staff Only." I knew if I followed, I'd lose any progress I might have made with him.

"By the way," he called over his shoulder, "I like the black rims on your car. Makes it look like some kind of covert vehicle."

My reeling mind screeched to a halt. *Black rims.*

Chris Hale.

. . .

I didn't remember driving home. I probably ran lights and would have a ticket in the mail. For all I knew, I could have outrun a cop. An offense that would only add to the list of things Todd would eventually nail me with. At least he didn't have murder. Yet.

Mousecop greeted me with his usual "feed-me-now" yowl. Too preoccupied for our standard snuggle, I shuffled to the kitchen and topped off his bowl.

Flipping off the lights, I kicked off my shoes and dropped my bag. I headed straight for the refrigerator and grabbed the last bottle of Stella. Then my acid medication from the counter.

Taking a long pull of the sweet beer and ignoring the instant fire in my gut, I sank into my favorite shabby recliner beneath the large dormer window and stared out into the bright lights of the city. Uncertainty bottled up my train of thoughts.

So Justin and I have a common thread. Who doesn't have mother issues? But what had he meant when he said "things were over the day he was born"? Had his father been the abuser? Is that why Todd refused to discuss it? And what about Justin's mother? Todd hated her, but that wasn't uncommon with stepparents.

Justin's mother was probably an emotional manipulator like my own. She could have enabled the abuse. Maybe Justin blamed her and rightly so if that were the case. *Still didn't justify his actions.*

But Justin hadn't tried to. In fact, he'd given me the distinct impression I was missing a much bigger piece of the puzzle than I realized. Which brought me to the true, burning question: why the hell was Chris following Justin? And why didn't he tell me? He'd told me his real identity, that his father was one of Pennsylvania's most notorious killers, and yet he'd kept this from me.

What was his interest in Justin, and more importantly, in me? He'd just popped into my life out of nowhere, talking crazy about being a sociopath and a killer garbage man.

Right before Kailey disappeared.

And Chris had been in the neighborhood the night before. Justin had reported the black car to his brother.

My blood turned to thick slush, slowing until my head ached.

What if he'd conned Kailey by saying her mother was hurt? Jenna Richardson was a nurse, and Chris was a paramedic, an authority figure to a child. Chris could have said her mom sent him to pick up Kailey.

I took another drink of the beer. Swallowing it felt like choking on a wooden block.

Chris knew about my past with Justin before I'd even told him. What if he'd just been playing me this entire time, keeping me busy with Justin while he had Kailey?

But why? I'm not law enforcement, and if Chris hadn't introduced himself to me, I wouldn't have even known he existed.

The sociopath's suit.

It's a sick game. Plus he gets to be part of the case, watching us all chase our tails.

I sat the bottle on the windowsill and buried my head against my knees, blocking out the world. *Maybe I'm over-thinking.* Justin was still the more logical suspect.

Except there was no physical evidence. And right now, I had as much reason to suspect Chris as anyone.

Chris could have been telling me all along exactly what he was. Or I could just be making crazy shit up to feel like I was doing something. Either way, I'd known there was more to Chris's motives in seeking me out. Tomorrow, I'd see if Kelly could find out about his shift the day Kailey disappeared. Have her dig into social media and newspapers. And while Kelly did her thing, I would channel my own mother and see if I could manipulate the truth from Chris.

I left a message for Todd, letting him know I thought Chris was the one following his brother and why, and that he might be a suspect in Kailey's disappearance. I'm sure he'd call me back and chew me out for talking to Justin, but I didn't care.

Now I had a plan. Tomorrow I would take control and execute it.

A bitter laugh escaped at the irony of the word and echoed around the silence of the apartment.

I went to bed.

SIXTEEN

"Brought you some scones and coffee from the place around the corner." I sat the box of goodies down on Kelly's crowded kitchen bar top. Her little studio was blazing warm, and I'd bundled up against the morning gale. I peeled off my coat and scarf before my face started sweating.

"Thank you. I need to get to the store, but I keep putting it off. Living on ramen and water the past couple of days." Kelly bit into the scone and gave a little moan of bliss. "So good."

"Do you have therapy this week?"

"Mmmhmm." Kelly licked the sugar off her slender fingertips. "Monday. Can't wait."

"It's good for you to get out."

"Yeah, yeah. So what's this epiphany you had? You sounded pretty stressed when you woke me up at the ass-crack of dawn."

"Sorry about that." I played with the lid of my caramel macchiato. "I think we need to dig deeper into Chris Hale."

"Why?"

I dug my fingernail into a tiny scratch on the countertop. "Because I think he's the one who was following Justin."

Her mouth barely moved. "I thought he was helping you."

"So did I, but after I spoke with Justin yesterday, I realized Chris lied."

Kelly's eyes were wide. "You saw Justin yesterday?"

I nodded, trying not to let the memory of Justin's misery cloud my judgment. "Chris's fancy car gave him away."

Kelly listened with wide-eyed interest at my theory of Chris's possible involvement in Kailey's abduction.

"Is there any way you could find out about his shift on the day she disappeared? He said he was going to work."

"I can try, but that's personal information. I can't exactly hack into the city's personnel database. Not without getting caught, that is." Kelly twisted her scone wrapper into a rope-like, wrinkled mess. "I've got a couple of contacts at District Seven's precinct. They might be able to find some stuff out for me. Todd's downtown in District Six, right?"

"Smack in the middle, yeah. And I left him a message he'll hopefully follow up on. But I can't count on Todd keeping me in the loop after my sneaking around to talk to Justin."

Kelly dumped the breakfast wrappings into the trash and started cleaning the counter. "You know, it's funny this all comes up because I've been thinking about Justin all morning."

"And?"

"I wonder if he's actually telling the truth. Maybe he didn't take Kailey."

"I don't know what to think," I admitted. "He seemed so sincere yesterday, and I got the feeling there's a lot more to his past than I imagined. But maybe that's all the more reason to suspect him."

"Why?"

"Whatever happened to him as a kid made him attack another child. You can't undo that kind of damage."

Kelly sat on the other bar stool, leaning close enough to me our knees touched. When Kelly laid her hand gently on my arm, I stared at her in amazement and didn't dare move. Kelly rarely initiated touching, and she shied away from any kind of intimate moment.

"Listen," she said. "I think I can safely say I'm your closest friend. I know you and the chemist have your occasional physical thing, but he doesn't know the things I do. I understand what drives you to make certain choices. And I say this with as much compassion as I can muster: you've got to stop pigeon-holing kids like Justin."

Calling me a coldhearted killer would have had less of an impact. I sucked in a hot breath, the macchiato still lingering on my tongue. "I... what?"

"Just because he was abused as a kid doesn't mean he'll be a monster. I was abused. But I don't hurt people."

I raised my eyebrow. "Not directly. But you've helped me hone in on my targets since I started."

Kelly shrugged. "So maybe I'm a hypocrite. But those aren't innocent people. Those are men who hurt little kids and work our screwed-up system so they can keep doing their filthy deeds. It's different, and you know it."

"So you're saying I'm not being fair to Justin?"

"Maybe. I know sex offenders don't change. But... his situation is different, Lucy. He was so young. Maybe the doctors got to him in time. Especially if there is more to his story."

"Or maybe, because he acted out at such a young age, he's more of a monster than we could imagine." The words sounded futile—tiny hopes dangling from the edge of a cliff. *Or maybe I'm the one hanging from the edge, clinging to some dirty root that refuses to budge.*

"It's possible. But it's not the only possibility here. There's Chris. And a couple of others too."

"You've found more suspects?" I brightened at the idea. At least I'd have something to do instead of chase my tail.

"Possibly. Let me show you something."

I followed her into the computer area, trying to reconcile Kelly's words.

"Before I forget..." Kelly cracked her knuckles and sat down at the system. "Slimy Steve, the pig you were after when Chris first approached you? His IP pinged in one of the sick sites last night. He's trolling. Don't know if you're still paying attention to him with all this going on, but I want to pass it on."

Of course he was. Probably never satiated. "Thanks. I'll see if I can find the time to track him down again."

Kelly logged onto her complicated-looking system. "I searched around various social media sites and found out you were right. Kailey does have an online profile, and I'd guess she's using it at the babysitter's."

"Did you get into her accounts?"

"There's a backdoor entrance for social media sites that only a select few in the hacking world know of," Kelly said. "Kailey's your typical kid. Looks like she mostly played games, but a couple of them have chat forums."

"Who did she talk to?"

"A few people, but only two of them regularly. Both claim to be kids, and as far as I can tell, they are." Kelly closed the window and swiveled to face me. "I called into my liaison at District Six. She's the one who assigns me cases to consult on. Told her I'd heard about Kailey's disappearance and wanted to know if I could help. We had the standard argument about the protocols of my coming into the station, and I reminded her that she makes exceptions for me because I've got major anxiety issues, but I'm so good she needs my help."

I grinned. "It's true."

"They've seized the babysitter's computer, and they're aware of Kailey's online stuff and checking the identities of everyone she talks to. She did let it slip they have another suspect."

Interesting. Most kids were taken by someone they know,

but a stranger was a definite possibility. Still, it was hard to imagine better suspects than Chris and Justin. "Who is he?"

"Couldn't get a name. But he lives three houses down, has served time for exposing himself to a minor and soliciting, and is out on parole. Lucy, he fits the profile as well as Justin. And from what I could get, his alibi is shaky. They're trying to get warrants for a full search."

I catalogued the information. "So we've got four possible leads: Justin, Chris, Brian Harrison, and the cops' suspect."

"The cops' suspect's off limits to me," Kelly said. "What about the Smiths?"

"I passed the lead to Todd, but I really don't think they're involved. Not after figuring out Chris is the one who's been following Justin. Speaking of Harrison, do you have anything?"

"I got into the dead brother's laptop." Kelly looked disgusted. "You made the right call on him. His hard drive was loaded with naked kids, and his browser history went to a couple of really disturbing websites. I hacked his email after a few hours of trying and managed to find an email address for Brian."

"What do you think?"

Kelly shrugged. "It's the best we've got. If he likes pre-teen girls, there were several of those on the hard drive. I can embed a remote access program into one and email it to Harrison. All he's got to do is click on the picture, and the program will be unleashed and installed in his system."

I stared blankly and felt stupid. "And it works how?"

"If Harrison is on the computer, I will be too, and see everything he does. If he's got anything there of Kailey, I can find it. The computer just needs to be on."

"I'm still not sure Kailey's his type," I said. "But I do think he'll have other girls, and if we get lucky, we can piece together his victims."

"What if he's not the guy who molested the girl in the vacant lot? What if he's just a looker and not a toucher?"

"He'll touch at some point. But we'll deal with that when we get the answer." I rolled my shoulders, trying in vain to ease the tension. "In the meantime, I'll stick with Justin and Chris, see if I can get anything. Maybe the cops will end up being right and their suspect is the one. But I doubt it."

"You need to worry more about Chris than Justin." Kelly pulled her knees into her chest and wrapped her arms around them while still balancing on the chair. The benefits of being a tiny, flexible thing. "The very fact that he knows about your cyanide excursions scares the shit out of me. You need to get to the bottom of his motive. If you're lucky—or unlucky, depending on how you look at it—you might find Kailey. Because, after all, that's the priority, right?"

I was getting tired of that question. "Of course."

"So you do what you can with what you've got. Justin's a dead end right now. Focus on Chris. I'll let you know if I get anything from Harrison."

After I left Kelly's, I decided to try Todd again. Straight to voicemail. I reminded him to check into Chris and to please call me and then ended the call, sinking into my cold, leather seats.

Every time I turned around, another complication reared its head, and I was no closer to finding Kailey. I didn't know what to think about Justin anymore. My judgment was clouded by my agenda and pride and suspicions about Chris.

My phone rang, and Chris's number popped onto the screen. I only debated a minute before answering. "Hello?"

"It's me." Chris sounded breathless. "I couldn't get back to sleep after my shift ended and decided to swing by Justin's work. Thanks for trusting me with that information, by the way."

As if he didn't already know everything about Justin by the time I came into the picture. "He took a personal day yesterday. Was he there?"

"Just briefly. I think he picked up his check, and then I followed him."

"Why?" I asked. "I thought you didn't think Justin took her."

"No idea, but it seemed like the right thing to do. Anyway, he's at a storage unit in Spring Garden right now, Lucy. I don't know what's inside, but I figured you'd want to know."

My heart leapt into my throat. Did Todd know about this unit? "Text me the address."

SEVENTEEN

I whipped through Spring Garden's residential area and turned onto a beautiful street lined with well-kept, three-story brownstone townhouses, most of them dating back to the nineteenth century. Newer condos stood on this street, though I much preferred the older homes. I caught sight of the sign for Spring Garden Storage and hit the brakes, careening into the parking lot.

Chris's Audi sat in the back behind a white van. I parked a few spaces down and hurried to join him. Getting into a car with Chris might just top my list of dumb things to do. But I'd already done it twice and survived. And I was on my guard. I could take care of myself.

He leaned across the passenger seat and opened the door for me. The car smelled like clean leather and Chris's musky cologne. He wore his glasses again, and they didn't hide the circles beneath his eyes.

"Must have been a slow shift if you couldn't sleep," I said.

"Not really. I just kept thinking about this whole mess." Chris shrugged, and the light caught his cheek just right, highlighting the scar along his jaw. "He's been inside about forty-five minutes."

I glanced at the storage area, noticing Chris had chosen a perfect spot. His car was mostly hidden by the van, but he still had a decent view of the red Honda Justin drove. I leaned back in the warm seat.

I grazed the scar with my index finger. "Did you fall on something? I've got a scar on my elbow from when I was about ten. Classic running with a stick. Tripped and jammed the wood into my arm. Lucky it wasn't my eye." I cringed at the memory. My sister had been the one to clean me up, staying calm while our mother worried what the doctors would think. The hypocrisy didn't dawn on me until after my sister's death.

"It was an accident." Chris stared straight ahead. A muscle in his jaw worked, tightening and flexing as the struggle to appear unfazed played out on his face.

I wanted to keep him talking, see if I could ferret out the lies in his story. "So, why'd you decide to be a paramedic? Not exactly a dream job for a sociopath."

"I'm trying to assimilate. Maybe even rehabilitate."

"Sociopaths don't want to rehabilitate. They don't see anything about them as being wrong. Then again, I'm not sure you're one at all." *Or you're the scariest one I've ever met. I'm just not going to tell you that.*

Leaning his head against the back of the seat, he turned lazily toward me. "I wish you were right."

Once again, his eyes betrayed him. Instead of flatness or uncaring, they shined with pain. His grin, meant to be charming, looked more like a choked-up grimace.

"Why do you think you're a sociopath?"

"Long story." Chris returned to watching the parking lot.

"We've got time."

"Actually"—he pointed—"we don't. Justin's heading to his car."

Walking with the same defeated slouch, Justin exited the unit alone and empty-handed. He glanced around but his gaze didn't linger in any direction. He headed west out of the parking lot, oblivious to the Audi.

"You know where Todd lives?" Chris asked.

"No clue. But I'd bet he's not home." I didn't want to tell him Justin was probably going to the shelter. The fact that I was protecting him didn't escape me, but I didn't have time to ponder its meaning. I'd do that at 3 a.m. when sleep eluded me.

Chris cleared his throat. "You know it's been more than forty-eight hours since she disappeared. After that long…"

"I'm aware." Little Kailey's life could have been snuffed out days ago. A tremor shot through me, whispers of the panic that sometimes crept up on me in the night. No child should have to face that nothingness.

"It's been almost two hours. What the hell did he do in there for so long?" Chris asked.

A myriad of horrible scenarios flashed through my mind, accompanied with the voices of the abused children I'd listened to over the past decade. "You don't want to know."

Whatever worries I had about Chris dropped to the back of my brain. Adrenaline flushed through me with a dizzying veracity, leaving me breathing in whistling gasps. "We need to get inside now. This is the perfect place to hide her."

"You're right," Chris said. "We've got to get inside and see if she's there. If he's hurt that kid, we take him down."

The conviction in his voice surprised me, not because he'd suggested killing Justin, but because his tone sang with empathy for Kailey.

"So let's go."

EIGHTEEN

Chris hung back as I worked the lock on Justin's unit.

"Where'd you learn how to pick a lock?"

"Googled it."

"Nice." The lock popped open, and Chris slowly lifted the door, which creaked and squalled as it rolled up. I shined my flashlight around the unit until I found the light switch. The hanging bulb was dim, and my eyes took a moment to adjust. When my vision finally sharpened, my knees turned to jelly. The unit was about the size of my childhood bedroom, and boxes and plastic bins lined the western wall. It was the rest of the room that made me feel woozy.

Justin had decorated the entire back wall with pictures of his mother. A few were snapshots, but most were his own drawings. Every one was done in pencil, and the detail was mesmerizing. Martha Beckett had always intimidated me, and these pictures were so lifelike I felt the same unease creeping over me. A tall woman with broad shoulders, manly hands, and nondescript facial features that made her expression perpetually tight, she resented me on sight. Justin's father drank too much and let Martha run the house. The woman had been furious that anyone—and I suspected my looks and the way Justin had taken to me also fueled Martha's ire—would insinuate anything was wrong with her son.

Martha's haughty eyes followed me as I examined the drawings. One thing quickly became clear: Justin Beckett hated his mother. Every depiction had her in an eerie position of power, as though she were standing over him in the flesh, brutish and domineering.

But the one that really struck me cold was the full body drawing of Martha from the back. Hair gathered at the back of her neck, her clothes were too tight around her thicker frame. Justin had drawn his mother so the right side of her face was partially visible, and again she was drawn from the position of someone looking up at her. The most chilling feature was the way her right eye glared, as though she had turned her back but still watched from the corner of her eye. If there was ever a boogeywoman, this drawing of Martha Beckett was the perfect representation.

I jumped when Chris's hand touched my shoulder. "Christ! I'd forgotten you were here."

"I could tell." He walked over to the cheap computer desk and folding chair set up in the corner. Various art supplies covered half the desk while newspaper clippings were scattered across the other half. "More drawings of the same woman. That his mother?"

"Martha Beckett."

Chris stared at the pictures taped to the wall. Peering closer, he gazed up at one of the close-up sketches of Martha's face with a look of intense concentration. He gave himself a shake. "She looks like a peach."

"She was rude and uncooperative. And when Justin was incarcerated, she spent more time being angry at her son than trying to understand him. From what I've been told, he hasn't seen her in years."

"Not sure I believe that."

"Why?"

"Look at the pictures." Chris pointed to the one at the far left that he'd been so caught up in. "She's younger there. And look at her hair. It's all big and poufy. All bangs. Like my aunt used to wear hers in the 90s." He walked along the wall, his hand hovering near the pictures. "She's younger in all of these." He stopped at the one portraying Martha from the back. "Harder to tell with this one, but I still say she's younger. And then look at these." He moved to the right. "She's thinner. Shoulders more stooped. Looks like she's got some gray. Maybe wrinkles."

"God, you're right."

"Doesn't mean he's seen her, though," Chris said. "He could be aging her simply because it makes sense to him. But—"

"If he hasn't seen her, and he holds this much obsession with her, he'd still draw her the way she looked when he was a kid." I went to the last picture in the haphazard line and studied it closely, looking past the threatening visage. "She's opening the door here. Her expression almost looks surprised."

"Maybe he was fantasizing about seeing her again and watching her shock."

"Maybe. Or maybe he's already seen her. When I spoke to him yesterday, I knew he had a lot of resentment toward her. I assumed she'd stood aside while he was being abused but now, I wonder."

Chris gingerly touched one of the pictures. "Wonder what?"

"If she didn't hurt him too. I assumed it was his father, but now I don't know." I glanced at Chris. "It's more common than people think, especially with sons. It's a control thing. Sometimes it's sexual. The way he shows her in positions of power makes me really nervous."

"What does it matter now?" Chris went back over to the

desk. "He's a grown man, and whatever damage she inflicted is firmly ingrained. A person can't recover from that sort of thing. Can they?" His tight, controlled voice sent a tremor through me, and I remembered I was talking to the son of the infamous Lancaster murderer.

"Every person is different," I said. "There are a lot of people out there who came from terrible backgrounds living productive lives. I think it's a matter of genetic makeup, of the wiring. Some people just can't cope. And he's obviously obsessed with her. And even if this is some form of therapy, Martha Beckett may be in danger."

"So what?" Chris dropped the pile of papers he'd been rifling through. "If she did hurt her son, she deserves whatever he's got planned for her. *He's* the victim. She's the monster. Isn't that your whole working concept, anyway? By your system, Martha should be dead. It's justice." His voice, loud and loaded with raw anger, rang in my ears. I thought of the things he must have seen as a child in Lancaster, and I knew in that moment he was more damaged than I'd imagined.

Chris stepped toward me, the thud of his boots against the concrete floor matching the tenseness in his body. "You can't be a vigilante killer of kid attackers and then worry about whether or not one of the pigs is in danger from the child they abused. Especially when it's their own kid. You can't have this shit both ways, Lucy."

His anger made the hair on my arms stand up. I suddenly realized I was in a small storage unit with a man I barely knew who might have more agendas than I realized, and my pepper spray was in my car. "You're right. But I don't know for sure she actually abused him. Maybe she just let it happen because she was too busy in her own life. Or because she was afraid. Or worried about what might happen to her."

"So that's the distinction? Enablers get the Lucy Kendall acquittal?"

"If they didn't, I'd have to take out my own mother." I gritted my teeth. I had no interest in telling Chris about my sister.

"You were abused?" Chris's eyes widened, his anger stepping down a notch. "By who?"

"Not me. My sister. Mom's boyfriend. Mom never wanted to hear the truth. And that's all I'm going to say. The point is, we don't know the whole story. And we're not here to worry about Martha Beckett. We're here to find out if Justin took Kailey. So let's start looking."

Chris looked like he wanted to argue, but he nodded. "Let's start with the desk first. He's got a lot of shit crammed onto the shelves."

We spent the next fifteen minutes in strained silence carefully sifting through Justin's workstation. Nothing related to Kailey. Or any kids, for that matter. A couple of pictures of himself and Todd when they were younger. One of his dad. None of Martha. I assumed they were all on the wall.

Most of the newspaper clippings were about Justin's crime and eventual release, save one. I held the yellowed paper underneath the desk lamp I'd turned on. My throat went dry. "The Lancaster Kidnappings."

Across the room, Chris dropped the box he'd been looking through. He knelt down and started throwing old clothes back in the box. "What did you say?"

"He's got an article on the 1991 Lancaster Kidnappings."

Chris strode across the room and snatched the paper. Anger resonated off him in hot waves. The silence felt heavy and dangerous, and I started to babble.

"I remember watching it on the news when I was a kid. It was the start of fifth grade." I'd gotten my period the same day, and my mother had been running around like a squawking chicken, upset that her baby was now a woman, and what did it mean for her?

"At least they've got the story right," Chris gritted out. In the yellow light of the unit, his blue eyes glowed almost feral. "My father was a mean bastard who abused his wife. The wife stopped taking it when she discovered a teenage girl in the barn. John Weston kidnapped and killed at least four girls over the years."

"You were too young to know what was going on." The words sounded small and stupid.

"My mother wasn't."

"But she was abused and never allowed in the barn. She had a victim's mindset, Chris."

"By all rights and your logic," Chris said, "I should be another predator roaming the streets."

I didn't know what to say, because I was afraid of exactly that. So I ignored the comment. "Why would Justin have information on this? It happened years before he was born."

"Because he's got problems. Maybe he likes researching cases where kids' parents royally screwed them up." He shoved the dilapidated box out of his way and opened a plastic storage bin, tossing the lid. It landed on the concrete floor with a loud clatter.

"Well, that's interesting." Chris held up a file, but before he could say anything more, the unit's door began to rise. I ducked behind the desk, but Chris didn't move. Face frozen in panic, he looked like he didn't know whether to duck or attack. *My ass he's done any of the shit he claims.*

I crouched, thinking fast. No spray, but I knew some self-defense moves. As long as Justin was alone and Chris got over his apparent stage fright, the two of us could take the scrawny kid. My pulse raced. What if he was bringing Kailey here? Maybe he'd moved her from some other location. I could save her, bring Justin in, show everyone I'd been right.

Carefully, I peeked around the desk.

It wasn't Justin who stood in the open doorway.

NINETEEN

Todd Beckett reminded me of Yosemite Sam when he'd been outsmarted by Bugs Bunny yet again. Between the red face and pulsing vein in his forehead, I thought his head might burst. He pointed his gun at Chris. "Hands in the air, Mr. Hale, isn't it?"

Oh shit. I hadn't even considered Todd knowing about the unit. Damn, damn, damn.

"Call me Chris." He obeyed.

"You want to tell me why you're in my brother's storage unit?"

"Looking to see if he took that little girl."

"Or maybe you're planting evidence to keep us off your tail."

"You think I took her?" Chris laughed. "Jesus. Kid doesn't have a chance in hell."

"Why are you so interested in my brother?"

"I just told you."

"See, here's the thing. He mentioned the car that's been following him had black rims. And when I got here, I noticed a fancy Audi with nice-looking black rims. Ran the plates. Guess who the Audi belongs to?"

"Fine. You got me. I've been keeping an eye on him for a while. Looks like I did a shitty job."

"So I'll ask you again, why have you been following Justin the past few weeks? Did someone put you up to it? A pushy redhead, maybe? Her car's in the parking lot too, so she might as well come out."

Chris didn't say anything.

So much for deception. "Don't shoot." I stood up slowly, keeping my hands above my head. "Justin was in here, and I thought he might have Kailey. I didn't know if you knew about this place or not."

"You have my phone number." Todd's voice sounded dangerous.

"I didn't know how soon you'd get the message."

"Unbelievable. You leave me a message you're concerned about this guy, and then you break in here with him?"

I glanced at Chris, inwardly cringing at having to play both sides of the fence. Made me feel too much like my mother, and I'd be damned if I wanted to turn into her.

Chris met my gaze, raising an eyebrow in challenge, reminding me exactly what he could tell Todd about me.

"It was my idea. I wanted to keep him close, and I wanted to get in here."

Chris glared at me, but if he was going to start telling Todd stories about me, I'd have to be ready to play ball. *Self-preservation.*

"You're both coming to the station."

"Are we under arrest?" Chris said.

"I haven't decided," Todd shot back. "You both ride with me, we have a chat downtown. Then we'll see if I book your meddling asses for trespassing." He glared at me. "Or worse."

. . .

Todd stuck Chris in a holding cell while he hauled me into an
interview room.

"Will you please take these off?" I held up my cuffed hands.
"Unless I'm being charged, and I'm sure Justin will be happy to
see that happen."

Todd leaned against the wall. "Not up to him. I own the
storage unit."

I couldn't stop the shock from playing out on my face. "Do
you know about his obsession with his mother?"

"That's none of your business. And I don't have time for
this." He sighed, looking even more exhausted than the last time
I'd seen him. "I'm supposed to be looking for a missing child."

Me too, but reminding him probably wasn't in my best
interests right now. "Still nothing?"

"We have a few leads of registered offenders in the area.
We're following those up. Thanks for the lead on Brian Harrison. Where did that come from, by the way?"

The ball of nerves in my stomach leached into the rest of
my body. I curled my toes to keep my legs from jerking. "I can't
reveal my sources. Anything pan out with him?"

Todd didn't answer for a second, and that small blip in time
felt like hours. "He's called in sick at school and isn't answering
my calls. Hasn't been at home, either. Given his priors, he might
be on a bender. Still worth looking into."

A blissful if temporary reprieve. Todd would talk to
Harrison soon enough, unless I got to him first. I focused on the
task at hand. "I needed to see what Justin was hiding in that
storage unit."

"Why?" Todd brought his hands down on the table. "You
know we're treating Justin like any other suspect. We've
turned up nothing. And yet you assume we're missing
something."

"Because he spent an hour in there today and came out with
nothing. I needed to be sure. And because if he did this, I'm

responsible. I should have done something different all those years ago."

Todd tossed his badge onto the table. "Stop trying to be a martyr. You're not infallible. Bad shit happens. You weren't the victim. Not even collateral damage. But you've twisted it around and made it about you at the expense of other people."

I knew he was right, knew it as much as I knew my own fears. I just didn't know if I could walk away. I sank into the seat, shame burrowing right through my skin and into my bones. "You're right. But I want to help find Kailey."

Todd pulled a set of keys from his pocket, motioning for my wrists. He removed the cuffs, his calloused fingers lingering on my hand. "That's the shittiest part of all this. However misguided you are, I know you believe you're doing what's right." He pulled his hand away. "Now, to Chris Hale. You left me a message about the black rims after you talked to my brother." He paused, letting me know he didn't appreciate that fact. "I checked with Justin, and Hale's Audi matches his description. How long have you two been dating?"

I shifted in the hard chair, choosing my words carefully. "We're not dating. He introduced himself to me the night before Kailey disappeared."

"What has he told you about himself?"

"He's a paramedic. He's complex." I couldn't very well tell him Chris believed he was a sociopath. I decided to hold the information on Chris's true identity until Todd showed his hand. "I may be wrong, but when I realized he was the one following Justin and hadn't said a thing, I got worried. I just thought you should know."

"Yet you went inside that unit with him. He could have attacked you."

I really wished he'd keep to the hardline cop routine. He was easier to deal with when he wasn't being nice. "A decision based on what I thought was a necessity."

"We've been sniffing around his firehouse. He did work the night Kailey disappeared, but there's a window of time unaccounted for. Trouble is, guy's got connections."

"Who?"

"Frank Hale. Assistant district attorney."

I should have known. He'd said his uncle was a lawyer. Why didn't Kelly's search turn that up? *Because you didn't have her look into family connections. You were too busy chasing Justin.*

"Tonight's stunt gives me a chance to grill his ass. At least until he calls his uncle. Which brings me to the next point. This is something you really need to know. Frank and Elizabeth Hale raised him as their own." Todd took a document out of the folder he was holding. "This is Chris Hale's birth certificate." He slid it across the table.

I read the certificate, trying to decide how to answer. "Christopher Alan Weston. Born in Lancaster, Pennsylvania in 1986."

"He was four years old when his mother discovered the girl in the barn and fled," Todd said. "According to the police reports, Chris heard crying, and insisted it wasn't the horses. Chris is the one who opened the barn door, running ahead of his mother. John Weston strictly forbade them from entering, and she was terrified they'd both get a beating. He saw the teenage victim, still alive, tied up and naked in an empty horse stall. She'd been beaten and sexually abused. His mother grabbed him up and ran down the road nearly a mile to a neighbor."

I sat speechless even as realizations I should have clued into days ago began to click. At the age of four, Chris had witnessed a heinous crime. And who knows how many beatings he'd been subjected to—or watched his mother receive.

He said he was a sociopath. Maybe he really is the very best of them. I wanted to see how much more Todd knew. "You said he was raised by his aunt and uncle? What about his mother?"

"Details are thin, but it says she gave up custody of him in 1993 due to inability to care for him because of the trauma caused by her husband."

"Makes sense."

"I don't have to tell you what kind of damage kids like him have." Todd took another photo out of the file. "This is the girl Mary Weston discovered. She was only fourteen. Look at her school photo."

I stared at the photo, my senses blasted again with shock. "This could be Kailey in five years." It was like looking at a disproportionate version of Kailey, as though the older features weren't quite as symmetrical. Her eyes were wider apart, the eyebrows more arched. This girl had lost her baby cheeks, and her lips glistened with lip gloss, making the beauty mark to the right of her upper lip stand out. Kailey had a similar mark.

"Oh my God." I dropped the picture and stared at Todd, who nodded grimly.

"That's Jenna Richardson. She was John Weston's last victim, and she barely survived."

TWENTY

"I shouldn't be sharing this information with you," Todd said. "Legally, my ass is on the line, but since you insist on butting into the case and you're caught up with Chris Hale, I'm telling you for your own safety."

"I really need a drink." I tried to reconcile everything I'd just learned. Did Chris know Jenna was the last victim? "Preferably strong."

"Old coffee's all we've got."

"I don't know how you do this job without a supply of bourbon."

"You see the worst of people too." Too bad I couldn't share my coping mechanism with Todd.

"I've talked to Jenna about her time with Weston," Todd said. "She doesn't remember the little boy who found her, and there isn't much she can tell us. She was kept blindfolded."

"So... you think..." My voice trailed off, my brain refusing to allow me to put everything into a cohesive sentence. It seemed I'd been on the right track but missing a wheel, and I was too dumbfounded to put it all together. "What do you think?"

"I think it's very possible Chris somehow found out where Jenna lived. He didn't take her but her daughter instead."

"Why? Just because he saw Jenna tied up all those years ago doesn't mean he'd act out now. He was a kid."

Todd barked a laugh. "What a hypocrite you are."

I jerked, the words stinging more than they should have. "Your brother's different. He actually acted out his rage once already, at a young age."

"Yeah, well. It's a big freaking coincidence that Chris introduces himself to you right before the daughter of his father's last victim is kidnapped. And he's been following my brother for at least two weeks. And for all we know, Chris could have been acting out for a long time, building up to this."

He told you what he was. Why didn't you listen? I still couldn't quite reconcile the idea of Chris being disturbed enough to fool me so thoroughly. "But why bring me into it?"

"Inserts himself into the investigation." Todd shrugged.

"Before I even got involved?"

"I think he knew my brother lived near Jenna Richardson. Justin's case was pretty big news a few months ago, and even though he's not a registered offender, his address had to be public. Part of the terms of his release. Negotiated by me. Chris finds out about you and your very vocal stance since you spoke at Justin's hearing. So he buddies up to you, knowing full well that you'd find out a kid in Justin's neighborhood went missing. And he'd have access to inside information. It's just a bonus that you're now a PI and you've asked him to help stalk Justin. Why did you do that, anyway?"

My cheeks burned with embarrassment. Had I really been taken in so completely by Chris? "I'm not stalking. And hell if I know."

"Well, you're going to stay away from both of them. I trust you're satisfied Justin isn't involved in the disappearance now?"

I didn't want to give the answer. Didn't want to admit defeat over my instincts. Guilt over the misery I'd caused Justin ate through my stomach lining. I still believed the neighborhood had the right to know he lived among them, but I'd allowed my own selfish need for atonement to control my decisions. And Justin wasn't the only one affected. Todd had been smacked with the shittiest end of my self-righteous stick.

"He told me what you said to him yesterday," Todd said. "And even though you are a gigantic pain in my ass, I know your heart is in the right place. So you tell me, after talking to Justin, how do you really feel about him?"

I swallowed hard. "I'm not sure anymore."

"Not a shred of evidence points to him, even with his previous contact with Kailey. We don't have anything concrete on Chris Hale yet, either, but we've got some nice circumstantial facts piling up. More than anything we've got on Justin."

"His uncle is the ADA," I said. "You can't go accusing him of anything without hard evidence. Frank Hale is one of the best."

Todd grunted. "I know. We'll get it if it's there."

"Let me help." Damned if I was going to let Chris use me like some easy pawn. If he had Kailey and had been wasting my time the past few days, playing on my guilt, I'd pour the cyanide straight down his throat.

"What?"

Righteous indignation cleared my clustered thoughts. I jumped up and started to pace, rubbing at my still-sore wrists. "You give Chris Hale any idea you suspect him, and he'll call his uncle. Which buys him time to move Kailey if he did take her." If she was still alive.

"I can handle it."

"So can I. Let me get closer to Chris. See if I can find anything you can use." I could do this. He wanted to know more about my lifestyle. About me. I'd tell him whatever I needed to in order to find Kailey. And if Chris started talking shit about me, I'd have to hope Todd took it as revenge ramblings, even though he wouldn't. He was too good of a cop.

"You are not a cop." Todd drew the words out for emphasis. "You need to stop trying to act like one."

"But I know how to manipulate people."

"Really? Well, that makes me feel great about trusting your judgment, then."

I flushed. "I'm not proud of it, but my mother is the queen bee of emotional manipulation. I've learned."

Todd took of his glasses and rubbed the indentation marks on the bridge of his nose. "Even if I agree to this, he knows you called me, concerned about him. You really think he's going to trust you now?"

If I play my cards right, hopefully he will. Even if I have to talk about my sister. Or my extracurricular activities for the last year. "At least let me try."

"I've already told him I know he followed Justin."

"So ask him about it and take his word. Or let him think you did. Let us go tonight, and give me twenty-four hours to find something else out."

Todd shook his head. "How do I know you're not playing me? You just admitted to being a mastermind player. What if you're hot for this Chris and want to help him out?"

I sat back down. "Because you know I want to find Kailey. Whatever mistakes I've made, that's been my goal."

Todd chewed on his lower lip until he broke the skin. "Twenty-four hours. And know that we're going to be investigating him as much as we can. I'm looking into his financials, his property records, anything I can find out. And if I try to hold him now, Uncle ADA will have him out, and probably make him shut off all communication with you."

"Absolutely." I wasn't sure how much pull Chris's uncle

had over his decisions, but now wasn't the time to argue with Todd.

"And..." Todd stood up and leaned over me. I didn't challenge his position of power, but I didn't shrink. "If it turns out you're trying to help him in any way, I will arrest you for trespassing, tampering with evidence, and if it turns out he did take the girl, conspiracy, not to mention accessory to kidnapping and murder if she's dead. Got it?"

"I've got it."

Sitting in the station's waiting area, I tried to relax. Todd should be finishing up with Chris soon, and I needed to be ready.

I didn't have a clue how I was going to keep myself from getting in his face and demanding the truth. Todd's theory about why Chris had been following Justin and me made sense, but something about it didn't feel right. Maybe it was my own pride, but Chris's story had a lot more pages.

Chris emerged from another interview room with Todd behind him. They shook hands, Todd's expression stoic. This had to be killing him. He said something to Chris, who looked surprised and then nodded. He raised his eyebrows when he saw me sitting on the bench.

"Figured you would have caught a cab home."

"I wanted to make sure you didn't get arrested."

"Really? Didn't sound like that earlier." He closed the distance between us and spoke quietly. "Maybe you're just making sure I didn't tell the detective anything about you."

So that's how I needed to play this. "I won't lie. I'm a little nervous."

"I don't sell out friends." He brushed past me, heading for the door. I hurried to keep up, a trickle of remorse sliding through me. Chris obliterated every natural instinct I had. He seemed so sincere, and yet common sense dictated Todd was right, that Chris was in this up to his neck.

"I'm sorry. Going head to head with Justin freaked me out. When I realized you were the one following him and you hadn't said anything, I didn't know what to think."

Chris zipped up his thick sweatshirt, slipping the hood over his head and effectively blocking me out. I realized we were headed for the street, presumably to hail a cab.

"Don't you have to go to impound for the Audi?"

"Nope. Mr. Detective didn't impound it. Gave me a pass. Figured I hooked up with you and let you talk me into doing you favors. Like following his brother and helping you break into the storage unit. I agreed."

Of course that's what Todd said. No doubt relishing every word. "That's because I told him that's what happened."

"So why didn't you get arrested?"

Because I knew how to play the game. "He's got other shit on his mind. And I had to grovel. Admit I was wrong about his precious brother."

Chris waved his hand to hail a cab. "You think so?"

"At this point, yes. Unless Kelly hears something, nothing points to Justin. I can't keep chasing shadows." Saying the words out loud felt strangely liberating, a weight moving off my shoulders.

A yellow cab squealed to a halt at the curb. Chris yanked open the door, and then turned to stare at me. "And what about me? You still think I took the little girl?"

Did I? Did I believe that his childhood could have made him a coldhearted criminal? Absolutely. It happens time and again. And Chris had lied to me, right? I realized he hadn't, not technically. He'd simply omitted following Justin. Everything else could have been the truth. I didn't know, and I didn't know what I believed.

"No."

"Why?"

"Because you're not that good of an actor," I lied. "You came to me to hear about my choices. My line of work. I'm the one who involved you in this business with the kidnapping."

He debated, the intensity of his gaze making me feel naked. "All right, then."

"But I do need the answer to one question." I glanced at the irritated-looking cabbie. "Why were you following Justin?"

"Same reason you're interested in him. I watch the news."

"So you decided to check him out months after his release?"

"Hey." The cabbie, a round man with a thick, graying beard and a wool cap, glared at us over the back of his worn leather seats. "I'm trying to make money here."

Chris pulled out his wallet and retrieved a twenty-dollar bill. He thrust it at the grumbling driver. "Just give me a few minutes." He turned back to me. "My schedule was full when he was first released. I wanted to see where he was living. When I found out there were kids around, I started watching more. Only wish I'd been there when the little girl went missing. Might give us more answers."

"Why only at night? When the kids were in bed and Justin wouldn't have access to them?"

He shrugged. "My work schedule, mostly. Plus, I thought he might be going into other neighborhoods. Not shitting where he eats, so to speak."

"Why didn't you just tell me that?"

"You didn't need to know."

"Todd thought it was me!"

"But you knew it wasn't. And he didn't have any proof," Chris said. "If he'd have kept harassing you about it, I would have stepped up. But I figured you were already creeped out enough by my following you."

"Yeah. I'd have been less creeped out about your following Justin. That reasoning I get. I still don't know why you decided to follow me. And I don't believe you saw me at a scene. I never did, actually. But I played along because I was afraid of what you'd do if I didn't."

He looked pleased. "So I intimidated you? Wasn't my intention."

"Where did you first see me?"

I was pretty sure I already knew the answer. He'd found out about me when he honed in on Justin, like Todd said. Whether or not he was using me, I hadn't decided yet. And his answer right now would go a long way towards that decision.

"During the media buzz when Justin was paroled," he said. "I saw your name and picture in the paper with the parents of the kid he attacked."

"That was a year and a half ago."

"When I decided to check up on him, I did the same with you. You interested me. And then I saw you at a scene—I didn't lie about that—and figured you out."

"How? Just because I happened to be—"

"It was the look on your face," he said. His eyes suddenly roamed over me, making me feel like I'd just been strip-searched. "Immense satisfaction. And then I knew. And I wanted to talk to you." His grin hinted at embarrassment, but his expression was apologetic. "It's kind of lonely being me. I thought you were someone I could talk to."

"But you believe you're a sociopath. Why did you want to talk?"

He pursed his lips, shaking his head. "I can't answer that. I just... did." His tone was so vulnerable, I was struck with the need to comfort him. I barely caught myself.

"All right, then." I echoed his earlier words, more confused than ever. "If you want to talk, we can talk."

"Thanks. But not tonight." He finally slid into the backseat of the taxi. The driver grumbled under his breath and gunned the engine. "It's late, I'm tired, and I still need to get my car. I came off a shift this morning, you know."

"Can I share your cab, then?" I shouldn't tell him where I lived. Of course, he probably knew already.

"I was raised right," he teased. "As long as you split the fare."

TWENTY-ONE

Too early the next morning, sitting at the breakfast table, I watched Philadelphia wake up. An untouched bowl of steel-cut oats sat cooling in front of me. I sipped coffee and wished I had an espresso maker. The extra boost would be extremely welcome right now. I should at least start buying stronger coffee, but I'm too cheap to buy the good stuff.

Mousecop warmed my lap, his legs dangling on either side. I ran my fingers through his silky fur, the feel of his happy purring easing my rampant nerves. This afternoon would mark ninety-six hours since Kailey's disappearance. Her mother had appeared on the news this morning, looking exhausted and pleading for her daughter's return. I was amazed the media hadn't realized who Jenna was. According to Todd, her family went to great lengths after she was returned home to establish a new identity for her, and that's why they hadn't made an appearance since Kailey had been taken. They wanted their daughter to be able to move on without anything more than her own memories hanging over her head. As if those weren't monsters enough. Todd hadn't even realized who she was until he found out Chris's real name and started checking out Jenna on a hunch.

Still, the media could smell a sensational story like a shark senses chum. They'd find out, and most likely soon. Probably from a source in the police department. I wondered how long it would take before they tracked Chris down. Then again, he had his uncle protecting him.

I prayed Chris didn't have Kailey. If he did, then my instincts had gone to complete shit. Last night, despite everything I'd learned and my own previous fears, I couldn't shake the feeling that Chris had nothing to do with the kidnapping. I had no real reason for this, other than a pure gut feeling, and that apparently wasn't very reliable anymore. But every time I thought about our talk in the parking lot, about the way he looked when he answered my questions, about his emotion when he spoke of Kailey, I couldn't swallow the idea he'd taken her.

And that needed to end right now. My business wasn't based in gut feelings. I worked with hard evidence. With every vigilante action I'd taken, I'd had hard proof the subject was still hurting children. This was no different. All I had to do was work the methodology. And get Chris to talk. By tonight.

The buzzing of the intercom nearly made me topple in the chair. Mousecop leapt off my lap and sauntered off, his bottle-brush tail sticking straight up. Hand to my pounding heart, I trudged to the speaker. "Yes?"

"It's Justin Beckett. I really need to talk to you."

My mouth dropped open. "How'd you get my address?"

"I spent the night at Todd's last night. He had it on file."

"He's got a file on me?" *Of course he does.*

"He thought you were following me."

"You thought I was following you," I corrected.

"Can you blame me?"

No, but still. I couldn't believe he'd shown up here. "What do you want?"

"Please. This is about Kailey. Todd won't listen, and I don't know who else to turn to."

Letting him in was stupid. But I couldn't say no, and he knew it. "Fine, but I'm texting a friend to let them know you're here."

"Whatever works."

I hit the entry button and then quickly texted Kelly to let her know what was going on, imagining the look on her face when she read it. Justin knocked on the door just as I hit the icon.

I tightened my robe. The tank top I wore beneath it had a built-in bra, but it was made for women with little on top. At least the robe went to my knees.

Taking a deep breath and bracing myself for defensive maneuvers, I opened the door.

"Thanks for seeing me." He'd gotten a haircut. He still slouched.

"Come in." I motioned for him to sit, making sure not to turn my back. Justin looked around and chewed his nails. Finally, he sat down only to jump back up again.

"You've been in the storage unit."

"I have." I stayed by the door. "You're a very talented artist."

"I hate her." Justin's expression mirrored his angry tone.

"She's the one, isn't she? The one who hurt you."

"She did more than hurt me. She ruined my life!" He closed his eyes, pressing his fingertips to his forehead. His body shook for a moment, and then he took a deep breath. "You said you wanted to understand. Did you mean that?"

"Yes." I stepped forward without thinking, half reaching for him. "Tell me what happened."

Justin pulled up the right sleeve of his navy sweatshirt to reveal a faded, thin scar along his inner forearm, on the sensitive skin on the underside of the wrist. "She did this to me when I was eight. Said I was a whiney, pretty boy. A baby."

I'd heard more stories like this than I wanted to admit, but every one still felt like a punch in the stomach. "Is that the first time she hurt you?"

"No. She disciplined me, as she liked to call it, since I was little. And the verbal abuse goes back as long as I can remember. But this"—he touched the scar—"this is when things changed."

"What did your father do? And Todd? He was a teenager. Old enough to help."

"Todd lived with his own mother most of the time. And my dad was a drunk. She controlled the house. And me. Never let me have any friends."

"I remember your being alone," I said. Anger surged through me. It's gender bias, but hearing about a mother abusing her child is worse than salt in a wound. How could a woman who shared her body with her child, who brought his life into this world, turn on him like that? It's despicable. And unforgivable. "I am so sorry I didn't help you."

"There was no physical proof," Justin said. "Because the beatings were reserved to my ass most of the time. The mental abuse was worse. She resented me, wanted to control me. And when I got a little older and started getting interested in girls..." His voice caught.

"You were eleven," I said. "That's still pretty young. And Layla was only ten."

"We were just playing around." Justin sat back down on my couch and dropped his head to his hands. "Layla saw her parents having sex the night before. She knew she wasn't allowed at my house, but she saw my mother leave for the store and snuck over. Layla told me what she saw, and then she decided to show me. I didn't know what to do, so I did what she told me to. I lay down; she climbed on top of me. She started bouncing around, and my body reacted. She wanted to see it, and I showed her. I knew it was wrong, but I was so curious. And she was the only thing close to a friend I had. Which is why my mother hated her."

He finally looked up. "She caught us."

"And then what?" My throat had gone dry. I sat down on the couch.

"My mom started screaming. Layla tried to run, but Mom knocked her down. Slammed Layla's head on the coffee table, and it started bleeding. Layla said she was going to tell her parents and my mom would go to jail." Justin's skin was gray. "Mom went ballistic. She grabbed Layla by the hair and started hitting her. The whole time screaming at me that this was my fault. She took off her belt and snapped it at me. I hated that belt. She blistered my ass with it once so bad I couldn't sit for days."

"She made you hit Layla."

Tears squeezed out of his eyes. "It was my punch that knocked her out. I'll never forget the look on her face when my fist came towards her. She was so scared and then shocked. Like she couldn't believe I would really do it. Then it got worse." He gulped air, his chest wheezing.

"My pants were still down. My mother grabbed me and squeezed so hard I dropped. She told me if I wanted to know what boys did to girls with that thing, she'd show me. I was rolling in pain, but I tried to get to the door while she went to the kitchen. She came back with a spoon. And she..." He swallowed and looked sick. He rubbed his face until it glowed red.

"Jesus Christ." I thought I might throw up myself. The police report had said Layla was abused with an object, and the theory had been because Justin couldn't get an erection, he'd used the object. Never in my darkest nightmares had I expected to hear this.

"When she was finished, she slammed Layla's head on the floor. Hard. There was blood everywhere. She wiped her hands on my clothes. I couldn't speak. I remember feeling like I was outside of my body. Like this was some dream I'd wake up from." His words came fast, his breath faster, practically on the verge of hyperventilating. I hurried to the kitchen and grabbed a bottle of water.

"Stop, take a drink. Catch your breath. Whatever happened is in the past, and you have however long you need to tell me the story."

He nodded, sucking down the water with such force the bottle made a sharp popping noise as the sides caved in. Justin breathed deeply and then rolled his shoulders back. "When it happened, the whole time she was smearing me with blood, she kept telling me I'd done this. Because I let the little whore stain me. I was the one who'd hurt her. My mother did what she had to do. It wasn't her fault. After my shirt was all bloodied, she yanked it off me and smothered Layla. Then she cleaned herself off and called the police."

Justin fell back against the couch, gangly body limp.

I stared. Anger and disgust and shame coursed through me, some targeted at Martha Beckett, the rest at myself. If I ever had the chance, I'd make her pay for the lives she'd ruined. "You never said anything. Why on earth didn't you speak up?"

"She told me she'd kill me if I did. And I believed her," Justin said. "I'd just witnessed her rape and kill my friend. And I'd spent years with her mental abuse. I was eleven. Do you really think it's such a stretch that I didn't say anything?"

I thought back to the days after Layla's murder. Justin had been catatonic for the first three. And then he'd simply said, "Yes, I did it. I wanted to touch her, and she wouldn't let me. I got angry." He'd never answered any more questions. And from what I knew, the intense therapy he'd undergone during his time in juvenile detention revolved around his anger issues. "Why are you telling me this now?"

"Because I think my mother took Kailey. And it's my fault."

I suppose I should have seen his words coming, but after the horror I'd just listened to, my brain took a few seconds to catch up. Justin waited, as if he knew I needed to process. Silent and pale, with his haunting eyes, he reminded me of the little boy I'd visited in the detention facility almost a decade ago. I remembered everything about that day. I hadn't been able to eat. The juvenile facility smelled like cleaning chemicals and hormones. A group of older boys played basketball in the courtyard, watched over by a dutiful, if not bored, guard. One of them stopped and stared as I walked past. He was cute. And then I felt like Mrs. Robinson and hurried inside.

Justin was under strict observation. A psychologist kept trying to get him to talk, and he did nothing but stare vacantly. Staff shook their heads and whispered about how impossible something like this was, that children don't kill children, that someone should have seen this all coming and done something to stop it.

At the time, I believed that someone should have been me. I slunk into the room and tried to get through to the little boy who'd seemed to like me just a few short weeks ago. He never spoke.

But his mother did.

Anger reverberated through me. I'd nearly forgotten how that woman had yelled at me. She'd charged toward me, her stride and ferocity so reminiscent of one of my childhood bullies I actually shrank back.

"Your mother blamed me." My voice sounded froggish.

"What?"

"I came to see you the day after you were arrested. You weren't speaking, and I wasn't sure you even knew I was there."

"I don't remember. But I don't remember much about those days."

"She came at me in the hallway. Said I should have seen the evil in you."

"She was a great actress," he said. "Sometimes I think she believed her own lies."

If anyone deserved my kind of justice, it was Martha Beckett. Just like Chris said. A woman looking the other way or putting her own visceral needs before her child is crime enough, but what Martha did was unspeakable. Unimaginable. Unforgivable. The parallels between Justin and Chris's early lives were painful and sadly ironic.

"She took Kailey," Justin repeated.

I trained my eyes on him. Vengeance could wait. "Why do you say that? And why are you telling me instead of your brother?"

"I have told him. He thinks I'm reaching, my version of acting out. I thought you might listen because Todd said you felt bad about suspecting me, and I don't have anyone else to go to. You said you want to help find her..."

"I'm listening," I said. "Tell me why you think your mother's involved."

"When you started following me—at least, I thought it was you—I got really pissed. It was bad enough you believed I was a monster, but to know you were checking up on me just ignited the hate. So I paid my mom a visit."

"How did you find her?"

"She's not exactly hiding. I hadn't seen her since I was twelve or so. She gave me up as a ward to the state, you know. Anyway, the look on her face when she opened the door to find me standing there... she was stunned. And pissed."

"Chris was right," I said. "That picture..."

"Yeah. I went right to the unit and drew it."

"Why did you do all that in the storage unit?"

"I have home visits with a court-appointed therapist." Justin shrugged his shoulders. "I don't want her to see that shit."

I could get behind that. "I suppose you guys still talk about your anger issues? Did you ever tell the therapist? Why didn't you ever speak out as you got older?"

"You think they'd believe me?" Justin's bitter laugh rang through the apartment. "Martha runs a popular business. She bakes, for Christ's sake. Everyone felt sorry for her. Do you know what that's like, to see the person responsible for all the shittiness in your life make herself the victim?"

If he only knew. At my sister's funeral, my grieving mother threw herself over the pink casket, asking how Lily could do this to her. I walked outside and dry-heaved.

"So you suffered in silence."

"Todd knows. He's been pushing me to tell the truth, expose her for what she is. But I kept thinking the damage was done. And it was my fault, in a way. I should have made my friend go home. I knew better." He dragged his hands through his short hair, digging his fingers into his scalp until they turned white.

"Spoken like a person who's been expertly manipulated his whole life. So you sought her out because you thought I was following you?"

"Yeah. It was like being thrown to the dogs all over again. And I wasn't going to take it." He glared past me, eyes hazy. Probably caught in the memory of his own injustice.

I tried not to let the idea that I'd somehow set all of this in motion take over. Chris had been the one following him. And this had to stop being about me. "What did Martha do when you showed up?"

"I hoped she'd have a heart attack. But she just glared like a constipated bulldog." He sneered. "I thought she wouldn't seem like such a giant, but she's still bigger than me."

"She let you inside."

"She had no reason to be afraid."

Apparently aging had done nothing to weaken Martha's confidence. Then again, she'd managed to keep Justin silent without speaking to him for years. Truly impressive to maintain control with no contact. My own mother would be jealous.

"What did you tell her?"

"That I was through with her messing up my life. Told her I'd been given a second chance, and I was going to make the best of it. She laughed." Justin's teeth dug into his lower lip until he drew blood. "And I said to laugh while she could, because I was going to tell the world what she did. Even if no one but my brother believed me, at least the truth would be out there. And she wouldn't be able to pity-trip her way through. No one would look at her the same again."

"You woke the sleeping beast," I said. "You think she took Kailey to discredit you before you could say anything?"

He nodded.

I crossed my legs and then remembered my robe. "It's possible, but that's a big stretch. If she did those things and got away with them, I'm not sure she'd believe your threat. She's been in power for so long, she may have assumed you were all talk."

Justin was already shaking his head before I finished my sentence. "My mother drove by my place two days before Kailey disappeared. Kailey and those two older girls who ignore her most of the time were hanging out front while I was painting. The older ones wanted to see my drawings. I told them no, to get home. I had my box of pencils sitting on the porch railing and knocked them off." He banged his fist to his forehead hard enough it had to hurt. "She saw Kailey pick them up and hand them to me with this big, shy smile on her face. That's when I saw the red car slow down."

"You're absolutely sure it was Martha?"

"She smiled and waved. Kailey disappeared the next day."

I wanted to bang my own head against the coffee table. "And you've told Todd all of this?"

"Yes, but he's been on my ass about my obsession with her. He thinks my going to her was a mistake. That I let her get in my head again. Thinks I imagined it. He said he'd check into her whereabouts, but he's already got a good suspect."

"Chris Hale. Speaking of which, why did you have newspaper articles on the Lancaster killings?"

"Weston," Justin corrected. He flushed and looked down at his toes. "Dunno. I guess because there was such a young kid involved, and he turned out okay. I thought that might mean I could too." He stared up at me with dark but hopeful eyes. He wanted me to agree.

"Of course there's hope for you." I spoke the last words I ever thought I'd say. "You were victimized in so many ways, and you're still fighting. There is always hope."

He swallowed, his Adam's apple bobbing, and then cleared his throat. "You really think Chris is more of a suspect than my mother?"

It felt like my head might explode. The voices whirled around me like a vortex, making it impossible to discern one voice from the other. The ever-thinning line keeping me on the right side of the law was disappearing. If I kept up with my own investigation, I'd use up Todd's leniency. I didn't need any focus on my extracurricular activities.

But as I stared at Justin's pleading, desperate face, I saw my sister. Her voice emerged from the din. The day she told my mother what my possibly soon-to-be stepfather was doing to her, our mother had cried, but not for my sister. For herself. She would never have such bad judgment. Lily was just a willful, bitter teenager, and how could she make such horrific accusations? She slapped Lily. My sister screamed and begged for her to believe her. She must have shouted the word "listen" a dozen times, and I swear, every time my heart shattered all over again. She was so sad. So hurt. And I couldn't help her.

My mother told her to go to her room and think about how selfish she was. Later, as I was trying to hide from my mother's self-pity, I poked my head in my sister's room. She lay on her side, facing the wall.

"I believe you, Lil," I said. "I believe you."

"You're not enough," Lily said. "You're just a kid." And then she turned to me, face swollen from crying and her eyes flat. "Don't ever let him touch you. If he does—if anyone touches you like that, you fight back. You do whatever it takes to protect yourself, Lucy. You're an innocent kid just like I was. And no one is going to protect you but yourself. Knife him if you have to. Run away. But don't submit."

Those were the last words my sister said to me.

My phone beeped, signaling a text from Kelly. I glanced at it, planning to let her know I was all right.

Info on Brian Harrison, the sex offender who lives near Kailey's place. Come when u can.

I wasn't sure how I'd find the alleged photo his brother had shared of me the night of our date—the night I'd killed Brian's brother. But Kailey had to be my first priority.

"Lucy." Justin's nervous voice brought me back to the present. "What do you think? Will you help me? Are you listening?"

My eyes snapped to his. "I'm listening. Can you give me until tonight?"

TWENTY-TWO

"Sorry to make you come over here," Kelly said. "But I couldn't email this shit. What did Justin want?"

I was still trying to reconcile Justin's confession. "Just to talk. I promise I'll tell you about it later, once I get it all sorted in my head. Tell me how you got this information again?"

One of the best things about Kelly is that she knows when not to push. "I sent Brian a picture he couldn't resist loaded with a virus that lets me remote into his computer."

Technical stuff that was above my head, but I trusted her. "What did you find out?"

"A lot. Brian Harrison doesn't hop around the child porn sites much, which probably explains why his computer security is so lax. He does, however, belong to a forum of pigs who think they should be allowed to have sex with pre-teen girls."

The familiar disgust rippled through me. "Of course he does. Anything you can do about that?"

Kelly shook her head. "They're not doing anything illegal, technically. They aren't posting pics or links or discussing how to meet. They're mostly just whining like bitches."

"Of course. God forbid our legal system stop something before it starts."

Fingers flying, Kelly went through a series of folders on her computer. "This is my temporary section. I trash all of this—permanently, so there's no trace—but while I'm stuck with the garbage, I've got it hidden as deep as possible."

"Prepare me. Are we going to see filth?"

"No. But it's creepy." She finally got to the hidden folder, and a series of images popped up on the screen. Obviously taken from a cellphone, and many from a distance, they were all of unsuspecting little girls just going about their lives. All of them had some sign of puberty: budding chests, shapely little hips, and innocent smiles. Many of them were wearing short shorts and tight shirts, which seemed to be the norm these days, and a few were teasing boys, already fully aware of their prowess. I felt a surge of disgust followed by a wave of sadness. *How has society changed so much that it is acceptable for little girls to dress like this?* It doesn't give pigs like Harrison the right to covet them. It just means they're growing up too fast, already sexualized and already putting more emphasis on their bodies than on their brains. That's a recipe for low self-esteem and lots of heartache.

One of the girls caught my eye. Long, dark brown hair, pink shorts to show off strong thighs and newly formed hips, with a white tank-top to display an emerging chest she was probably very proud of. She was pretty, and her face still had the roundness of childhood. The picture caught her mid-laugh, clapping her hands, and she looked like a child stuck in a woman's body.

Anger boomed in my head with the fury of a bass drum. *Josie.* I'd been right. She didn't want to go to the vacant lot because Brian Harrison had attacked her there, and she couldn't escape him at school. That's why she didn't want to go there, either. She'd rather be dead than endure.

My molars ground together with the force of my gnashing

jaw. A sizzling bolt of energy rolled through me. "That's Josie Henderson, one of the girls who walks Kailey home. I think he molested her in the lot."

"Shit," Kelly said. "She's Harrison's star. Most of the pictures are taken in the neighborhood, with her friends. But a couple at the pool. Kailey isn't in a single one."

"Are there any taken in the fall? Ones that are more recent?"

Kelly scrolled through the pictures, and the result sent me into a fury. Josie and another girl, likely Bridget, in the vacant lot, lost in a conversation. Both girls wore jackets, and the weeds were yellowed and coarse. "This is the vacant lot, isn't it?"

Sly Lyle had likely seen Harrison attacking Josie there. Had he honed in on Kailey next? The age difference nagged at me, but it wasn't impossible for a predator to change preferences. At any rate, I had all the information I needed. "Yes. I'm going to need to talk to Brian Harrison."

Normally, when I chose a target, I tailed them for a few weeks, getting to know routine, habits, hangouts. I chose the best place to seal the deal; it had to be crowded, loud, and if I was going to spill cyanide, alcohol had to be served. One thing I never did was waffle on my decision. I might spend hours wearing a path on my carpet worrying about the logistics, but once I had the evidence, I never second-guessed myself.

But Brian Harrison needed to be dealt with right away. I'd find out if he took Kailey, save my own ass, and end his chances of making another child suffer. If he actually did have Kailey and I continued to sit back on my heels, I might as well have attacked her myself.

Cyanide was the best solution for my Brian Harrison dilemma. It presented like a heart attack and left few traces, with the exception of the almond odor, and that wasn't always noticeable. Most medical examiners aren't looking for cyanide, and since Brian Harrison was a known drug user, a heart attack wouldn't be out of the ordinary. He and his mouth would be out of my way, and Josie's molester would get his due justice.

One phone call from an untraceable, prepaid cell was all it had taken to get him to an empty parking garage in Southwest Philly. This area of the city is dangerous, but since the majority of it resembles a post-apocalyptic wasteland and is in terminal decline, it's the best place to find privacy.

My message to Brian Harrison was short and sweet.

"I know what you did to that girl in the vacant lot. I've got the pictures to prove it. Get your ass to the empty parking garage on Island Avenue in Southwest Philly, or I'll go to the police."

I didn't have a plan B if he didn't take the bait, and I didn't need one. I watched Brian Harrison arrive. He looked gaunt and nervous. He'd replaced his janitor's uniform with dirty jeans and well-worn, steel-toed boots. Weapons, I reminded myself. I already had my latex gloves on beneath my wool ones. The vial of cyanide was in my pocket, my hand clutching it for fast reaction. I needed to give my chemist a call. Once I took care of Slimy Steve, I'd be out.

He'd arrived alone, as I'd told him. I knew he would. He didn't have friends, his neighbors thought he was a pedophile, and he couldn't exactly ask for backup tonight without telling someone what he was being accused of. I had the advantage.

He didn't see me approach. Leaning against a pylon, shivering in his thin jacket, he lit a cigarette and took a long pull. His hand shook. Up close, his pale skin was splotchy red. I took stock of his clothes: a thin jacket with the buttons only partially buttoned and a V-necked undershirt. Easy access. I wouldn't have to worry about the stuff seeping through his clothes. I would, however, have to approach this one differently. I couldn't pretend to spill my martini on his lap. This would be direct contact, and I needed to hit his skin.

There's a first time for everything.

"Hello, Brian."

He whirled around, nearly dropping his cigarette. I'd donned a wool cap to cover most of my hair, but enough of it stuck out that he quickly made the connection, just like I wanted him to. The twisted part of me that longs for vengeance —the part I rarely acknowledged—wanted Brian Harrison to know the same woman who'd brought his brother to justice was about to do the same to him.

"You killed my brother." His fear turned to anger, eyes thinning into slits and his cheeks breaking out in red splotches. He took a step toward me, flexing his thick hands, his muscles straining against the sleeves of his jacket. I held my ground.

"I knew your brother. He was a pedophile like you."

"I don't know what you're talking about." He licked his dry lips and squared his shoulders, pulling back an arm. I clutched the small vial of cyanide tightly.

"Save it. I've seen the pictures on your computer. Lots of little girls, but Josie was the star. Seems you especially liked her pink shorts. You took lots of pictures on those days."

His newfound bravado wilted like a limp flower. He leaned against the pylon, glancing around the vacant garage with nervous, darting looks. "What do you want?"

"Kailey Richardson. Do you know anything about her?"

"The little girl from Kipling Elementary who's missing?" He stood straighter, obviously relieved. "No, I already talked to the cops when they were going round the neighborhood."

I took out a picture. "Kailey walked home with Josie and her friend. You see her at school every day. What happened? Did you get tired of Josie and want a younger version?" I tasted bile at the words.

His bulbous head rocked from side to side. "Kailey's just a little kid."

"Josie's a little kid, too."

"She's a teenager."

"She's twelve." I warned myself not to grip the bottle too tightly. Harrison deserved the stuff poured down his throat.

"Looks like a teenager."

"Did you have anything to do with Kailey's disappearance?"

"No. I'm not into little kids."

And this was why pedophiles can't change. There's something in their chemical makeup, something that keeps them from seeing the world through the same lens the rest of us have. "Just because a little girl is starting to look like a woman doesn't mean she's fair game for creeps like you."

"She didn't seem to think that."

Another part of the sickness. The child who doesn't understand her own sexuality somehow asked to be attacked. "The witness I spoke to said Josie looked terrified."

He swallowed hard, losing his brief confidence. "Can't be no witness."

"You think you're the only person who goes to that vacant lot?" I smirked, enjoying the white fear that flashed across his face. Even the most vile serial killers have morals about sexually abusing kids.

Harrison took another drag off the rapidly burning cigarette, hand shaking so badly I thought he'd drop it. "I didn't do anything to the little girl. She's too young. The other girl was different."

I wished I could crawl inside his mind and pick it apart, study the slivers of his brain that made him think his actions were okay. "If you tell me where Kailey is, or anything you might know, I'll forget about those pictures. Let this whole thing drop."

"I don't like little girls." The words came as though he were biting down on each one. His white face had now turned purple and a thick vein on his forehead pulsed.

I believed him. He didn't have any pictures of Kailey.

I softened my voice. "Do you know anyone in her neighborhood who does?"

"Rumor is the child killer did it, the one no one knew about living across the street."

"Why is that a rumor?"

"'Cause he was living there without any of the parents having a clue about who he was," Harrison said. "Then the kid disappears. Ain't rocket science. And it ain't right, his not having to tell parents what a scumbag he is."

He reeked of self-righteous arrogance, rigid in his belief that his sexual urges were natural. Justified. People like him are the gutter of our society. Brian Harrison calling Justin a scumbag just breaths after defending his own actions—another part of his incurable disease. He simply can't see his actions as wrong, because in his mind, his system is the correct one. Societal rules don't matter.

And I am the same.

The realization shocked me to momentary paralysis. Multicolored dots flashed in front of my eyes, dancing around Brian Harrison's pale, ugly face like painted dust motes. He sensed the shift in my confidence and stepped closer, a vile grin spreading across his face and showing the yellowed tips of his teeth.

I snapped back into alertness. "Is he a different kind of scumbag than you?" The container in my hand seemed to grow hot. Carefully, with a practiced hand, I unzipped the plastic bag and unscrewed the cap. I knew I took my life in my hands every time I used the cyanide. I took precautions covering my skin, but accidents happen. Still, I didn't know how to do this any other way.

"I don't kill kids."

"No, you just steal their youth."

He rolled his shoulders back in defiance. The cords in his neck bulged, his blond chest hairs trying to escape through the collar of his shirt. Jaw taut, eyes barely open, he had the balls to be offended at my accusation.

The man who abused my sister was just like Brian Harrison. When he showed up at our house months after her death, he'd come to see me. He knew I was home alone. My mother had broken up with him more out of mortification than anything, and he still lived in the neighborhood, walking around a free man while my sister rotted in her grave.

"She wasn't a little kid, you know," he explained to me that horrible day. "When we started, she was just like you. Had this body she didn't know how to use, and she wanted me to see it. Like they all do." His eyes slid over my chest; I'd gotten my first bra that summer, and its lines were visible beneath my shirt. He stepped toward me, licked his lips. "How old are you again, Lucy?"

I went for the baseball bat and cracked his skull. My juvenile record was expunged, and my sister's abuser left us alone. He's still out there somewhere, probably hurting other little girls. Maybe one day I will find him.

"I want those pictures," Harrison said.

"They're in your computer."

"Then how'd you get them?"

"I have my ways." My right hand was still in my pocket. I assume Brian thought I had pepper spray ready. With the cap between my thumb and forefinger and the vial clenched in my fingers, I withdrew my hand.

He watched, a bemused expression on his face. I'm sure, in this darkened parking garage, a two-hundred-pound man didn't believe he had anything to fear from an average-sized woman.

"What you got there?"

Self-control kept me from throwing it on his face. Instead,

with a smooth flick of my wrist, I tossed the cyanide directly at his chest, watching the liquid splash onto his shirt and exposed skin. A droplet lingered on one of his chest hairs.

"You dumb bitch." He looked down at himself in disgust. "What the fuck? What is this shit?"

I said nothing. Some of the poison had made direct contact with his skin. This wasn't going to take long.

If I were a polite murderer, I would have offered him a hand. Maybe told him to sit down so he didn't fall and hit his head. At least offer him some comfort in the last moments of his life. After all, it wasn't his fault he was like this. It was something wired in his brain, maybe mixed with some lousy childhood experience.

"Were you and Cody abused?" I asked. "Did someone sexually assault you both? Is that why you became deviants?" The cold abruptness of the question surprised me. Shouldn't I feel some sort of empathy for what was about to happen? Normally, by this time, I was nearly back to my car, long away from the scene of the crime. So logic would dictate I have some sort of empathy or remorse at this moment. But I felt nothing but anger and disgust. I expected self-preservation to kick in, the warning that I needed to run, to keep from seeing the result of my actions. Instead, I stood rooted to the spot and watched the cyanide take effect.

Maybe I'm the sociopath.

I'll think about that later.

"What?" Brian breathed as though he'd just finished a marathon. He leaned against the pylon.

"You and your brother are both child molesters. Or, in Cody's case, were. Why? It's unusual that both of you would be so screwed-up, unless you experienced something really bad in childhood. So I'm asking you what it was."

"None of your business."

I shrugged. "So something did happen to you. It's almost

always that way. A combination of nature and nurture. That's why it's a vicious cycle."

Harder breaths now, coming on like a speeding freight train. Glistening sweat dotted his forehead, with a few droplets dribbling down his face. He shivered. "What are you talking about?" His knees jerked as if he'd been kicked, and his shaking body slipped down the pylon.

"How can you want to touch them? They're babies. My sister was just a baby. How can you justify taking that from her?"

His meaty fingers dug into his left arm. "I don't know your sister. I think I'm having a heart attack."

He didn't know Lily—none of them did. But every sicko was of the same breed connected by some sort of corrupt DNA thread that required eradication. "That's only what it feels like."

"It? What?" His eyes widened, and his breaths were long and ragged like shards of glass. "What did you throw on me?"

"Cyanide." My matter-of-fact tone sounded like it belonged to someone else. I should be in my car, feeling remorse, reminding myself that this person needed to be put down like a rabid animal. "It presents like a heart attack. Since it made direct contact with your skin, this won't take long. I'd apologize for your suffering, but truly, I'm not sorry."

Shock flickered across his face, and then panic. He tried to get up, gasped, still clutching his arm. His eyes were wild now, darting past me, searching for someone to help. There wouldn't be anyone. I'd chosen this parking garage well.

"You're killing me. Like you killed Cody."

"I am."

I expected him to beg. Cry. I could deal with those things because I believed he didn't deserve them. Didn't have the right to plead for anything. He didn't listen to his victims' plea.

"I deserve to die."

The iron case around my heart weakened. "You don't believe that."

"Yes, I do. I've always known it. Me and my brother... we never had a chance. Least, that's what he said. I always believed him. And I did..." He gasped again. "I did try to be good. But I never could manage it. Every time I thought I'd beaten it, the urge came back worse than before."

"It's impossible." *Shut up. Don't try to be a human now. Don't make me feel for you.*

His skin paled, tinged with the blue of a corpse.

"So I should be put down. Like a rabid dog." He'd gone into my mind, yanked out my own words. Maybe we were the same, just with different addictions. My addiction was my twisted need to make things right, to squash some of the torment that kept me up at night.

I'm killing him for myself too.

Another breath, this one more labored. "No more trying to fight it. No more worrying about getting caught. Maybe I'll see Cody in hell too."

He closed his eyes and said nothing more, nursing his breathing.

My own breath grew unsteady. My heartbeat ramped up until my head hurt. A voice I usually kept locked up roared in my head.

What gives you the right? How can you do this? This man is dying. You're a killer. A screwed-up mind seeking solace, just like all the other murderers on death row.

"I'm doing what any parent would." I spoke out loud to no one. Brian was beyond listening. His eyes rolled back in his head, saliva pooling at the corner of his mouth. "Every parent of an abused child would kill the person responsible if they thought they could get away with it. I'm doing that for them. For all the Josies of the world."

Brian groaned, then mumbled something I couldn't understand. The color had drained from his face like someone turning a colored photograph into a black and white one. He coughed, once, hard. His body began to shake, most likely a seizure, and his eyes flew open. They were filled with a terror I would never forget. He reached for me, his hand flailing for some kind of human contact. He was going into the void. Did he see darkness? Was it slithering over him like an immovable veil?

I gave him my gloved hand. *I'll have to burn these.*

His gaze locked with mine, his grip tight enough to cut off circulation. A final shudder, and then stillness. His unseeing eyes still seemed focused on me, accusing in their opacity. There was no sense of peace, no feeling that his soul had left. Just utter stillness.

He's nothing now.

I pulled my hand free of his and ran to the car.

TWENTY-THREE

I shouldn't have just shown up at Kelly's door, but she didn't seem surprised. I must have looked terrible; she ushered me right in and put the teapot on to boil. Her little place smelled of orange tea, and the scent made me feel less like crawling out of my skin.

"I thought I might see you again tonight."

"Why?"

"Because you couldn't walk away until it was done this time." Kelly sat the cup of tea in front of me. Chin on her hand, she looked young and sweet. Innocent. But her mind and body knew horrors because of someone like Brian Harrison.

I did the right thing. Killing Brian Harrison is for Kelly and Josie and kids like them. His terrified eyes flashed in my vision once more, and I rubbed my temples as if to extricate the memory.

I didn't give her any details. She didn't need any more sinister images to keep her awake at night. "He thought he was at peace with death. Like it was the best thing. I think that's what threw me."

"You watched a man die. At your hands. If you didn't feel something, I'd be worried about you."

But I didn't feel anything for him at first. What does that say about me? I couldn't bring myself to ask her.

I took a drink of the steaming tea, wincing as it burned my throat. I took another drink and let it burn my lips. "It's not that I didn't fully understand the consequences of my decisions. Seeing them in action, watching the life literally leave his eyes... I don't know how to explain it."

"Because you can't. Human life is vibrant—an energy. Even if that energy is dark and twisted and needs to be extinguished, it's a tangible force. Watching its destruction makes us all realize how fragile we are. And when you're the wrecking ball..." Her voice trailed off.

"It's the nothingness, Kel." My voice was barely audible. "Whenever life ends, it just quits. We literally cease to exist. Every single one of us. It's not even blackness. It's literally nothing." The pulverizing fear rushed me, yanking the breath out of my shaking body. "I bring the nothingness to people."

The cold, stark reality of what I'd become seeped into my bones. I may be a nice person. I'm loyal, a good friend, I help families, help children. I want to make this world a better place, truly. But I'm a killer, just like Chris said. I'd convinced myself I didn't belong on Murderers' Row because I was doing a good service, and so I really wasn't the same. For the past few months, until the day Chris barged into my life, I really believed I was at peace with my decision.

But that's wrong. Being at peace with it would make me a true monster, and I don't want to become a monster. Accept the decision and consequences, fine. Continue on the path I've chosen because I believe I'm helping, all right. But never at peace. That's a reprieve I don't deserve, and a punishment I'll take.

"Are you going to be okay?" The gentle pressure of Kelly's hand on my shoulder soothed me.

"Yeah. I just need to process. You know me."

She smiled. "Better than anyone, I think."

We sat in silence for a few minutes, but I kept seeing Brian's eyes, dead and accusatory. Then his face morphed into the five other men I'd killed and to the one I should have killed, my sister's abuser, and finally to my own cold, dead face. I needed to talk about something else. Kelly beat me to it, however.

"So I've got some good news on Slimy Steve, the scumbag you were watching at Chetter's when Chris interrupted you. My contact at the police department told me about an electronics scam they're working on. Some guy is stealing tablets and laptops, filing the serial numbers off, and selling them in an online action. Guess who one of the prime suspects is?"

"Steve," I said. "Are they building a decent case against him?"

"My contact thinks so. Apparently it's quite a network. Maybe you'll get lucky, and they'll take him off the streets for you."

That would be a blessing. I didn't want to think about tracking anyone else right now. "I hope so. Listen, I need to tell you Justin's story from this morning."

Kelly sat in stunned silence as I told her everything Justin had confessed. Part of the reason I'd put off telling her was because I knew how much it had to hurt her to hear. She knew what it was like to have a parent use her for his own sick means. I hated having to dump it all on her, but she was the only person in my life I fully trusted. And if I didn't get the words out, I would explode.

"Jesus Christ," she finally said. "That poor kid."

"I'm sorry to dump this on you."

"I can handle it." She squirmed in her seat, looking queasy.

"And I should have listened to you. You were right about Justin."

"Stop worrying about what you should have done and do something now."

"I don't know what to do." Hopelessness slid over me. "There are plenty of things I want to do, but they all have consequences, and I don't know which sucks less."

Kelly sighed. "What's the first thing you want to do?"

The answer required no thinking. "I want to confront Justin's mother. I want to make her admit everything she did to him and force her to tell me if she took Kailey. Then I'd like to drop a cup of cyanide down her throat."

"Let's save that second part for later," Kelly said. "Why not confront her, especially if she did take Kailey?"

"She thinks she's got the upper hand. That Justin's shaking in his boots. If she found out he confided in someone else—in me, particularly—she might bolt. If she has Kailey..."

"Yeah, okay. Plan B?" She paused. "And what's Todd got to say about all of this?"

"Todd says she checks out, but Justin doesn't buy it. That's why he came to me." I rubbed my temples, trying to squash the images still tormenting me. "Her bakery and house are in Fishtown. She could easily be hiding Kailey in either one of those places, but try to find out if she's got any other property."

"You need to get into her house. That's where she'd have her," Kelly said. "Even if she doesn't have any employees, keeping the kid at her business is a big risk. You've got deliveries, customers. Easier to be discovered."

"You're right, of course," I said. "Justin doesn't know her schedule, but we're planning on heading to her house tonight. If she steps out the door, we're going in."

Kelly was silent.

"What?"

"Well, I believe him. But I don't like the idea of you going off with him and doing this. I mean, you've gone from thinking he's the devil to being alone with him."

"I don't have much choice if I want to find Kailey."

"Can't you go to Todd? Tell him you believe Justin? And what about Chris? Aren't you supposed to be getting into his head? Have you just abandoned the idea he could be the guy?"

I stared into my tea. "Todd will tell me to back off, and Justin doesn't want him to know he'd spoken to me. As for Chris..." I hesitated, knowing Kelly wasn't going to like this part. "I really need his help getting into Martha Beckett's house. Justin's young and skittish. Going into his mother's home is going to be really tough on him. I need a backup."

"You're taking both of them?" Kelly's voice went shrill. "Are you nuts? What if Chris is the guy? Or what if they both flake out and get you caught?"

She had a point, and I was too worn out to shuffle through my mental file of Chris's possible motives. "You know what? I've got his address. I'm going to pay him a surprise visit and flat-out ask him."

Kelly coughed, nearly spitting out her tea. "What?"

"Kailey is running out of time. Martha Beckett looks like a better suspect than Chris. The only way to rule him out is to lay everything I know on him and hope I can make a judgment call."

"And what if he lies, and you run into big trouble? Like, I don't know, his attacking you?" She wiped her mouth with a napkin, hands shaking.

"If Chris gets out of line, I'll wing it."

"You've lost your mind."

To be honest, I'm not sure my mind's been fully put together for a long time. I've never been one to believe in any kind of fate, but it's hard not to look back at my life and wonder. Why did Chris come into it when he did? Is he part of some larger plan—a notion I really don't believe in—that I'm not understanding? Maybe Chris showed up so I could see myself for who and what I really am.

I see it now.

But the more likely explanation is that I'm just making excuses for my bad choices. "You're probably right. But I'm done dancing with him."

TWENTY-FOUR

My ballsy plan might be for nothing if Chris wasn't home. I was out of my element. My routine was to follow, to observe, to research, and then judge. Impulsivity was not a part of the Lucy Kendall justice system. But sometimes improvisation is a necessary evil.

As usual, Center City teemed with nightlife. College kids and singles huddled outside the popular bars, laughing and flirting. One of my favorite cheese shops boasted a wine-tasting sign, and I longed to go inside, find a corner, and drink until I passed out.

I ignored the normal people and drove straight to Chris's condominium, located in one of the newer buildings in the area. I wondered if he even had a trust fund or his uncle just bankrolled him.

"Lucy?" His voiced cracked over the speaker, and I secretly smiled with glee at taking him off guard for once. "What are you doing here? Did something happen with the little girl?"

"Her name is Kailey. And I need to talk to you right away."

I half-expected him to refuse, but he hit the buzzer, and I found myself on the elevator to the third floor. My stomach twisted into hard knots, and my jaw ached from grinding my teeth. I wrapped my coat more tightly around me, as if it would protect me from whatever shitstorm I was about to insert myself into. I pocketed the nerves and knocked on Chris's door, a pristine white slab of wood with a gold number three in the middle, just above the peephole.

"Hey." He looked as casual as I'd ever seen him, wearing black track pants and a white, fitted long-sleeved shirt. The black glasses had returned. His sandy hair was tousled, adding to his rugged look. "Come in, but my place is kind of messy. I don't get a lot of visitors."

"Thanks." I quickly took stock of my surroundings. Messy was the wrong adjective, unless you counted too much stuff on the counters and the sweatshirt hanging off the back of a kitchen chair. Chris's condo was an open floor plan, with lots of neutral furniture and a nice granite bar. Artwork hung on a couple of walls, and I think there were some family pictures on a side table, but I barely registered them.

"So what's going on?"

My heart jumped around against my ribs. My mouth went dry.

"Did you know Jenna Richardson is your father's last victim?" The words came out before I considered them.

Chris sank onto a bar stool. His coloring actually went from normal to pallid in about two seconds. A single tremor wracked his lean frame. "The girl in the barn?"

Empathy for what he must have gone through swelled through me. "Yes, Jenna is the girl you found in the barn. Kailey looks a lot like her. Didn't you see the resemblance?"

"I don't remember the girl in the barn's face. I just remember her being chained. Dirty. And crying." He looked at the floor. His shoulders were rigid as he took a long breath.

"And you were following Justin. And me." I kept pushing.

"Were you actually following Justin? Or were you coveting Kailey?"

"What?" His head shot up, surprise replacing his pale shock.

"You see what this looks like, right? You had a childhood trauma—the kind that can significantly alter a personality. Kailey looks like your father's last victim. You were young enough then you may have seen more than just what happened in the barn. Do you follow?"

His thick eyebrows knitted together, forming deep lines across his forehead. "You think I took Kailey? Because of what I was exposed to, I'm somehow following in my father's footsteps?"

"It's possible," I said. "I think you decided to follow Justin because he was released. And then you saw Jenna. Maybe you snapped."

"I didn't follow Justin because he got released." He slid off the bar stool, hands in his hair. His shirt slid up to reveal the toned muscles of his stomach. I purposely looked away.

"So you lied about that too." I bottled my anger and fought to keep my tone even. "If you want me to trust you, tell me everything right now. And that includes why you even stepped into my life. Because I gotta tell you, it really looks like you're using us all as pawns while you hide an innocent child."

Chris held up his hands. "Fine, fine. I guess it's time I laid it all out anyway." He sighed and paced. "My uncle was close to the prosecuting attorney in Justin's case," Chris said. "It was a big deal in our house. I was finishing up school and getting ready for paramedic training. And I kept hearing my uncle say the same things you did about Justin. That he was likely to repeat the behavior if he got out. My aunt always felt he deserved a second chance. And your name came up several times during the trial."

"It did?"

He shot me a keen glance. "You were there at the trial every day. And you visited Justin a few times. The district attorney always talked about how personal you took it. He used to be afraid you would never be able to fully separate yourself from your cases."

I swallowed hard but made no other comment. "Go on."

"So when talk of his release came up, you can imagine my uncle," Chris said. "He was beside himself, and so was the DA. We all followed the case. And I saw you again, on television." His eyes softened a bit as he looked at me." You looked so different than you did ten years ago. Not aged, but seasoned. Hardened. I read what you said in court, that you disagreed with the psychologist's assessment and you felt Justin would repeat. And I felt bad when the judge blew you off."

I didn't like to remember that day. The judge was irritated with me, calling me a crusader and an emotional liability. I'd almost gotten a contempt of court charge. "He said that while he appreciated my extensive experience with Child Protective Services, I wasn't qualified to make judgments on an adult's mental health. He only granted me a chance to speak at the request of the victim's family."

"Did you really think they'd let him out?"

I shook my head. "No. Sometimes. Late at night, you know? When I would try to sleep. I'd get that gut feeling, and then I'd talk myself out of it."

"My uncle cried."

"That's the day I snapped," I said. "I couldn't believe it. I walked out of the courthouse and away from everyone. I walked for hours until I realized I had blisters on my feet. By the time I finally got home, I'd made my decision."

"To be a vigilante."

I nodded. "But this is about you. Why did you start following me?"

He sat back down again, this time on a chocolate-colored

settee that looked like a great place to curl up and read. "You know how many times I've heard my uncle say that people like Justin are destined to be monsters? How many cases of abused kids he's dealt with who turn out to be abusers themselves?" He passed a shaking hand over his hair. "I was just a little kid when I saw that girl in the barn. But there was so much more. Memories I blocked out that only came back years later, in flashes. Things that I witnessed..." Chris looked up at me with pleading eyes. "Lucy, I'm no different than Justin. And if he's destined to be a killer, then shouldn't I be too?"

I caught my breath. So this was his issue. And it was valid. What could I say? "Plenty of abused people go on to lead healthy lives."

He took a tremulous breath. "You don't know what I've seen. It's not just the girl in the barn—Jenna. I have this memory of another girl. She's got dark brown hair. She's in the barn, too. And she's begging me for help. There's blood on her face and between her legs. I know she's not very old. She had braces. And a locket with the initial 'S' on it. My father is in the background, laughing." His voice cracked. "I think I saw more girls."

I felt a hot ball of sickness in the pit of my stomach. "It might not be a real memory," I said, feeling desperate. "You could have read about the case, and your mind filled in the blanks."

"It happened at my birthday party. I remember hearing my uncle say he'd be surprised if I didn't grow up a sociopath." He laughed, bitter and short. "I always hoped he was wrong, but I don't think he was. There are days I don't feel anything. And I don't want anyone in my life unless I can benefit from them. As for why I followed you, I really just wanted to talk to you at first."

He took his glasses off, rubbing them vigorously. He cleared his throat, and I gave him the time to get control over his emotions. I didn't want to see him cry any more than he wanted to cry in front of me. "I wanted to tell you who I was. And what I'm so afraid of."

"Of being like your father?" I finally stepped away from the door and into the room, closing the distance between us. I leaned against the bar stool he'd abandoned.

"Of being nothing. Nothing but a product of my past. I wanted to know if you really believed we don't have a choice in who we are. I wanted you to tell me the difference between me and Justin. And then I realized what you were doing after I saw you at that scene. And I wanted to be like you. I thought, if I could take out the trash like you do, then maybe I'd fulfill my destiny in a way that didn't hurt innocent people. That maybe I wouldn't end up being... nothing."

I blinked against the tears welling up at his words. They hit too close to home. "You've never killed anyone."

He shook his head.

"You're not a sociopath, not that I ever really believed you were. Sociopaths are coldly rational; they don't feel empathy. They either fake it or feel sorry for themselves, but not for anyone else. They're pathological liars, and manipulating people comes natural to them." A sharp needle of cold pierced through my calm. I could have been describing myself.

I couldn't think about that right now.

"Then what am I?"

"Someone with a lot of baggage, like most of humanity." I didn't know what comfort to offer, or even if I should. "Do you remember anything else?"

He looked back down at the floor. "I don't want to talk about that now. I should have told someone a long time ago, and now it doesn't matter."

I decided not to push him. He was a victim, just like the kids I worked with. He needed to trust me to tell me more. "And why did you follow Justin?"

"I wanted to see if he repeated, for my own sake. If there was hope for him, there was hope for me."

The silence deepened between us as I thought over everything Chris had told me.

"You didn't take Kailey." He hadn't really said anything to clear himself, but I knew it in my gut just as I knew my own killing would have to be answered for.

He came to stand in front of me, close enough I smelled his cologne. "I swear to you, I didn't. But I don't blame you if you don't believe me. God knows I've lied enough."

We all have make or break moments. The ones we know we might regret. I've always thought that's part of human nature. We simply go with our gut instincts until we get burned.

"I believe you. And I need your help."

TWENTY-FIVE

Two hours later, Chris parked down the road from Martha Beckett's house. She lived in a small, older but nicely kept A-frame house on the edge of Fishtown. I didn't see a garage, and her property wasn't large enough for any kind of storage. Justin fidgeted in the back seat, and I wondered why I'd let Chris talk me into driving.

"You know, we were arrested less than twenty-four hours ago for this very thing," Chris said.

"Detained, never charged," I corrected him. I craned my neck to face the backseat. "You're sure of this?"

Justin nodded. "The last two days, she's gone out at this time." It was nearing midnight, and my eyelids felt heavy. Martha had better leave soon.

"Doesn't mean she will tonight," Chris said. "You know where she went?"

"No."

Chris cocked his head toward the backseat. "Why didn't you follow her?"

"I didn't have the guts."

No one said anything else. Chris didn't like Justin coming,

and Justin was pissed I'd told Chris. I really didn't care what either one of them thought. I wasn't doing this myself. Too much had happened in the last twenty-four hours.

"You seem really calm." Justin leaned between the front seats of Chris's Audi. I almost laughed at the comical twitch of Chris's upper lip. "My brother thinks you've got your own set of secrets, you know."

"Everyone has secrets." *It's all in the keeping of them,* I wanted to add.

Justin rested his chin on my headrest. "Secrets are toxic, eating away at your insides. Even though it doesn't really change anything, I feel better since I told you the truth."

"It changes everything," I said. "Martha's going to be exposed for what she is. And you can move forward. With the right kind of therapy." I gave him a pointed look. "You need to tell the truth to your doctor so he can actually help you."

"You've helped me." His eyes filled with adoration. "You know how long I wanted to tell you the truth? When you spoke against me to the judge last year, I wanted to fucking cry. My brother believed me, and that was great. But he's supposed to. He's the only family I've got. But you're the only person—the only female—who ever came close to treating me with real compassion. Hearing you condemn me was gutting."

I was reminded again that he was no more than a man-child, a little boy with stunted emotional growth trapped in an adult's body. The woman who should have shielded and loved him had done things most people never dream of, and Justin had paid the price. Growing up in a juvenile facility should have hardened him. That's the sort of thing that turns wide-eyed boys into men. And yet Justin was trapped in a sort of personal purgatory, driven not by the need for revenge, but for acceptance and approval. He would never get it from the woman who should have cherished him. His expression told me he was desperate to have it from me.

"I'm very sorry for what you went through," I said.

Chris coughed a hard, obviously fake cough and glared out the windshield. I ignored him. "I didn't know the truth. I'd like to say I should have dug until I got it, but I can't change what's in the past. All I can do is work with the present. And I'll help you however I can."

"Thank you." Justin's voice thickened, and he slouched back in his seat. I pretended he wasn't about to cry.

Chris continued to scowl out of the window. "Hope you know what you're doing." His hissed words were still loud enough for Justin to hear.

"He could say the same about you," I said.

"Yeah, I could. I know who you are. We have a lot in common," Justin piped up. "My brother told me."

Chris twisted in the seat to face him, face bright with rage. "Listen, don't worry about who I am, you got it? And we are nothing alike."

"Enough," I said. "You guys need to trust each other, or at least my judgment, until we're done here."

"Sorry," Justin said meekly.

"What if we don't find anything?" Chris asked.

"I've got to call Todd anyway. Tell him what I found out about you. If we don't find anything, I'll tell him Justin filled me in"—I ignored Justin's protest from the backseat—"and that I believe him. See if I can push him into finally following up on Martha."

Chris huffed. He hadn't been surprised when I'd told him my plan to manipulate information from him. "You going to tell him we took a stroll through Martha's house?"

"Only if I find something worth using."

"Look." Justin spoke tensely. "There she is."

My fingers dug into the dash as I got my first look at Martha since Justin was a child. She was still tall, still broad shouldered. But like Justin's drawing, she stooped. From the distance, her shoes looked like orthotics. She chugged down the steps.

"She still wears her hair up." A whisper was all I could manage. I'd like to say I was filled with rage and thus purpose, but I really couldn't think clearly. I've come across all kinds of people in this life, and Martha Beckett is the only woman who ever truly scared me. I used to think it was because I was just as materialistic as the next person, and she wasn't a feminine ideal. But now I knew it was more than that. True evil puts out an energy all its own.

"She hated me on sight," I said. The memory of that day in the small apartment in North Philly came back to me. Todd was at his own mother's and Justin's father supposedly asleep from working the late shift, but the bedroom reeked of beer. Doe-eyed Justin took my hand and invited me to sit while his mother glowered in the kitchen doorway. That day in front of Martha, I was too naïve and inexperienced to trust my gut instinct. But I'd had it. I'd sensed the cruelty within her, but I didn't trust myself. I wouldn't make that mistake again.

"She hated every female," Justin said.

"Does she always wear a dress?" Chris spoke for the first time since Martha came outside.

"Yes," Justin and I both answered at once.

"Religious thing?"

"No. Martha never talked about God," Justin said. "Just that women should never wear anything above the knee. No shirts with sleeves shorter than the elbow."

Chris folded his hands on the steering wheel and watched Martha climb into her car. She backed out onto the street and drove east.

"How long was she gone last night?" I asked Justin.

"Just over an hour."

I looked at Chris. His face had hardened into a grim mask. "Let's go."

. . .

Martha's lock was surprisingly easy to pick. Her lack of security system was a stroke of luck. The three of us slipped inside the front door. No one spoke. A strong, musky scent greeted us, accompanied by blasting heat. My eyes watered.

"She likes incense." Chris stated the obvious.

"Always did," Justin said. "I hate that shit."

"Me too."

I took charge. "Justin and I will go upstairs. Chris, you check down here. Basement first."

He left to search for it, and Justin and I headed upstairs. "This house is pretty small," I said. As I suspected, it was a two bedroom, and both bedrooms had those annoying slanted ceilings that some people found charming.

"Be careful not to leave anything different than you found it."

Justin went to the right, and I took the room to the left. Despite the heavy dark, the streetlight provided enough light to maneuver. A twin bed and a nightstand, along with a clothes rack, were the room's only items. The closet was tucked under the eaves, and with the exception of a few hangers, it was empty. I got down on my hands and knees, testing for loose boards or hidden compartments.

"Did you find anything?" Justin's sudden appearance made me jump. I needed to settle down and stay alert.

"No. You?"

"Nothing." He shook his head. "Closet's empty. But I'm not surprised."

"Why?"

"Martha doesn't like second floors. She hated our apartment when I was little because it was on the second floor. Something that happened when she was a kid."

You might have told me that earlier rushed to my tongue, but

I swallowed the words back. I got to my feet and headed for the door. Dampness pooled between my shoulder blades. I squirmed; I hated sweating. "Let's get downstairs and help Chris."

Justin blocked my path. "Wait."

"We don't have much time."

"There's something I want to say. And I don't want to say it in front of your buddy."

Sweat beads broke out on my forehead. "What is it?"

He looked down at the floor. Then back up at me. I couldn't see his eyes, but I saw the set of his jaw. Determination. "I'm not interested in little girls."

"I understand that now."

"And I don't know how to deal with women I am interested in."

"You haven't exactly had a level playing field. But you'll learn."

"Until a woman finds out about my past. And then she'll bolt."

I suppose I should tell him there's someone out there for everyone, but I don't believe that. Some people are unlovable. And some people have so much baggage they won't allow anyone to take a chance on them. We didn't have time to discuss it right now. I gave his shoulder a squeeze. "You deal with that if it happens. Get out there first, test the waters."

He grabbed my hand, his grip clammy and tight. "I'm still a virgin." He let my hand go and stared at the floor. Despite the dark room, the heat of embarrassment seemed to emanate from his slumped figure. *Poor damned kid.*

"Don't let that stop you from dating. And some girls will find that endearing. You'll get past the inexperience too. In time."

"I need someone I can trust. Someone who won't make me feel dirty or stupid or weak." His voice lowered, and he finally looked up to meet my gaze. "Someone who cares about me."

All of a sudden I realized where this was going, and I wanted to crawl into the empty closet. I was out of my depth psychologically, but I knew enough to know the reasons behind his impending proposition were entirely unhealthy. I couldn't very well lecture him on that when he'd bared his secrets with me, and I didn't want to hurt his feelings. Stalling him gave me some time to think. "I know you need to talk right now, and I'm not trying to blow you off, but we have got to get downstairs. We'll pick this up later, I promise."

He nodded vigorously, and I bolted for the stairs, wondering what the hell I would say to him when later came.

"Chris?"

The living room was dark and silent, but a beam of faint blue glowed from the kitchen. I hurried across the house, with Justin close behind.

In the kitchen, the blue light seeped from the opened basement door. "Chris?"

"I'm downstairs." His voice was stretched taut, and my heart shot into my throat. Had he found her? Why hadn't he called me right away?

"Did you find..." I couldn't finish the thought.

"I need you to come down here."

Justin and I hurried down the narrow steps. I flicked on my own flashlight and desperately cast the beam around the space, feeling out of breath and ready to burst at the same time. Chris was in the corner, on his knees. A cardboard box was opened beside him.

"Kailey's not down here," he said. "Doesn't look like she ever was, best I can tell."

"Did you find anything in those boxes?" Justin asked.

"I hoped to find something about another property or storage." Chris stared down at the open box. "And then I saw this."

I took a step closer. Chris's head shot up and his eyes met mine. Their usual blue was overrun with tiny streaks of red. Dread slithered down my spine. "What did you find?"

He held up his clenched fist. A gold locket dangled from his hand.

"Old jewelry?" Justin sounded far away. My attention was caught in the cold, frightened gaze of Chris's eyes. I'd seen that look before, just after people have been given the worst news of their lives.

Chris's lips barely moved. "With the letter 'S' engraved."

A low buzz built in my head. The other girl in the barn with the locket, the one he'd remembered after his mother left him with his uncle. "What else is in the box?"

"More jewelry. A tiny ankle bracelet that would never fit Martha." Chris shoved the box away as if it were contaminated. "Pictures."

"Of who?" But I knew the answer. As impossible as it was, I knew the answer.

"Of *me*."

TWENTY-SIX

Dead silence, broken only by the groan of the furnace kicking back on. Chris's chest heaved. He kept staring into my eyes, his grief and tension pulling me toward him as though we were attached, like two parts of a broken toy. I knew he expected me to say something. But what the hell could I say?

"Are you sure?"

"Yes. I remember when this one"—he grabbed a wrinkled picture from the box—"was taken. There was an old well on the farm. I hated it. But my mother made me sit on the edge and take this picture. I was terrified I'd fall in." His large hand shook, but his low voice was deadly calm.

"How is this possible?" I asked.

"I haven't seen my mother since I was five years old. She gave custody to my aunt and uncle. A few Christmas cards, but they dried up a long time ago."

"What's going on?" Justin finally spoke. I'd completely forgotten he was there.

"I think I knew it when I saw your drawings," Chris said. "She looks different. But the eyes were the same. Same cold, sneering indifference. I told myself it was my imagination. And then when I saw her tonight—the dress and the shoes. The fucking incense! The bed in the dining room because she hates sleeping upstairs."

"But your mother is Mary Weston," Justin stammered. "She can't look that different unless she had—" He stopped cold. His mouth dropped open in a way that would have been comical in different circumstances.

"What?" I asked.

"It happened before I was born," Justin said. "Before she met my dad. She had reconstructive surgery after a car accident."

The locket clattered to the concrete floor, and Chris's head went to his knees, his body wavering. I dropped in front of him and put my hands on his shoulders.

"Just breathe. It's all right."

"Don't you see?" His red eyes and twisted expression resembled a man being torn apart. "All these years, I *knew*. I knew she lied. Little by little, I remembered things—her laughing at the girls, taunting them. But I didn't want to believe it." He dumped the box onto the floor. Several other pieces of jewelry fell out, including the tiny ankle bracelet he'd mentioned. A ring rolled to my hand, and it was so small it would have barely fit my own slender fingers.

I picked up a delicate cross with a diamond chip in the center. My heart actually clenched. "My sister had one of these."

"I kept telling myself my memories were just mixed up."

Justin came to stand beside me. "What are these things?"

"Trophies," I said. "The locket is one Chris remembers a girl in his father's barn wearing. I assume the rest are trinkets from the other girls." Martha Beckett used her son to escape the hell she'd created with her husband and then started her horrors all over again with a new family.

"Do you get it now?" Chris glared up at the younger man.

"We're half-brothers?" Justin looked between the two of us.

Chris jumped to his feet. "Good job. Keep thinking. Martha killed a girl in front of you. But that wasn't the first time."

"Oh shit." Justin's voice trembled. "My mother is Mary Weston. And she was behind the Lancaster attacks all along."

Chris pressed his hands to his head as if he were trying to shut out everything. "I should have said something. Made my uncle listen to me."

"It's not your fault," I said. "You were so young."

"So was he!" Chris pointed to Justin. "And you said his age of exposure meant he was destined for terrible things. I witnessed just as much, if not more. What does that say about me, Lucy?" His raspy voice broke on my name.

I took his shoulders. "That's when I thought he'd killed another kid. That's what made me think he was destined for terrible things, not the fact he was abused. And I was wrong, okay? He didn't hurt Layla. He's as much of a victim as she was. Look, I know you've both suffered terrible things I can't begin to imagine, but that doesn't mean you can't lead productive lives. You already are." I looked between the two of them, searching for the right words. "This is bad, I know. And I'll try to help you both in whatever way I can. But right now, we've got to get out of here before Martha comes back. Then we call Todd and let him know we have proof that Mary Weston helped her husband commit the Lancaster murders. And she just happens to be your mother too."

"Let's go." I nudged Chris. He stood motionless, and I could only imagine his poisonous thoughts. I didn't know what to say. I wasn't a nurturer—not when it came to adults, anyway—and we didn't have time to discuss it now. Theme of the night, apparently.

Before I could say another word, a noise from above paralyzed me. The muted squeal of a door opening and closing, followed by heavy, uneven footsteps. How in the hell had I slipped this much? I prided myself on subterfuge and now twice in the last week I was about to be busted with breaking and entering. At least we had enough evidence on Martha to hopefully keep Todd from throwing us in jail. That is, if we could keep Martha from killing us.

We hastily switched off our flashlights, and heavy darkness descended. Despite my attempt at stifling my breathing, the noise seemed to swell and encompass the entire basement. Surely Martha would hear us and come raging down the steps. I gripped my sturdy flashlight and prepared to fight.

Justin's hand dug into my arm, his lips at my ear. "I shut the basement door."

Smart kid. Had we disturbed anything upstairs? I didn't think so, but I wasn't sure if Chris had left anything in his wake. That's when I realized Chris's entire body had tensed like a coiled snake. I snagged his upper arm just as he started to lunge, as though I had a chance at keeping him from going after his mother.

"Get off," he hissed.

"You can't."

"I don't care if we get arrested."

"I can't get arrested," Justin whispered.

"Shut up," I said, keeping my voice low. "Chris, think. Forget about your pain for a minute and think about Kailey. If we screw up and Martha gets away, or if you do something really stupid, like break her neck, we'll never find Kailey."

"I don't care." He took a step forward. Above us, Martha's heavy tread stopped. A series of rumbles followed, like she was digging in a drawer. Probably for a knife to deal with the loud intruders in the basement. If I managed to get out of this, I was going solo from now on.

I blocked Chris's path, literally wrapping my arms around his waist. I couldn't see, but I felt the warm, rigid muscles in his chest and smelled his minty breath on my face. "Get off."

"I trusted you," I hissed. "Now you trust me." Playing that card seemed like a low blow, but I was desperate. Martha was moving around again, and it sounded like she was getting dangerously close to the door. If she didn't have a gun, the three of us could take her. "Please, Chris. I promise I'll help you get her. But let's be smart."

Something inside him broke. I felt it through his warm skin and his thick coat, felt the muscles loosen, his breath lengthen, his resolve wane. He reached around, grabbed my hands, and squeezed them hard. "Promise me."

I knew what he was asking. I didn't hesitate.

"Yes."

A beat passed. Justin shifted, brushing against me. Martha was still in the kitchen, and from the clinking noises, I guessed she was rummaging in the refrigerator.

"Fine." Chris dropped my hands. I stepped back from his heat and turned around blocking his path to the steps.

"Now what?" Justin whispered.

"Now we shut up and wait," I hissed back. "If she doesn't come down here, we try to get out when she's asleep."

"I could text my brother," Justin said.

I shook my head.

"Stupid." Chris's voice was low, his body close to mine. A new sort of connection smoldered between us, unspoken and powerful. "Anything we have right now is illegally obtained. He can't use it. Be quiet."

Justin said nothing else.

Martha kept shuffling around from one room to another. I tried to picture her uneven walk and her stern, almost hateful expression, but all I saw was my own mother. It's funny how we categorize people like that. If anyone in our life wrongs us, even in the most minute way, he or she becomes a villain. We waste time thinking of all the things we'd like to say if we had the chance to throw decorum out the window, if only we could lower ourselves to the same pathetic level. Because the villain is such a bad person. Trouble is, we don't realize until we come across someone like Martha Beckett that all the other wrongs in our lives are nothing more than blips on life's radar. Martha is true evil, cruelty personified right now down to her stature and sour expression.

Behind me, Chris's hand came to rest on my shoulder. It was large and warm. I didn't know if I should grab it, if he needed that comfort, or if he just needed to remind himself I was there. I reached back, intending to merely pat his hand, but he pinned my fingers to his.

Martha started walking toward the living room. The jingling of keys pierced our dark prison. Could she really be leaving?

The answer came seconds later, when the front door once again open and closed.

"Shit," Justin said.

"Shh," I said. "Give it a minute."

Chris still held my hand hostage. I hoped he would let go before Justin saw him. I'd almost forgotten about the kid wanting me to take his virginity. My stomach burned. How was I going to make him understand he deserved better?

"I counted to seventy-five," Justin said. "She's gone."

His blue flashlight suddenly shined in my face. Chris released my hand, and I blocked my eyes. "Jesus, point that thing somewhere else."

I turned my own light on and then looked at Chris. His face was pale, his expression resolute. He pulled out his phone. "Let's take as many pictures as we can to show Todd. He won't be able to use a damn one for evidence, but at least he'll have to believe us."

TWENTY-SEVEN

Justin called Todd. He'd gone home to get a few hours of rest, and I could hear him yelling over the phone. He ordered us to his house, and the words "felony," "dumbass," and "pushy private investigator" echoed out of the phone. The ride was silent, each of us lost in our own web of thoughts.

"Your cologne," I said as we pulled up in front of Todd's Spring Garden condo.

"What?" Chris said.

"It leaves a trace. Why didn't she catch it?"

"Her sense of smell was damaged in the accident," Justin said. "Reconstructive surgery can't help that."

"How convenient for her." I slammed the car door and followed Justin.

"Too bad she didn't die," Chris said.

"Yeah," Justin said. "Then I wouldn't be here, and no one else would have gotten hurt."

Chris looked down, and I didn't know what to say. We'd reached Todd's door, and it flew open before anyone knocked. He was dressed in gym shorts and a sweatshirt. Strange to see him in anything other than a suit.

He looked from Justin, to me, to Chris, and then back to me again. "Some days I really hate you, Lucy Kendall."

Todd looked through the pictures on Chris's phone three times before saying anything else. "While I was waiting for you, I looked up the Weston victims. There were four known girls: Lena Ryan, Carrie Anderson, Sarah Jane, and Jenna Pine, now known as Richardson." He held up the locket. "Sarah's family mentioned a locket she was wearing when she disappeared. John Weston led police to the three bodies, but the locket wasn't with Sarah. Neither was the ankle bracelet Carrie Anderson's parents had given her."

"Is it the one in the picture?" I asked.

"I can't access closed files from home," Todd said. "But from what I managed to dig up online, yes, it's very similar." He turned to Chris, who'd listened to the entire exchange in silence. "Tell me what you remember about your mother."

"It's hard to explain," Chris said. "I've spent a lot of years trying to forget."

"But you do remember," Justin said. "You said you've had several things—"

"Just give me a minute." He sat next to me on the couch, closer than I would have expected. Our legs and shoulders touched, the connection still alive. Todd eyed the two of us, and Justin sat on the floor looking petulant.

"I remember the girl with the locket," Chris said. "I had nightmares for years about her. Her forehead was cut and blood kept staining her braces. My father laughed about it and yelled at her for crying. But I used to hear my mother too. I always told myself it was my imagination.

"But then there were other things. My mother cackling and saying things like, 'Poor little girl, you shouldn't have done that.' And she had this blue scarf. One of those silky ones. Old-fashioned. She wore it a lot, and I used to have dreams of her waving this scarf with this menacing smile on her face."

"Autopsy report said the first victim was strangled with a blue nylon material."

Chris's chin dropped to his chest. He jerked his head back and forth.

"Maybe you witnessed it," I said. "She probably figured you were so little it didn't matter."

"I used to sneak around the house," he said. "At night. Because of the noises in their bedroom. I kept hearing my mother harping, snapping at my father. Giving orders."

"There were videos," Todd said. "When your mother took you and called the police, her story was that you two had stumbled onto the girl in the barn. She claimed her husband abused her. She had bruises. So did you. When police raided the farmhouse, they found videotapes." Todd looked embarrassed. "Of a sexual nature. What your father was doing backed up her story. And when he admitted to everything, there was no real reason to suspect her. He's serving life in prison and has never once implicated his ex-wife."

"Why didn't Jenna say anything?" I asked.

"She was traumatized," Todd said. "And if we're right, Mary—or Martha—was very smart. She never let Jenna see her. Jenna was blindfolded at all times."

"Her voice was deep," Chris said suddenly. "Sometimes I used to have trouble figuring out if it was her or my father speaking. But she was always angry. Like her hate of everyone and everything simmered under the surface. I don't have a single memory of her being affectionate."

"If she was that smart," I said, "then she likely set your father up with the tapes. A backup plan."

"My uncle hates her," Chris said. "He's never said much except marrying that woman was my dad's downfall. Then he always reassured me I was the only thing good to come out of it."

"He's your father's brother?" Todd asked.

Chris nodded. "My father got life in exchange for telling where the girls were buried."

"I need to talk to him," Todd said. "You have any idea of your mother's last known address?"

"We were just there," Chris snapped.

"Her paper trail."

"No."

"I'll see what I can find out. Meanwhile..." He looked at Justin. "I guess you were right after all. I'm sorry I didn't believe you."

Justin shrugged. "How are you going to find Kailey?"

"There was no sign of her in that house, Todd," I said. "If Martha took her, she's got her somewhere else."

"It's entirely possible, and frankly, the best lead we've got. Every known offender in the area has checked out," Todd said. "She was taken by someone who didn't stand out, someone who knew how to manipulate a kid, fast."

"You guys aren't discussing the obvious." Chris spoke in a monotone. "We keep talking about how Justin's taunting Martha set her off, but I don't buy that."

"Why not?" Justin sounded indignant.

Chris addressed Todd, ignoring his new brother. "Are we supposed to believe it's a coincidence that the same woman who put Mary Weston's husband in prison and ruined her game now has her daughter stolen?"

New lines festered in Todd's forehead. "You're absolutely right. If Martha is the kidnapper, she's been planning this."

"Of course." I wanted to slap myself on the forehead. "She tracked Jenna down. Decided to have some revenge and was just biding her time. Or maybe she kept tabs on Justin and then found out about Jenna that way. Whatever the case, Justin showing up on her doorstep just made Martha decide to act."

"Exactly," Chris said. He went back to staring at his shoes.

"So what are you going to do?" I looked at Todd.

"I can't use any of your information," Todd said. "Right now, all I can do is stake out Martha's home and business and see what she does. And you two"—he looked between them—"need to get a DNA test. We get that, and with the information you both remember, and maybe getting your dad to talk, we might have a case. If we can bring her in, that is."

Chris and I rose to leave. Justin stood too, but Todd motioned for him to sit back down. "You're staying here tonight. No arguments. I'll walk you two out."

Justin shrank down to the couch, red-faced. He glanced at me and shrugged.

I felt badly for him, but the shriveling woman hidden deep inside me—the one who looked in the mirror weekly for new wrinkles or fresh gray hairs—secretly rejoiced. Forget the twelve-year age difference and the massive pile of baggage parked between us. Every damned woman loves the attention of a younger man, and if she says she doesn't, she's lying.

Justin's gaze strayed to Chris, a mixture of curiosity and transparent jealousy crossing his sharp features. I strained to see any resemblance between the two men. Neither one resembled his mother. Both were tall. Chris's eyes were the unsettling blue of water, changing colors as the waves of emotion crossed them. Justin's were just a pretty blue. His cheekbones were more accentuated; Chris had kissable lips. Chris was self-assured, almost smug at times, the kind of guy who exudes sexuality yet makes a woman nervous about giving him anything because he's probably got another girl or two lined up for later. Yet there was something, a sense of familiarity that had bugged me about Justin since he'd approached me the other day.

Justin's next words surprised me. "Hey, Chris."

Chris looked at him for the first time since leaving Martha's, I realized. He'd steadily avoided facing Justin, putting his face down every time he spoke.

"I'm sorry," Justin said. "For your finding out this way. But it's nice not to be the only one who really gets how horrible she is."

Chris stared at his newly found half-brother for so long the silence felt like a boa constrictor tightening around my ribcage.

"See you later," Chris finally said. He headed for the door. I followed Chris, trying to put myself in his shoes. He had to be burning right now, all twisted in pain and betrayal and anger. I wished I could think of something to say that would actually make a difference.

"I almost forgot," Todd said as we reached the door. "I spoke with Brian Harrison yesterday morning."

My stomach cartwheeled. I'd known this was coming. "What did he have to say?"

"He's got an alibi for Kailey's disappearance," Todd said.

"At least you know for sure." I waited for the blade to fall. Chris leaned against the door, eyes on Todd's scuffed hardwood floor, but I could see the set of his jaw. He knew it was coming too.

"Harrison had some interesting things to say, though," Todd said. "Seems his brother died a few months ago from a suspected overdose. But Brian doesn't believe it. He says his brother was murdered by the woman he was dating at the time."

I made my eyes go wide and hoped my pounding heart wasn't audible. "Sounds like he's in denial."

Todd cocked his head to the side. "I thought that as well, but here's the crazy part. He claims the woman showed up at Kailey's school the day after she disappeared. And she matches your description."

We stared at each other. My insides rolled and tried to crawl up my throat. I could handle this. Harrison had no physical evidence, and he was dead now too. Of course, when Todd discovered that, I'd have a whole new barrel of rotten to deal with. But until then, I'd keep calm and focus on Kailey. "You're kidding me, right?"

Todd shook his head. "He swore up and down the same woman at the school was the woman his brother dated, and he believes she killed his brother."

"Poor guy," I said. "I'm sorry he's so deluded."

"His brother was a junkie, right?" Chris cut in.

"Heroin," Todd said. "But Brian Harrison claims the brother had been clean for a while."

"You know how many ODs I see from addicts who've been clean for a few weeks?" Chris said. "The body is so shocked it can't handle the drug, the heart goes into cardiac arrest. That's one of the most common times to overdose."

"I'm aware." Todd's eyes remained on me. "I just found Harrison's insistence on the redheaded female killer very interesting, especially since Lucy's the one who showed up at the school that day."

I needed to get out of there. My ability to act like I wasn't freaking out had worn down to a nub. "Well, I can safely say he's off his rocker. But at least we know he didn't take Kailey. That's all that matters."

"For now," Todd agreed. "For now."

TWENTY-EIGHT

"Shit." I dropped into the passenger seat.

Chris peeled out onto the street. "You knew it was coming. But there's no real evidence against you, is there?"

"Not since I took Cody Harrison's computer." My palms felt clammy. I rubbed them against my jeans until the skin burned. "But Brian Harrison molested one of the girls Kailey walked home with. And God knows how many others."

I let the words hang between us and stared straight ahead. Out of the corner of my eye, I glimpsed Chris's gaze. Gooseflesh spread over my arms, and I again felt like my sense of self was being stripped.

"You killed Brian Harrison, didn't you?"

"Yes."

"Christ."

"You knew this about me." I still couldn't look at him. "This is who I am. So don't act surprised."

"No," he said. "This is who you choose to be."

He said nothing more, and I stewed. I couldn't tell him how much I hated myself sometimes, how much I worried nothing I did would ever make any difference, that my actions were doing nothing but destroying me. I wanted to tell him all of these things. Maybe I even wanted to tell him I was thinking about quitting. I'd chosen the wrong path for justice. But I never said a word until we drove by Jenna Richardson's apartment building.

"What are you doing?"

"I want to talk to Jenna." He pulled into the parking lot and killed the engine while I scrambled to think of the right words to stop him.

"Listen, don't do that to her. She's already had to relive this with Todd, and her kid is missing."

"I know. And feel free to call me a selfish asshole. But I need to talk to her."

"Why?"

"Because I *need* to." His voice cracked, and he stared at me, pleading. I couldn't imagine his pain. He must feel abandoned, angry, betrayed... the list of adjectives was endless. But Jenna Richardson was suffering too. I should keep telling him no, make him listen to me the way I had in Martha's basement, but the truth is, I simply couldn't. I couldn't contribute to the burning torment.

"Please."

His desperate, almost childish plea made something click in my head, and I saw the resemblance between him and Justin. The thing that bound them together was more than mutual suffering: it was the loss of childhood innocence, of never being able to see the world through the rainbow glasses a kid should be allowed to wear. And I recognized it because the very same darkness resided in my own heart. I just harnessed mine differently.

"All right," I said. "But if she won't let us in, then don't push it. Give her that much."

His answer was a mere grunt.

I prayed Jenna Richardson didn't answer the door.

. . .

Jenna Richardson tried to shut the door in our faces, but Chris stuck his foot in the door. "I'm Chris Weston. John Weston's son. I found you in the barn."

She staggered back, hands out in front of her like a trapped animal ready to fight whatever monster had it cornered. Then she saw me.

"Why would you bring him here?"

"I'm sorry, Jenna, but he came all on his own. I'm just trying to make sure he uses common sense."

"I've told Detective Beckett everything I can from that night." I saw her senses snap back into place, almost heard the connection pop in her brain. She glared at Chris with white-hot hatred. "He thought you might have taken my daughter."

She lunged at Chris before either of us could react, her small fists pummeling him. I tried to step between them, the five-foot-seven-inch woman defending a six-foot man, and one of Jenna's fists landed square on my lip.

"Damn." Tears welled in my eyes. I blinked away the dancing stars.

Chris had her by the wrists. "I'm cleared. He talked to my boss—I was on duty. I didn't take Kailey!"

She looked at me, and, rubbing my swelling lower lip, I nodded.

Jenna yanked away from Chris. "Then why are you here?"

Good question. I licked my lip and tasted blood.

"I found some things out, and I really need to talk to you," Chris said.

"This isn't about Kailey?"

Chris hesitated, and I hoped he had enough sense not to say anything about Mary being Martha and all the other immensely screwed-up things we'd found out tonight.

"No. I'm sorry. I know this is shitty timing. But I really need to talk to you." He glanced at me. "And she's bleeding."

"Sorry about that," Jenna said. "I'll get you some ice. But you're not staying long. I don't need to relive that time right now."

Her apartment no longer smelled like pumpkin spice. It had been replaced by the staleness that comes with despair. The scent is a special mixture that permeates a home touched by tragedy, getting in the clothes and furniture and embedding into the carpet. The stagnancy was heightened by the warm temperature. Jenna's appearance matched the atmosphere: gray yoga pants and a wrinkled blue, long-sleeved Philly Fitness sweatshirt two sizes too big and sporting a coffee stain. The only color on her face was in the circles beneath her eyes. Her hair was greasy. I didn't blame her.

She handed me a baggie full of ice wrapped in a towel, and I pressed it to my lip. The tingly cold hurt and relieved at the same time.

"Why should I tell you anything?" Jenna glared at Chris.

"You shouldn't, but I'm desperate. I've spent years trying to remember what happened in that barn, and when I heard you were the girl... I know I'm an asshole. But I'm begging you. Just a few questions."

She bit her lip so hard blood came to the surface. "Five minutes."

"Do you remember me?"

"I remember a child's voice. I guess it was yours."

She closed her eyes, presumably finding her happy place. Mine was the memory of my sister letting me crawl in her bed during a thunderstorm and telling me nursery rhymes until I fell asleep. "I've built a new life, and I don't want people finding out. And Kailey, when she comes home, I don't want her to hear about it."

"It won't leave this room," Chris said. "I didn't know everything my father did until tonight."

"I suppose the detective told you?" Her bloodshot eyes blazed, and I realized Todd could get into deep shit for sharing her personal information with us.

"No," I said. "I've got a friend who specializes in information. She dug it up."

Jenna sank onto the couch, the oversized cushions making her look even more petite. "The day you found me, your father had been gone for only fifteen minutes. I know this because I counted. It was the only way to keep sane. And he had a routine. Morning, when the sun shined between the barn cracks, and night, when the coyotes made too much noise. He never came in between."

"What happened?" I asked.

"I heard the door open, and I wet myself. I couldn't take any more. And then I heard a kid scream. It was the most awful and wonderful sound I'd ever heard."

"Did you hear anyone else?" Chris asked.

"Someone—an adult, I thought—shouted at you to get out of the barn. You were screaming about me."

"Did the person you heard sound surprised to see you?" Chris choked. "Or afraid because I'd found you?"

"I don't remember," Jenna said. "I was injured and exhausted. Next thing I heard were tires spinning out. And then suddenly the police were there."

Chris raked his hand through his hair, looking as though he wanted to shake the memories out of Jenna.

"Jenna, have you ever had any hypnosis or anything else to jog your memory?" I asked.

"No. I remember plenty."

"Not enough," Chris said.

I shot him a disapproving look. "Is it possible someone besides John Weston was involved?"

"I only heard his voice. But sometimes..." She looked away from me and stared blankly into the kitchen. "Sometimes he used things other than his penis in me."

"I'm sorry," I said.

"Did you ever hear laughter? A woman?"

Jenna grimaced, her upper lip curling into her nose. Her eyes were wet. "I heard laughter every time he attacked me. Sometimes it was close, other times it sounded far away. But I tried to go far away into my mind, so what I remember is sketchy."

"Chris," I said, "she's not going to give you the answers you're looking for. There's a reason why things worked out the way they did." And that reason was Martha herself. How manipulative had she been to get her husband to take the fall?

He took out his phone. "Look at these, please, and then I promise you, we'll leave. Do you recognize anything?"

Eyeing him warily, she took the phone and started scrolling through the pictures. Suddenly, her whole body went still. She was the trapped animal again. "That's my ring. Where did you get this?"

"Illegally obtained," Chris said. "But I promise, you'll have the full story soon. We're just making sure the case is solid."

"What case?" Jenna looked between the two of us. "John Weston's in prison for what he did."

"But my mother isn't," Chris said. "And she may know about you. And Kailey."

Whatever energy Jenna had left evaporated. Drained right from her skin until it was pale as a corpse. Her shock resonated throughout the apartment, temporarily freezing us all. Then she was on her feet, pacing. "Does she have my daughter?"

"We don't know," I said.

Jenna's hands went into her hair, as if she were trying to smash the images out of her head. "It can't be. This can't be happening to Kailey. My baby."

"Detective Beckett's aware of this information," I said. "He's doing everything he can to track Chris's mother down. And we may be wrong."

Jenna went limp. "Please leave."

"I'll find Kailey." Chris took the phone, put it in his pocket, and looked down at Jenna with determination. "I will find her."

TWENTY-NINE

"You shouldn't make promises you can't keep. And Todd's going to have your ass for mentioning that to her." We were almost to my building in Northern Liberties. Neither of us had spoken since leaving Jenna's, and I was glad. My brain needed some time to decompress and figure out the next move. Trouble was, I couldn't connect the various live wires of information in my head. I was too distracted by the pain of the man sitting next to me, too worried about the lost little girl I was beginning to feel we would never find. The lack of control over my thoughts and emotions only added to my mental clusterfuck.

It was hard to believe that just a few short hours ago, I'd accosted Chris, demanding to know if he was involved in Kailey's kidnapping.

"This is my place."

He parked the Audi, but I didn't make any move to get out. I knew I should say something to him, but what? Females are supposed to be nurturing and compassionate. My mother once said it was our job to make life less harsh and more beautiful. A nice word can go a long way, she'd lecture. Ironic coming from a person who could tear an individual down with a few well-placed verbal barbs. Still, I couldn't disagree. In the end, woman are the fairer sex, and if anyone can soften the misery of life's shitstorm, it should be us, right? My problem was I'd only ever been able to do that with kids.

"You ever have a moment when the bottom falls out?" Chris said. He stared ahead, slumped in his seat. I had no idea how to help him or even what to say. "Like you think you're just getting a handle on your life, whatever's left of it, and then suddenly everything has disintegrated?"

"When you want to crawl under the bed and hide?" I said softly. "Or maybe end your own suffering because you just don't see how anything could be right again?"

The car idled, its exhaust trailing into the street and glowing like misty fog beneath the streetlight. It drifted up, twisting into a cyclone-like shape, and then faded away as quickly as it had emerged.

"Is that what happened to you when you heard Justin was released?"

"No. I had that realization much earlier in life. When my sister died."

"What happened to her?"

I'd rather have told him about the first time I'd killed a man. But sharing my darkest moment seemed only fair after tonight. "Lily was four years older than me. My father left when I was a baby, and my mother didn't like to be alone. So there was always a man in our lives. I didn't mind, but my sister resented it. The last boyfriend, she really hated. He was around for four years. He liked Lily a lot."

"He molested her."

"Between the ages of twelve and fifteen. And she kept her mouth shut, because Mom was happy, and there was nothing worse than Mom being unhappy. She's good at making you feel like it's your fault. But finally, Lily decided to tell Mom. And she didn't believe her." I tasted the bitterness as strongly as I had when I'd heard my mother yelling at Lily. "Ostracized her for telling such terrible lies. I believed her. I told her I'd help her, and she made me promise to never let him touch me."

"Did you keep your promise?"

"With a vengeance." A smiled played on my lips. "The one time he tried to touch me, I took a baseball bat to his head. Put him in the hospital for three days and earned myself a juvenile record."

The day I found Lily is as fresh as any memory. Late October, just like now. But the temperature was unseasonably warm, and I'd gone without a jacket. Walking home, I'd basked in the sunshine and looked for shapes in the fat, low-hanging clouds. One particular cloud looked like an angel, I'd told my friend.

"Lily skipped school the day after our mother blew her off. When I came home, the house was quiet. Like heavy quiet, when you're listening for someone's breathing. I went to Lily's room, but she wasn't there. The bathroom door was closed. I stared at it, and somehow I knew what I'd find." Blazing with fresh pain, the images flashed through my head. I'd replayed that day so many times, and yet the pain never ebbed. "She'd cut her wrists—with his razors, of course. I didn't scream or throw up, or even cry. I just stood there thinking it wasn't happening but knowing it was because I could smell the coppery blood and her bowels." A hollow ache consumed my already tired body. "Her hair—it was the prettiest, silkiest blond —was fixed in curls, the way my mother liked it. They used to fight over that. Her eyes were like glass. Opaque and vacant. She was gone. My life as I knew it was gone." I blew out a hard breath as if that would dull the hurt.

"I called my mother. She said to make sure Lily had on clean underwear before the paramedics came. Presentation always mattered most to her." An acrid taste came with the words. "I hated her for a long time for that."

"Do you still hate her?"

I honestly didn't know how to answer. "Some days. Some days I want to get right in her face and call her out for not listening to Lily, for every cruel, manipulative thing she's ever said. It's a special fantasy of mine. Nose to nose, her cowering away from me with the same kind of fear I imagine Lily felt every time that bastard came for her. For once, I would do the talking. Tell her how her manipulation makes me feel, how her need for attention from men and her thirst for control ruined our family and that I hate her with everything I have. But other days I just feel sorry for her."

"I can't say the same for my mother." He cleared his throat. "I resented her for leaving me with my uncle for a while, but not because I missed her. I think I felt that way because it was how I was supposed to feel, you know? Kids whose parents choose their personal lives over them are supposed to be full of angst. But I got bored with that. And I always had the creeping fear that I didn't understand my mother at all. That more had happened at that farm than I allowed myself to remember." His hand, resting on the gearshift, clenched into a white fist.

"You were really young." I laid my fingers on his trembling hand. He relaxed but still held the shift too tightly. "Kids that age compartmentalize. The mind's got a way of protecting itself. Your mind scrubbed away as much of your misery as it could. It did you a favor."

"How do you figure?"

"Your aunt and uncle are good to you—that's obvious from the way you speak about them. You grew up in a nice area of town, safe. Yeah, you had the occasional nightmare about Mother Mary, but your mind protected you from the worst and let you grow up relatively normal."

"A sociopath."

I suddenly didn't like that word. It made me feel twisted and dark, like some sort of infection was creeping through me. "That needs to stop," I said. "You're not a sociopath. That's an excuse you've used to justify some of your feelings. Or lack of. But no sociopath cares as much about people as you do. Look what you just promised Jenna."

"I promised her for myself." He sounded like he was trying to convince himself. "To absolve myself of guilt."

"Keep telling yourself that if it makes you feel better."

He suddenly took my hand, his skin hot and clammy. Twisting in his seat, he leaned close to me, disrupting my personal safe space, and stared at me with incandescent eyes. "I need you to promise me you won't stop looking for Kailey."

Between the street light and the glowing dash lights, an eerie sort of aura framed Chris. He looked on the verge of either breaking down sobbing or attacking me. Maybe both.

"I won't give up until Kailey's found. One way or the other." I couldn't bring myself to say the word "dead."

"That's not what I mean."

A heady sense of dread swept over me, cooling my toes and worming its way up my body until my heart felt like it was pumping ice. "If Mary doesn't come home, if Todd can't find her, promise me you won't give up searching for her. And Kailey."

"The police—Todd," I clarified. "He's already got an unmarked unit watching the house. He's got his own grudge, and now that he knows everything, it's going to be damn hard for her to hide unless she goes completely off the grid. And she's probably developed a false sense of security after all these years. Todd will find her."

"Or she's been preparing for a moment like this. She'll sniff out the cops and take off."

I didn't want to agree. "If the police can't find her, I don't know that I can. As good as my computer specialist is, she's limited. Police aren't. They can even call in the FBI if they want."

"I want *you* to find her."

I'm pretty sure I actually saw my life-altering moment as it happened, almost like I was peering in the car's window and spying on myself. The transition seeped into the car and surrounded me, its grip as strong as my fear of death. My throat dried up. My lungs struggled for air. And my brain screamed to flee. But that wasn't an option, and even if I ran now, Chris would keep coming at me until I gave him an answer.

"You're really asking me to kill her."

"Administer Lucy Kendall justice."

I dragged my fingernails over my forehead as if I could claw my way out of my head. "This isn't how I work."

"What?"

"Mother Mary—she's a pig. She deserves to be brought to justice. But I... I choose people. I keep a mental list. It's neat and tidy."

"So add her to the list."

It wasn't that easy. I couldn't allow it to be that easy. I worked mostly alone. Kelly gave me information, and I had a chemist in my back pocket, but that was it. Chris wasn't going to be a sideliner in this endeavor. The decision to end someone is very personal. And it's mine alone. Agreeing to act as nothing more than a hit woman was not part of my system. And after watching Brian Harrison die, I honestly wasn't sure I could do it again.

"Chris."

He jerked toward me, and for a moment I thought he was going to grab my shoulders. "She took Kailey. What do you think she's doing to her? What do you think she did to those other girls?"

"I know what she did. That's not the reason."

"Is it control? Because you don't take requests?"

No, it was because I was afraid that every time I killed someone, it got easier. I became less human. Another twist of the seeping infection. "Something like that."

Chris drummed his fingers on the steering wheel. I still felt stuck in the game changer, standing on the precipice of something I wanted no part of. Yet I knew I couldn't turn back.

"Then I'll do it," he said.

"What?"

"You let me in your circle. Help me find her. Guide me. I'll kill her myself."

His tone was so hard, so full of venom, that I knew he meant it. Every one of us can be pushed to the edge. And those of us who decide to take matters into our own hands all have a defining moment—the time when we snapped. Mine had been Justin's release into society and the free ride of anonymity. I'd never thought myself capable of hurting another human being until that day.

"Chris, I killed a man earlier. I knew he hadn't taken Kailey. But he'd molested one of her friends, and I killed him. With cyanide."

"I know. And you've done that before."

"But I had to stay with him." Revulsion pounded at my chest. "I had to watch him die. And until that moment, I didn't grasp the severity of my decision. Of the piece of my soul or humanity, or whatever you want to call it, that I've forfeited." And I'd made that decision, based my entire moral code on a truth that turned out to be a lie: Justin wasn't a sexual predator that had been released to attack again. "Are you sure you really want to do the same thing? And to the woman who gave birth to you, no matter how diabolical she is? Because even if it's by my hand, it's at your request. And you're one step closer to being just like me. Is that what you really want?"

"I want her dead. You kill her or I will."

I couldn't let him do it. I wouldn't let him do it. There's still hope for Chris. He didn't deserve to be a statistic. I had already sinned too deeply to change my fate.

"I'll do it," I said. "On one condition."

"What?"

I reached for his face, grazing the scruff on his chin. "Don't let Mother Mary destroy you."

"How do I do that?" His eyes watered.

"I don't know. But we'll find a way."

THIRTY

Five days since Kailey went missing. Sleep deprived and anxious, I sat next to Kelly in her cramped office and tried not to lose my patience. Or faith. She'd spent the last hour making phone calls, using up every source she had with the Philadelphia PD, trying to find out some details about the Weston case that might lead us to Martha's whereabouts. Nothing we found could be used in trial, but that was the least of my concerns. Chris had promised Jenna he'd find her daughter, and then I'd quite possibly made a deal with the devil by agreeing to help him bring his mother to justice.

"I can't believe you brought him here." Kelly still fumed. She glanced behind her, where Chris leaned in the doorway. He'd shown up on my doorstep this morning, just as I was heading over to Kelly's. I should have told him to go home, but his red-rimmed eyes and pale skin made him look especially pathetic. I'd had to beg her to let him stand in the doorway.

"At least I called first."

"If he screws us, Luce…"

"He won't." I prayed my instinct was right.

"I'm not going to turn you guys in," Chris said. "Lucy told you everything."

"Big deal." Kelly swiveled in her cheap office chair. "You don't have anything invested, do you? So you want to kill your mother. But you haven't done anything yet. Yet you know our dirty deeds. All you have to do is say we suckered you into it. And we don't have shit to keep you quiet."

Grim-faced, Chris took out his wallet. He handed Kelly a wrinkled paper with some numbers on it. "I figured you might say that. When they adopted me, my uncle set up a trust fund. I'd like to say I'm too noble to use it, but I supplement my paramedic salary with it. I like living in Center City and driving a nice car. I like a good lifestyle. There's almost a million dollars in there, and that's all the information you need to get into my account."

Kelly and I both stared at him.

"You're right. I've done nothing like what you two have. If I had, I'd give you something to hang me with so we could be even. But this is the best I've got, and believe me, I'd rather not lose my trust fund." He looked at Kelly. "I'm sure, with that information, you could take everything I have."

Kelly studied the paper. "I'll have to validate the account number, of course."

"Of course."

She glanced at me, and I shrugged. My head was still spinning over the million-dollar trust fund.

Kelly put the information in her desk drawer. "Just so you know, I don't have to steal your money to ruin your life."

A grudging smile played at the corners of his mouth. "Point taken."

I breathed a sigh of what should have been relief, but anxiety continued to restrict my lungs like a vice. "Have you found out anything, Kel?"

"Nothing different than what Todd said this morning:

Chris's father is refusing visitors. The district attorney is going to force him, but that takes time. Red tape and all. But they can't make him talk. Todd's staked out your mom's house. So far, she hasn't come back. And there's no chance of a search warrant without your matching DNA, and even then, it will be tough. All that proves is she had another kid."

"We need to figure out where she's gone," I said.

"Police are watching her store," Kelly said. "Place hasn't opened today."

"She could be anywhere," Chris said. "If she masterminded taking Kailey, then she had a contingency plan."

"You guys really think she took Kailey?" Kelly asked. "You have no real evidence other than this theory."

"I don't know," I said. "But right now, I've got nothing else to go on. And you have to admit, it's a pretty good theory. It's no coincidence Kailey is the one who went missing right after her mother's former captor drove by her apartment."

Kelly looked unconvinced. "All right. So what about her contingency plan?"

"Todd said they flagged Martha Beckett's passport," I said, "They couldn't find one for Mary Weston."

"If they couldn't get a search warrant, how can they flag her passport?" Chris asked.

"Easy. She's wanted for questioning in the disappearance of a child," I said, inwardly smiling at his naivety. "Police could even say Justin named her as an accomplice. It's a lie, but it would be enough. Don't be fooled. Police break rules all the time. As long as what they're doing doesn't affect a court outcome, they'll go for it."

"Great system."

I could have laughed. "Don't get me started."

"Call Justin," Kelly said. "See if he knows of any other place his parents may have owned. Or somewhere his mother could have gone, like a special place. Anything he may have mentioned."

"You don't think Todd's already done that?" I asked. "I'm sure he's picked that kid's brain clean."

"Right." She raked her fingers through her short hair until it stood on end, not unlike a porcupine. "What about you?" She directed the question at Chris. "Do you have any memory of any place with your parents other than the farm?"

"Every memory I have of my parents is there," he said. "I was never allowed in the barn, but I remember the house. To a kid, it seemed like a giant, crumbling mansion. I used to imagine it was haunted. I never had any friends, but sometimes my dad would play hide and seek with me. Mother Mary always got pissed because she was restoring the house on her own. She worried I'd knock over paint or do something else to ruin her project."

"She's a monster." That's why I couldn't allow myself to lose respect for my choice to end lives. I couldn't be lumped into the same pot as someone like Martha Beckett.

"I remember one time," Chris continued, "probably not too long before Dad's arrest. I fell down the stairs—they were spiral, and I was running too fast. Fell the last five steps and cut my chin on the jagged woodwork. She'd been working on the trim." He traced the faint scar along his chin. "That's how I got this. At first she was pissed, because I was stupid, and I'd torn off the old trim. Then she realized I was cut pretty bad and had to go to the doctor. She was nice to me there."

"For show?"

"Of course. But when you're a little kid and your mother acts like you're a pain in her ass, you'll take any affection you can get."

"She loved the house." Kelly was tapping away on her keyboard. "I wonder..."

Chris and I crowded behind her chair, waiting to see what

exactly she wondered. A Pennsylvania real estate site popped up, and soon we were looking at a rambling farmhouse. It was painted a cheery yellow, with black shutters. Planters hung from the front porch, and the chimney smoked. A hint of snow on the brown grass showed the picture had to have been taken before last spring. We hadn't had any snow yet.

The hairs on the back of my neck stood up, and my pulse quickened.

"That's my house." Chris sounded strangled.

"I know. It was bought at auction two months ago." Kelly typed some more, searching property records on the public site I never could figure out how to manage.

"By who?"

"Give me a minute."

Tap, tap, tap on the keyboard. Chris's heavy, uneven breathing next to me. The rushing of my own heart. I could barely hear my own thoughts.

"M. Alan Lee." Kelly had the answer. "Do you know that name?"

Chris staggered back. "Alan is my middle name, and Lee was Mary's maiden name."

THIRTY-ONE

Like a man on a suicide mission, Chris weaved through mid-afternoon traffic, jumping onto Interstate 76 and driving fast enough for a huge ticket. He'd barely given me time to stop at my place and pick up my hidden supplies. Mousecop watched me rush around the apartment with a look of disdain on his face, licking his paws and sitting next to his almost full food bowl.

"Listen to me," I said. "We have to be objective here. If she's got Kailey, we get her first. If we can safely rescue her and still take care of your mother, and come up with a plausible story for the cops, then we will. But you may have to accept letting them arrest her."

His answer was a brisk nod. "But we at least try it our way."

Our way. The man probably never did an illegal thing in his life before he met me. Let alone made the decision to take another's life. You don't make those decisions rashly. I'd been fantasizing about the idea long before Justin's release, rationalizing the action. And I now know the consequences of going down this road: I'm a killer. If there truly is a God, I don't expect him to give me a pass because I took out the scum of the earth. God himself—or herself, for that matter—never condoned vigilantism that I know of.

Even worse, I had put my own freedom at stake. But after all the kids I'd seen slip through the system's gaping cracks while filthy creeps bent our bureaucracy to their best advantage, I chose the dark path. I was willing to sacrifice for what I believed was right. That didn't come without a mountain of punishment. And dumping a glass of cyanide on an unsuspecting man, no matter how evil his acts, took its toll on a person.

The drive to Lancaster County had the glass-covered features of a dream; our mission seemed surreal, while the landscape shined with the stark reality of the coming winter. The heavily populated areas gradually turned to fields of harvested corn, their brown, short stalks looking piteous. Crumpled and withered, the stalks blended together, whipping past until I saw nothing but decay. Houses thinned out, replaced by farmland and long stretches of winter-brown fields. I wished it were summer. The ugly scenery was a perfect accompaniment.

Chris plugged the address into his GPS, and like every piece of modern technology, it wasn't without its kinks. The route took us the long way around Lancaster, bypassing the city but getting us stuck on a two-lane road behind a grain truck and an Amish carriage.

I snapped a picture of the Amish family with my smartphone. The kids smiled and waved while their bearded driver looked irritated. I suppose they did get tired of being a tourist attraction.

"I think I could be Amish." I stuck the phone back in my bag.

Chris snorted. "Says the girl with the most expensive smartphone on the market."

"Okay, giving up stuff would be tough. Probably impossible.

But if I'd been born into it, I think I would have stayed. There's something safe and beautiful in their simplicity."

"Simplicity is an illusion. Everyone has problems. And most of the time, the ones we expect have it easy are dealing with the worst shit."

I couldn't argue with that, so I shut up and gripped the door handle as he yanked the car into the right lane and passed yet another semi.

"You can't kill your mother if you're dead."

The sunshine had given way to thick, gray clouds that looked full enough to burst. Rain might work to our advantage, however.

The grating female drone on the GPS announced we needed to turn in a quarter of a mile, and Chris barely slowed down enough to make it.

"Jesus!" I braced my hand on the dash. "Get a grip right now. This thing says we're five miles away, so we need to pull over and collect ourselves. We need a plan. We can't just go barreling in the front door."

"Why not?" He eased off the accelerator.

"You realize you're going back into the lion's den of your memory, right? You don't know how you're going to react when you see that barn, or the house, and God knows what you'll remember. If you break down, I can't handle Martha on my own. Not without some kind of distraction. Translation: we need a plan, and I'm in charge."

He scowled and pulled the car over. "Fine. What is the plan?"

"If you can keep it together, you go to the front door and knock. Let's pray she won't recognize you. Say you're broken down and your cell reception sucks. Anything to get in the house. While you're doing that, I'll check the barn. If I don't see anything, I'll come around to the back door and find a way inside. Put your phone on silent. If I can't get inside, I'll text you."

"What if you find Kailey in the barn?"

"I'll send two texts."

"What am I supposed to say to her?" He shouted the words.

I laid my hand on his arm. "Relax. I just told you."

"You know what I mean."

"Just keep her occupied. Try not to say anything about yourself or Kailey until you hear from me."

"You make it sound easy."

"I know it won't be. And if you can't do this, it's okay. I'll figure out plan B." That was bullshit. Plan B would be calling the police. I was out of my element, with little preparation and in an unfamiliar place. If Chris couldn't perform, I'd make sure we'd found Martha and call Todd.

"I can handle it."

He put the car back in gear and pulled onto the road. That's when I realized how truly isolated we were; no one had passed while we idled on the shoulder, and no one lingered behind us now. The road quickly turned to gravel, cutting through a woody countryside. The fat clouds still hovered overhead, but they'd become a more ominous gray, almost as though they were sucking up the dead grasses and fields.

I stared as one cloud grew larger, billowing into a brilliant haze until it pulsated like a racing heart on the operating table.

"Oh my God." The words lodged in my throat as if I'd inhaled smoke. "That's a fire."

THIRTY-TWO

I once saw a fire department demonstration on how fast a fire can overtake a room. They'd set up a room of sorts, complete with Goodwill furniture and decor, on the lawn of a church hosting a community event. I don't remember the exact dimensions of the room, but it was a pretty standard size. And the fire turned deadly in exactly twenty-two seconds. The fire chief warned about the importance of smoke detectors, because with the right accelerant, a fire can double in size every thirty seconds.

By the time we reached the farmhouse, long streaks of fire jetted out the busted windows, and the entire house was surrounded by black smoke. I called 911, but someone must have beat me to it, because the engines squealed past us not more than a minute later.

We played the lost card, saying we were out for an afternoon tour after some stress in the city. Once they were sure we had nothing to do with starting the fire, the police told us to get lost and set up a perimeter while the firefighters fought the blaze.

We drove a half mile down the road and watched.

Neither of us spoke. Nothing to say. Nothing to do but wait. Everything—and anyone—in the house was lost, and the goal was stopping the fire from spreading to neighboring farms. The barn wasn't on fire, and it didn't look like anyone had been recovered from it.

At some point, I called Todd. He yelled at me for several minutes and then said he'd call Lancaster County and put them on the lookout for the body of a young girl.

"Maybe the house is empty," I tried to say. I felt like I'd inhaled a roomful of smoke, although I'd barely been out of the car before Chris and I both decided heroism was no more than a death sentence.

Sometime after seven, when the sun had rescinded and the blaze was finally ebbing, a dusty-looking SUV pulled up beside us. My heart sank into oblivion. The vehicle bore the Lancaster County Coroner's logo. The passenger window slid down revealing an unshaven, pissed-off-looking Todd.

"I didn't expect to see you," I said. "This isn't your jurisdiction."

"I've got a friend at the Lancaster precinct. When I told him what was going on, he invited me out."

"Is it a kid?"

He gave me single curt nod. "I got the call on the way from the city, caught the coroner as she was leaving. Place has been empty," Todd said, "except for the occasional contractor's truck. No one's met the new owner, but the gossip is that he was from the city and working on the house."

"He?" Chris spoke for the first time in hours.

"Lancaster PD said the only person ever spotted out here was a man," Todd said. "But the owner is listed as female, age fifty-six."

"I don't even know my mother's birthdate."

"We're having trouble locating her birth certificate," Todd said. "Everything we know about Mary Weston says that she was born poor, married off to your father young. She was in her early thirties when he was arrested, so the age fits."

"How many bodies are in the house?" I asked.

"Two." Todd's dismal tone reflected my own sorrow. Whether it turned out to be Kailey in the house or not, people had died, burned to death. And one was a child. *I'll never understand the cruelty of life.*

Todd turned and said something to the driver, who I presumed was the coroner. "I'll be back as soon as I can."

Everything became very hazy after that. Time stood still while Chris and I hung out on the fringes. The air reeked of burnt wood, and when the wind gusted just right, the rancid scent of pot roast that had been barbequed to a dry pulp on a charcoal grill.

Todd mostly ignored us, talking alternately on his phone and with the local police. At times, his voice raised, and I wondered who he was arguing with.

The coroner and a man I presumed was her assistant brought out the bodies one by one. The smaller one came first, tightly sealed in a shapeless, black body bag.

Chris walked back to the car.

I started to cry.

Surely this was a dream. I was still in bed, never having brought Chris to see Kelly, my twisted mind only making up the details of the house and its owner. If it weren't for the anguish coursing through me at the smallest movement, I might have actually convinced myself.

Later, when I was in a weird haze, weaving like a drunk, Todd appeared in front of me.

"What?" Chris had evidently returned at some point. My shoulders felt weighed down. I realized Chris's black jacket was slung over them.

"Two bodies," Todd said. "One is definitely an adult, but it's so damned burned up the coroner can't tell gender. Fire inspector says it looks like the accelerant was dumped straight onto the body. And no, without an autopsy, we don't know if the victim was alive or dead when the body caught fire. We'll have to wait on dental records for an ID."

"What about the child?" The words came out of my own mouth, but I couldn't feel myself speaking. I wasn't sure I could feel anything. The only real sense I had was sight, vivid and unrelenting. The house still smoking, its foundation littered with red embers; firemen hustling about, water still spraying; police lights flashing; Todd's drawn, broken expression.

"The child isn't as badly burned. Believed to be a female between nine and twelve. Brown hair. Pink shoes."

Pink shoes.

I felt more wetness on my lips. Chris's arm came around my shoulders. Todd cleared his throat, his own eyes glistening. "Lots of little girls have pink shoes."

He sounded as empty as I felt.

"It doesn't really matter, does it? A child lost her life." I went back to the car and waited for Chris.

THIRTY-THREE

"Do you think she killed herself too?" Chris finally spoke when we were halfway back to the city.

Sitting with my head against the cool glass of the window, watching the dark night rush by, I thought of nothing else but the smell of that little girl's—Kailey's—burning body.

"No."

"Me neither."

My mind was too trashed to reconstruct what Mother Mary had done, but no way had that woman killed herself. She'd managed to escape punishment for her crimes once and had been living an unsuspecting life. Justin had never truly stood up to her—she had no reason to believe he'd have any impact now. And if the accelerant had been dumped on the adult body like the fire inspector believed, the person either magically stumbled into a vat of gasoline or had it thrown on the body. My gut told me Mary had done the throwing, lit the match, and then took off.

"You heard what Todd said about there being a man around here, working."

"A new man at her beck and call. She had a kid stashed

here. But why burn the place now? How could she possibly know we were getting close?"

Hell if I know. "She took a child. Her stepson was on the case. Maybe she thinks Justin would eventually put Todd on her. Or maybe she figured the damage for Justin was done and decided to get rid of the evidence. Or maybe she's just a cruel, paranoid bitch."

"We'll get her, Luce. If I have to spend every dime I have tracking her down, I'll find her."

"Oh shut up," I said savagely. "Stop thinking about your own personal revenge and appreciate what's happened here. A child is dead. Burned like a piece of fucking meat. A mother's life is ruined."

"I know that."

"Do you? Because all I hear is 'I.' All about how you'll even your own score. Do you ever think that maybe the woman should be brought up on charges? That maybe killing's too good for her?" I was screaming, the sound high and guttural, coming from some dark place inside me I'd kept it bottled. Now, it unleashed on Chris. "What about the victims' families? The ones who think your mother's innocent of killing their daughters? Don't you think they should have the right to see her sentenced? What about Jenna? Doesn't she have the right to confront Mother Mary face to face? Look what she's done to her."

"You're kidding, right?" His snort of laughter made me want to wrap my hands around his throat. "Do you know what a hypocrite you are?"

"No. The men I've targeted were all pedophiles who somehow charmed the system. Given third, fourth, fifth chances. Released on mistrial." I spit the words at him like snake venom. "But every kid—every family—got the right to face their accuser. My actions were never based on personal needs."

"Bullshit. Everything you've done is based on personal need." His voice sounded as angry as I felt. "On personal failures. You feel guilty for not being able to help your sister. Convinced yourself that once you'd grown up, you'd save the children." He took his eyes off the road to smirk at me. *Pompous sonofabitch.* "Only you get inside the system and see how things really work. It eats at you, gnawing at your guilt and your pride until you're ready to explode. Then Justin gets out and you snap. Not for the children, but for yourself. To alleviate your own sense of hopelessness."

I hated him. Exhaustion and a tight seatbelt kept me from launching myself and pummeling his perfect face. "You know nothing about my choices. You're an outsider, an arrogant, rich boy know-it-all, one of the saved kids who tried to tell himself he understood what the others had gone through, but the truth is, you don't have a damned clue." Spurred by hot self-right-eousness, I twisted in my seat until I fully faced him and jammed my finger into his shoulder. "You got out. You don't have the memories of Mother Mary that Justin has. Giving you to your uncle was the kindest thing she ever did."

Chris's jaw clenched so tightly I half-expected his teeth to break and go flying into the dashboard. The wheel jerked to the side and the car careened off the pavement. Chris snapped it back onto the road.

"You may be right. But you're just as self-centered as I am, and you know it."

Something untamed boiled inside me—a rage I recognized. It was the same anger I summoned to attack chosen predators. The first time I felt it was when my sister's molester showed up at our house and tried to put the moves on me while my mother went to the store. He reached for me, his slimy hand on my knee, and my sister's voice screamed in my head. My baseball bat was in the corner; I'd been practicing with the neighbor kid earlier. Without thinking, I jumped up, grabbed the bat, and swung it as hard as I could.

The long-simmering rage erupted, and had my mother not returned home, I'd have killed him. I glanced at the bag at my feet. The cyanide was in its container. Chris concentrated on the road, weaving through thick Philadelphia traffic. Rain had started sheeting down a while back. I could open the container and throw it on him before he could stop me. He might wreck us, but what did that matter? If I died, so what? I'd failed Kailey, just like my sister and Justin.

But Chris hadn't hurt anyone. He hadn't done anything but point out the horribly painful truth I'd been trying to suppress.

It was still raining when he pulled up to my building. I'd brooded in silence for the last half an hour, and I wasn't ready to tell him he was right or admit defeat.

"What about Kailey?" I asked. "Do you care at all that she's probably gone? Or are you a sociopath after all?"

He didn't respond.

I got out of the car, slammed the door, and let the icy rain drench me.

THIRTY-FOUR

I didn't have any more alcohol in the house. It was hard on my stomach, and I don't have the willpower not to enjoy a glass of wine if it's available. Wretchedness kept me from venturing into the rain and buying a bottle from the nearest convenience store.

My sister had an open coffin. It was pink, lined with even pinker silk. My mother put Lily in a white dress she'd always hated. The long sleeves covered up the gashes on her wrists. The condition of her body terrified me. Not only was she stiff and cold, but her skin looked even more delicate and smooth than it had in life. Her cheeks were rosier than usual, her unfeeling lips curved up in a peaceful smile.

A lie. She'd died in a horrible way, and here she was, looking happy to be dead. The funeral director had suggested a closed casket since seeing children can be especially hard, but my mother insisted mourners got to say goodbye. I'd always believed she wanted to have as much attention as possible.

For years, I'd asked myself why Lily believed death was better than life. Why hadn't she run away? Tried to tell an adult at school? Yelled until someone heard her? It was only as I got older and realized how truly traumatic sexual abuse was that I understood. Yet she must have had second thoughts in those final moments. As the blood drained from her body, had she panicked before losing consciousness? It didn't look like she'd tried to stop the bleeding when I found her, with her arms spread evenly at her sides. But surely, she'd had at least a moment when she knew she'd made the wrong decision. Had she at least stopped to think about everything she was leaving behind? About who she left.

She'd left me alone with our mother.

I hated her for a long time.

That's really the crux of my guilt. Chris didn't suddenly open my eyes. I've wrestled with that knowledge for most of my adult life.

Chris had been right on the guilt factor, and that infuriated me. But my shame went deeper than not being able to save my sister or anyone else. I blamed her. Despite seeing her pain and watching her withdraw into herself, I blamed her for not doing what I thought she should have. I believed I would have handled things differently. I told myself I'd never have allowed him to touch me, and that if he did, it would have only happened once. Lily was scared and weak, and she took the easy way out, leaving me to pick up the pieces.

I remember the exact moment I realized how selfish I'd been.

My freshman year in college, I took a child psychology class and read an account of child abuse, both from the victim and the therapist. I finally understood the true impact of sexual abuse, the way it can mentally stunt a child's ability to gain perspective over events in life and his or her decisions. My sister didn't have a prayer.

I didn't sleep for two days. Then I went to church—the first and only time in years—and prayed to Lily for forgiveness. I don't know if she granted it, but I know I've never forgiven myself. Everything that happened after that realization was just more acid in the wound.

A stream of images assaulted me. Lily, before the devil showed up, and then after. My mother, resolutely looking the other way. Lily in her pink and white coffin.

Kailey's casket would be closed.

The blinking of my phone jarred me back to the present. I'd forgotten to take it off vibrate, and the blue flash made my head hurt. Kelly's number flashed on the screen.

"Hey," was the best greeting I could muster.

"Chris called me. He was worried about you."

I didn't voice my surprise or acknowledge the warm sensation creeping through me. "I'm okay."

"It might not be her, Luce."

"Even if it isn't, it's still somebody."

"Chris said Todd wasn't giving up."

"Did he tell you Todd also had to inform Jenna Richardson?" I asked. "Because he had to ask for Kailey's dental records?"

"Yeah. But maybe..."

"Right," I repeated.

"Do you want me to come over?"

Kelly hated going outside, especially at night. The knowledge that she cared enough for me to do it finally broke the last of my reserve. I burst into tears.

"I'll take the bus and be there as soon as I can."

"No," I managed to choke out. "It's raining, it's late. I won't let you put yourself through that."

"You shouldn't be alone."

"I'm not the one who's lost my child," I said. "I'll be fine."

"Come over in the morning and hang out with me," Kelly said. "We'll eat something really fattening and watch movies. You can pretend to forget about all of this, at least for a few hours."

"Sounds like a plan." I wrestled my tears under control. "Thanks for offering to come over here. That means a lot."

"You're welcome. Oh, before I forget, I have a bit of good news. Well, it's not good, but it's better than what's going on."

"What's that?"

"Slimy Steve got himself busted at work."

"The electronics scam?"

"I wish. He got caught spying on the girls' locker room at the gym where he works. Apparently he'd found a way to peek at the youth swim team girls."

"Was he arrested?"

"Nope. Gym declined to press charges, but hopefully one of the parents will get their head out of their asses."

Sudden, unrelenting exhaustion cascaded over me. "I suppose we'll call that a positive for the day. Thanks for telling me."

"Get some rest," Kelly said.

"I promise to try."

Zombie-like, I stumbled to the bedroom, threw my smoke-laden clothes in the hamper, and collapsed on the bed.

At precisely 2:22 a.m., my eyes flew open. Through a confused tangle of thoughts, I wondered, for a brief moment, if I'd been out drinking and the events of the last twelve hours were no more than a hangover-induced nightmare.

I'd been dreaming about Slimy Steve swaggering through Chetter's this summer, wearing a too-tight shirt meant to show off his toned body. The shirt bore the name of a gym. He'd bragged to the bartender about his job allowing him to see hot women sweat.

I'd left my phone in the living room. Half-naked and shaking, I managed to cross the dark apartment without falling.

"Lucy?" Kelly's groggy tone was laced with worry. "What's wrong?"

"Slimy Steve's gym," I rattled. "What's the name of it?"

"Philly Fitness. Why?"

"Jenna Richardson had a members' sweatshirt. I saw it when Chris and I were there the other night."

THIRTY-FIVE

I'd like to say everything happened very quickly after that, just like in the movies. But instead of a radiant burst of light, the realization was more like a hazy forty-watt bulb hanging in a dingy basement. Motionless, wearing nothing but my underwear and still smelling vaguely of smoke, I stared into the emptiness of my apartment. I tried to tell myself this was all painful coincidence, that Occam's razor was full of shit, but even as I tried to push the idea away, every fiber of intuition I had left screamed for attention.

The most logical explanation is usually the correct one.

Right under our noses, while I scrambled around chasing leads created by my own demons.

"Lucy."

I'd forgotten Kelly was on the phone.

"Do you really think it's possible?"

Jenna's words flooded back to me. "Kailey took swim lessons over the summer. Jenna has a picture of the two of them, when she finished her lessons. I don't know if it was at the same gym, but she loved the water."

I couldn't think straight. My brain stalled on the idea that

I'd let Steve get away the night before Kailey disappeared. Fortunately, Kelly picked up the slack.

"I can call my contact at the department, see if I can find out which Philly Fitness location Steve worked at. If that doesn't work, I can backdoor my way onto his Facebook page. He's always been careful not to post anything suspicious on there, but it may have work information. And we've got to find out which location Jenna attends."

"How long will that take? And how are you going to find out which gym Jenna went to?"

"I'm not. You're going to ask her."

I didn't want to go near Jenna right now. Giving her a false sliver of hope seemed incredibly cruel. "I can't. Now that there's a body, police aren't holding out a lot of hope. She's been told her daughter is likely dead. We could be wrong. I can't get her hopes up like that. But she works at Girard Medical Center. It's not very far from her place in Poplar, and I think there's a Philly Fitness around there."

"Everything I do is going to take time, and I doubt I can find out anything about Jenna." Kelly refused to budge. "You're either going to have to ask around or ask her. Wait." In that single word, Kelly's business-like tone turned unsteady. "Did you say Girard Medical Center?"

My nerves ratcheted to the sky. "Yes, why?"

"Because that borders West Girard Avenue. Steve's apartment—the one he keeps up and we always figured was his child porn palace—is on North Marshall. I don't know the neighborhoods like you do, but I remember that night this past summer, when you tailed Steve to his place. You called me from a little deli at the corner of Marshall and Girard and went on and on about their chocolate pie. Steve had gone in to eat, remember?"

I did remember. Nothing about the restaurant was special; in fact, their floors were dirty and the napkin holders had a month's worth of grime. But the pie had been delicious. I'd parked my car and followed Steve on foot that night, from his place to the restaurant and back.

My heart cartwheeled against my ribcage. "He walked along West Girard." My voice was toneless. "Which is only a few blocks from Kailey's street in Poplar. Their neighborhoods border each other." The facts piled up in my mind like a teetering Jenga tower: Steve working at the same gym, spying on the swimmers, Kailey's swim lessons, her age fitting his preferences, the proximity of their homes. "God, it's been right in front of me!"

"We don't know that for sure. I'll call my contact at the station, the guy who told me about Steve's being fired."

"Wake his ass up." I glanced at the clock. Anger at my failure spurred me out of bed. "It's almost 3 a.m. A lot of gyms open at five. Once you know for sure, I'll go in and see if I can find out exactly where Jenna's membership is. If I can't, then I'll ask Jenna."

"The more time we waste—"

"Believe me, I know. I've already wasted too much. But I've got to know we're right about the Philly Fitness location before I talk to Jenna. Find it, please."

"What are you going to do? Why don't you call Todd?"

"And tell him what? How can I explain what we know without getting us in trouble? And we don't know anything for sure."

"So what are you going to do?" Kelly demanded. "You can't go over to Steve's alone."

"I'm not going alone."

THIRTY-SIX

Rain sheeted against my windshield. Wipers on high, I sped through a sleeping downtown, cursing at the small numbers of cars out who dared to slow me down. I didn't have any right to ask for Chris's help, but I planned to do it anyway. He hadn't answered his phone, which didn't surprise me.

Guilt kept trying to creep into my head, to scream at me for not seeing who had taken Kailey all along, but I shoved it aside. I needed confidence right now.

I parked as closely to Chris's building as possible, but I'd forgotten my umbrella, and by the time I got to the door, I was soaked and freezing. The rain was heavy and cold, stinging me like miniature icicles. I rang his buzzer repeatedly.

"Who is it?"

"It's me."

"You have got to be kidding. It's something like 4 a.m. Not to mention what a mean hyp—"

"I don't think your mother took Kailey," I cut him off. "It was Steve, the guy I was after when you first met me. The one at Chetter's. He works at Jenna Richardson's gym, Philly Fitness. And he just got fired for peeping in the girls' locker room during swim practice. Kailey took lessons at Philly Fitness last summer. We need to find out if it's the same location Steve worked at." Breathless, I waited.

Maybe I was reaching, refusing to admit defeat. Maybe this was all a string of ugly coincidences.

"I'll be down in five minutes." Chris's growl was replaced by brisk control.

"My car's parked down the block on the right."

Five minutes later, he banged on my passenger window, and I quickly unlocked the door. He dropped into the seat, soaked as well. His hair stuck to his head, his glasses fogged and dripping. He pulled the hem of a white T-shirt out of his hoodie and quickly cleaned them off. "What's the plan?"

"I just heard from Kelly. Steve worked at the Philly Fitness on Girard, directly across from Girard Medical Center, where Jenna works." My stomach knotted at the words. I should have stayed on Steve, shouldn't have been so preoccupied with Justin that I didn't make the connection when I saw Jenna's sweatshirt.

No time for a pity party right now.

"Is that the gym she's a member of?"

"That's what we need to find out. Kelly is having trouble hacking into Philly Fitness's database. It'll be faster if we do the legwork."

Chris agreed we should avoid talking to Jenna unless we had to. He also thought we should go straight to Todd.

"Not yet," I said.

"If we find Kailey and you take care of Steve, how are you going to come out of this unscathed?"

"I don't know. We can move quicker than Todd. He can

talk to Steve, but he needs the damned warrant to find out anything. Even if he can get it, that'll take a few hours. We could have Kailey by then." I'd deal with the repercussions later. This wasn't about my winning or redeeming myself. This was about saving Kailey—if she was still alive—as quickly as possible.

"Fine. Then promise me once we know he's got Kailey and she's safe, you'll call Todd. That you won't use Lucy Kendall justice."

I shot him my nastiest glare. "You were all for my justice a few hours ago."

"This is different. You do that, and there's no way you're not busted."

"Would you really care?"

His mouth slipped into his signature cocky grin. "Very much so."

Pushing back my emotions, I turned onto Girard Avenue. "Keep an eye out for Philly Fitness. And don't worry, I don't plan on going to jail."

The gym was easy to find, its lights already on at 5 a.m. Across the street, an ambulance sat in Girard Medical Center's emergency bay, lights flashing and medical staff rushing around. Probably an early morning accident aided by the rain.

"They can't give out member information," Chris said as we headed inside.

"I know. But hopefully one of us can charm it out of them." I jerked my chin toward him, and he rolled his eyes. But his surly expression flashed to sweetness as soon as we opened the doors.

The girl at the desk looked young, college-aged, and extremely tired. She smiled at us, her eyes lingering on Chris. I nudged his elbow.

"Hi," he said to the girl. Erica, her name tag read. "I wondered if you could tell me if my friend is a member here?"

"Sorry, that's against the rules."

"Yeah, I figured." He leaned across the counter, licking his lips and smiling at the girl. Her hand fluttered to her collarbone. "But I just need to know if this is the right place. We're thinking of paying for a month's worth of yoga classes for her birthday. She's a single mom."

"That's really sweet."

"Anything I can do to help her out."

Erica's hands inched toward the keyboard. "I just, I really can't."

I took my cellphone out of my pocket and scrolled to the copy I'd taken of the picture of Jenna and Kailey at the pool. "See this little girl? She's missing. This is her mother, Jenna. She's a nurse across the street, and she's frantic about her daughter. Now, you don't have to tell me if she's a member here. But have you seen this woman in this gym?"

Erica looked at Chris, who nodded. She glanced around.

"I've seen her, working out in the morning, two or three times a week, every week for the past year. But not in the last week."

I'd almost hoped this would be another dead end. I'd be partially absolved, and I wouldn't have the toughest decision of my life ahead of me. "Thank you."

We raced back into the rain.

"Now what?" Chris's eyes watched me with trepidation. "Do we call Todd?"

"Not yet," I said. "We've only got circumstantial evidence, and I don't want to pull him away from Martha just yet. Let's get something concrete first."

"So?"

"Now we head to Steve's apartment."

THIRTY-SEVEN

There is an adrenaline rush that comes with closing in on a predator. The hours spent researching, figuring out his routine, deciding on the best time to attack are a buildup of aggression, so that when it comes time to strike, I wasn't thinking about anything but completing the job. At least, that's how it worked before I watched Brian Harrison die. Now I was a jumble of nerves, all knotted up with worry. I felt frail and yet jacked up.

"Are you just planning on knocking on the door?" Chris drove. I'd handed him the keys without a word. I needed to clear my head, figure out the best move.

"Yes. He lives in an old complex. Cheap rent, he's not always there. Kelly and I think he uses it for his den of sin. Perfect place to keep Kailey."

"We can't ask him to buzz us in."

"No. We'll have to play it up, pretend to be new residents. Get someone to hold the door for us."

"That could take a while," Chris said.

"Then we wait. Turn left on Marshall."

My phone rang with Kelly's call. A sliver of instinct flared;

Kelly preferred to text. She'd found something big. I didn't bother with false preamble. "Yeah?"

"Lucy!" Kelly's voice was shrill, shaking. "I found Kailey. On a website. He's selling her, right now."

Scalding terror rushed through me, stealing my breath and making my stomach burn. "Chris, pull over. Kelly, how?"

"I was trolling, looking to see if I could find anything in the Philadelphia area, any connection to Steve. One link led to another, and there's a site, an auction site. Sellers upload pictures and videos, and buyers get to choose."

"Videos?" Acid boiled in my stomach, making my throat burn. "Of what?"

"Different things. None are overtly sexual—they're careful. There's a lot of talk about natural habitat. That's what Kailey's video is about. Here, I'll email you the video. Just... prepare yourself. Call me back."

"What is it?" Chris pulled the car into a parking lot.

I could barely manage to spit the words out. "Kelly found a video of Kailey. She's for sale."

He stared. My phone beeped, signaling the email. Wordlessly, I cued up the video, leaned closer to Chris so that he could see, and pressed play.

A second or two of nothing, and then, a blurry image of a room brought into sharp focus. It was very small, maybe eight feet by four feet. A closet, I realized. Bedding was carefully arranged on the floor: pillows, quilts, and sheets in varying shades of pink. A little lamp sat in the corner, the only source of light. Several toys were scattered in the small space, and sitting in the middle of it all was Kailey Richardson.

She wore different clothes than the ones she'd been wearing when she was abducted. A summer dress revealed her muscled legs, and her hair was down around her shoulders, carefully brushed to a shine. She sat with her chin resting on her drawn-up knees, arms tight around her legs. A protective little ball. Eyes large and filled with fear, face pale and tear-streaked.

Lettering flashed at the bottom of the video. *Bidding ends at 8 a.m. Eastern Standard Time. Cash only, pickup arranged by seller.*

Vomit shot up my throat. I opened the door and dry heaved, dropping my phone onto Chris's lap. The cold, wet air rushed into my lungs, and I turned my face skyward, welcoming the misting rain.

"Jesus Christ," Chris said. "How could someone do that?"

"They're inhuman. That's why we need to put them all down." I slammed the door and took the phone back, quickly calling Kelly.

"It makes sense, doesn't it?" She jumped right back into our conversation. "The electronic scam he's being investigated for is just a tiny part of his empire. You've got to call Todd right now. All the information about the website is included in the email for the police techs. Implicate me if you have to, I don't care. We can't let this little girl be sold."

I felt like I was standing on the precipice of a dark hole and trying to decide whether to jump in or find something to walk across. "The email you sent it from, have you protected it? Is it traceable back to you?"

"I don't think so. The IP address isn't local, but there are ways around that," Kelly said. "We don't have time for me to go into them, but trust me. I'd bet my life he's got her right there in that shitty apartment."

I didn't have a choice. This was beyond my twisted need for justice. No way was Kailey Steve's first sell. "I'll call Todd, and I'll forward the email." I checked the time. "But I'm not waiting around for them to get their legalities lined up. We've only got an hour and a half before the sale is over."

"Just be careful."

I promised her I would.

"Todd won't sit on this," Chris said as soon as I ended the call.

"He'll have to get a warrant," I said. "Even if he lights a fire under a judge's ass, we can be quicker. And the evidence I've got on Steve is circumstantial, especially since we can't prove this feed is from the city. His techs can try to trace the signal, but that takes time. She doesn't have it."

I called Todd and prayed he'd answer.

"Lucy," he grouched into the phone. "I really don't have time for this. We're waiting on the DNA results of the child from the fire and—"

"It's not Kailey. She's alive."

A beat of silence. "How can you possibly know that?"

I described the video in detail. "The feed is a live countdown. My friend just took a few minutes' worth of video. She can't tell where the source is coming from, and I've sent all the information to you in the hope that your techs can. But Kailey doesn't have time, and I know who took her."

"I'm listening."

"His name is Steve Simon. He's a known offender and in the system. He just got fired from Philly Fitness across from Girard Medical Center for spying on the girls' locker room during junior swim team practice. That's the same gym Jenna Richardson is a member of and where Kailey took swimming lessons last year. And Steve's previous convictions involve girls Kailey's age." My words tumbled so fast I just hoped I made sense.

Todd let out a low whistle. "I'm looking at the email. My God."

"No question it's her. He's auctioning her off like a piece of equipment."

"I'll get my tech people on it." The shuffling of papers accompanied Todd's words. "Give me the name of your computer geek who—"

"No. She stays out of it. In the email is all the information she has. If you have questions, you can go through me. I'm not exposing her."

"Fine. I'll look into Steve right away, see if I can verify your information and push through a warrant. Do you have his address?"

"517 North Marshall. Prairie Woods Apartments." I braced myself for the incoming argument. "Kailey doesn't have time for a warrant. She's down to eighty-two minutes. If we don't get to her at Steve's, we may never find her."

"I'm on the website." Todd sounded queasy. "There are seven bids, well into the thousands. So much for the public misconception that child molestation is a class issue. And it's eighty minutes."

"I'm going to Steve's apartment and getting Kailey myself."

"You are not a police officer," Todd snapped. "I'm sending officers right now, and I'll be right behind them."

"I'm not losing her."

"You're not qualified to go barging in there," Todd said. "You could get hurt, or worse, Kailey could get hurt. Steve could get spooked and run. Wait for my guys."

"I know the layout of his place. Won't let it happen."

Todd sighed. "I don't even want to know why you know the layout. But you do this, you're setting yourself up for interfering with a police investigation, maybe even obstructing justice, losing your private investigator's license. And don't think I've forgotten about the Harrison brother. Are you prepared to face those consequences?"

"Yes."

"Lucy, I'm begging you not to do this."

I didn't have a choice. "There's no time. I can't sit back and wait. You get to work and do what you can. So will I."

THIRTY-EIGHT

Chris pulled into the parking lot of Steve's complex. It consisted of four aging buildings painted light brown and trimmed in mud brown. The paint peeled in various areas, and the complex's two dumpsters overflowed with trash. Several bicycles were chained to a rack, which was pretty brave of the owners.

"He's in building three, apartment two."

Steve's building looked to be the oldest and least maintained, with scattered graffiti along its front. My heart began to thrum in my head, batting my nerves like a tennis ball. I checked my pockets, the bottle of poison giving me a sense of control. I'd found it hidden deep in a compartment in my closet before I'd taken off for Chris's. It must have rolled back and been forgotten, as if it were destined for Steve all along.

I couldn't use it. Todd would know everything if I did. But right now I really didn't give a damn.

"We need to think this through." Chris caught my arm. His grip was firm and warm. A brief sense of calm rushed over me, and then my energy started a new race.

"We can't wait for the police."

"I know, I know. But we need to realize what we're getting into. Do you have any kind of weapon?"

I glanced at him, then at my pocket. He swallowed. "Besides that."

"I don't carry a gun. There's a tire iron in the trunk."

"Good thing I wore my big sweatshirt." Chris found the button and popped the trunk. I scrambled out of the car after him.

The morning had dawned dull and rainy, and the place was quiet. I blocked him from view while he slipped the tire iron into his sweatshirt.

"What are you going to say?" he asked.

"Whatever I can think of to get into the door. Right now, we've got to get into the building first."

We hurried up to the door, slipping on the wet pavement. My hair was wet again, but I was grateful for the cool water and brisk air. Kept my head clear. I ran my hand down the list of names. All of them were laminated except for apartment two. I hit the buzzer and crossed my fingers.

"Hello?" a groggy, male voice answered.

"Um, hi. This is your third-floor neighbor. I'm just getting back from my shift, and I left my stupid key at the hospital. Is there any way you could buzz me in?"

"Sure." The buzzer sounded, and I pulled the door open. We stepped into a small entryway, with threadbare carpet and the lingering smell of vomit and fruit-scented cleaner.

"What if he'd asked you how you planned to get into your actual apartment without the key?" Chris asked.

"My boyfriend never hears the buzzer, but he'll hear me knocking."

"Your ability to lie is pretty impressive."

"It's an acquired skill." I headed up the stairs, and he caught me by the arm again.

"Let me go first. And don't even think about using that stuff in your pocket."

"Why the hell not? If anyone deserves it, it's this pig."

"You'll go to prison."

Killing Steve might be worth prison.

Chris stepped ahead of me, taking two stairs at a time, his broad shoulders tight and tense. His right hand tucked into the bottom of his sweatshirt, clutching the tire iron.

"I need to do the talking," I said as we reached the fifth floor. "He's not going to let you in."

"I've got the weapon."

"Then be ready to strike. But I need to get us inside."

Steve's door loomed ahead. "You need to stay off to the side, where he can't see you."

Savage, feral anger stung my insides, making me feel like I was breathing fire, and pounded against my temples. I clenched the vial in my pocket so tightly I could have broken it. With a deep, burning breath, I let the bottle go and knocked on the door.

Chris stood just to the left of the door, his blue eyes lit up like bright crystal, focused solely on me. A tiny bit of my tension eased, enough for me to think clearly.

"Who is it?" Steve barked through the door.

I smiled sweetly, knowing he was looking through the peephole. My fingernails dug into the tender flesh of my hands. "Hi. I'm your new neighbor, and I'm just off a shift at the hospital. I forgot my key. May I use your phone?"

"You don't have a cellphone?"

I bit my lower lip and shrugged my shoulders. "I forgot to charge it. Please, I won't stay long. I've just got to get hold of the super. I need to shower and change before I pick up my daughter. It's my day with her, and I don't want to be late."

"You don't have your daughter full time?" Steve's voice dropped a fraction.

"Not yet," I said. "Since I work nights, it's tough to find a decent babysitter who will stay over, so she stays at her dad's. It sucks, but it's really hard finding someone to trust, and my daughter's at the age, you know? Eight years old and already developing in ways that make me feel really old."

Chris's face twisted in disgust at what I was doing.

"Yeah," Steve said. "You say you're new to the building?"

"Yep. I moved in last week. Single mom and all. Work so much I haven't had the chance to introduce myself. So can I please use your phone to call the super?"

"Yeah, just... let me get some clothes on."

I glanced at Chris. He unzipped the sweatshirt, gripping the tire iron with both hands. A single nod told me he was ready.

"Come in behind me," I whispered.

The lock clicked, and the door opened enough for Steve to wedge himself between it and the frame. He was unshaven, wearing another tight shirt and track pants. He handed me his phone. I made a calculated decision and dialed Todd's number.

"Hello?"

"Hi, it's Lucy Kendall, your new tenant." Todd knew where Steve lived. He'd get here soon enough. "I'm here at the apartments, and I forgot my key. Is there any way you could come help me out?"

"Lucy," Todd growled. "Walk away."

"Please," I said. "I don't have much time. I'm lucky my new neighbor is nice enough to let me use his phone. I'll see you soon." I ended the call and handed it back to Steve. "Thanks so much."

"No problem." He started to shut the door, but I casually leaned against it, making sure to block his view of Chris.

"You work at Philly Fitness?" I motioned to his tight shirt.

"Uh, yeah."

"That's right across from the hospital where I work. I'm a

respiratory therapist. Do you know if Philly fitness has kids' sports?"

"What do you mean?"

"Well, my daughter's a gymnast. She's got the perfect build for it, I swear, long and lean. I'd love to get her into a more structured training, and I know some of the city gyms offer it."

A very fine sheen of sweat appeared on Steve's forehead. "Um, not sure. I know they've got swimming."

"She loves to swim too. I might have to check that out." I gave him a coy smile. "Don't suppose you could get us a discount? Since we're neighbors and all?"

"Probably not."

"That's okay." I leaned toward him, trying not to grimace at the smell of his sweat and bad breath. "If you could, I'd be really grateful." I licked my bottom lip.

He looked increasingly uncomfortable. Shifting from foot to foot, he ran a finger through his cropped hair. "I'm not... I don't..."

"Oh, I'm sorry, are you gay?"

"What? No! I just—" He glanced behind him, and I moved closer. We were now toe to toe, my chest pushing up against his. Steve stared at me. I braced myself against the doorframe, and motioned to Chris behind my back.

"What are you doing?" Steve stammered.

In one move, I jammed my fist into his windpipe. His knees buckled, and he staggered back in surprise. "I'm here for Kailey, you bastard."

THIRTY-NINE

Chris swung around behind me, and Steve fumbled around, gasping for breath and trying to run. Chris dipped a shoulder into him, knocking him inside the apartment, and I quietly shut the door behind me.

Recovering, Steve swung at Chris, who deflected with the tire iron. I heard the snap of Steve's wrist and hoped it was broken. Their scuffle was brief. Men like Steve are neither brave nor buff. When faced with real opposition, they are likely to fold and beg for mercy.

Pinned beneath Chris's knee, with the tire iron at his chest, Steve already looked close to begging. "Please don't hurt me."

"I'm here for Kailey," I repeated. "And I'm not paying a fucking penny for her."

"Who's Kailey?" His left eye twitched, his entire face now soaked with sweat.

"The little girl you're hiding in a closet, filming for your sick auction." I looked at my watch. "Which ends in fifty-seven minutes, right?"

He shook his head. "You're crazy."

"No. You're the one who's screwed-up. But your little business ends today."

My phone rang. I knew who it was. Never taking my eyes off Steve, I answered.

"Hi, Todd."

"Damnit, Lucy." He sounded like he'd been running. "You're something else."

"I was right."

"We're en route," Todd said. "Please, for the love of God, don't do anything else."

"What else would I do?" I listened to the sound of Todd breathing and stared at Slimy Steve, still pinned by Chris and the crowbar.

"We'll discuss it later, but I think you have an idea. Right now, I've got you for interfering with an investigation," Todd said. "Don't make it any worse."

"We'll be waiting for you." I hit end. Todd likely knew about Brian Harrison. I'd deal with that death sentence later.

"The police are on their way."

Steve began to struggle, but Chris sank the tire iron deeper into his throat. "I will strangle you."

"It's over, Steve," I said. "Get ready to be a prison bitch. Tell me where she is."

He refused to speak, but his eyes flickered to the closed door off the kitchen. The room was surprisingly clean, although stacked high with various boxes and plastic crates. I stopped at the sink, slipped the vial of cyanide out of my jacket, and emptied it down the drain, making sure to rinse all the residue. I slipped the bag and vial into my tall boot, and then headed into the bedroom. In the far corner was a large walk-in closet with a bungee cord securing the knobs together.

I yanked off the cords and opened the door.

Kailey still sat in the middle of the makeshift bed, in a very similar position as earlier. She blinked at the intrusive light and then skittered back against the wall. The wide-eyed, trusting innocence of youth was long gone from her face, replaced by sour-smelling terror. She'd wet her pants. *Poor baby girl.*

"Hi," I said. "My name is Lucy. I know your mom, Jenna. I'm going to help you get home to her."

Kailey shook her head. "He told me that too."

"He lied. He's a very bad man, but he's not going to hurt you anymore. The police will be here any minute."

I took out my phone and handed it to her. "Why don't you call your mommy and tell her you'll be seeing her soon."

She stared, obviously trying to ascertain if I was tricking her. I laid the phone on the pile of blankets and stepped back from the doorway, giving her room to come out if she wanted to. Finally, slowly, like a cat trying to sneak up on a mouse, her spindly, little arm reached out and snatched the phone. Gaze darting between the numbers and me, she punched in her mother's number.

I will never forget the sound of her frightened, broken little voice saying, "Mommy!"

FORTY

Todd arrived a few minutes later, and I was shunted aside as paramedics closed in on Kailey.

"Don't crowd her," I said. "She's been through enough."

A heavy grip on my arm pulled me out of the bedroom. "Let them work, Lucy."

Todd's tone was surprisingly gentle, his words sounding choked. I imagined he was feeling the same mix of relief and bitter heartache at finding Kailey. She would never be the same. But her mother was a survivor. Kailey would be too.

I allowed him to guide me into the living room, where Chris sat on the couch. Steve was handcuffed, still pinned face down to the floor. He sounded like he was crying, and if it weren't for Todd's hold on my arm, I would have stomped his face into the dirty carpet.

"How is she?" Chris asked.

"She's alive," I said. "As for the rest, only time will tell." I turned to Todd. "I let her call her mother."

"Jenna's meeting us at the hospital across the street," Todd said. "But I've got to deal with you two first."

"You could always just let us go and deal with the real criminal." Chris came to stand beside me. I leaned against him, suddenly exhausted.

Todd bristled. "At the very least, I have you both for interfering in a police investigation. I told you specifically not to come here, and yet you did it anyway."

"How close were you to getting the warrant?" I asked. "You may have been on the way, but you didn't have the right to enter, did you? Would it have come through in time to get her before the auction ended?"

"Beside the point." His mustache twitched.

"No," I said. "That's exactly the point. Your hands were tied, ours weren't. And he let us in."

"Here's what's going to happen," Todd said. "You two are riding with a uniform to the station, where you will once again be separated while I deal with this. Only then will I talk to you and decide what to do with you."

"We can drive," I said. "I promise we'll go straight there. We'll wait as long as you want."

"Your car will be impounded. I'm not giving you any more time to match up your stories." He motioned to a young uniformed officer standing in the doorway. I realized it was the same one I'd charmed the first day I spoke with Jenna. I smiled, and he looked away, blushing red.

"Can I ride up front?" I asked.

I spent the better part of the day waiting in a windowless interrogation room while Chris sat in the other. I didn't care. As long as I kept from getting arrested, I'd avoid a pat-down. And I was pretty sure Todd would call my hours on hold enough penance since I'd saved the girl's life. Most of the time, I dozed, caught up in living dreams. You know, the kind you could swear are actually happening. They sped by on fast forward, with bright colors and bone-chilling fear I could never completely

seize. Several times I jerked awake, unsure of why I was terrified, but wanting to hide under the table.

At 6:07 that evening, Todd finally entered. He'd taken the
time to shower and shave, leaving only his unsightly mustache. I
smiled. He was a good cop.

"How is she?"

"Physically, she'll be all right. Eventually. Sexually
assaulted more than once. But nothing that won't heal." He
spoke in a monotone, keeping the necessary detachment. The
horror of child sex abuse will eat a person alive without it.
"Mentally? She's not great."

"Is she speaking?"

"To her mother, thank God. She's the only person she'll
allow near her. The examination was a struggle."

"Jenna will help her. She knows how."

"Do you believe in curses? Or fate?" Todd sat down across
from me.

"Hell if I know, Detective."

"I mean, Jesus. First Jenna's ordeal, and then years later,
Kailey's. Martha wasn't involved in Kailey's abduction at all.
How can it happen in a family like that when the abuser isn't
related?"

"Some people have really shitty luck," I said. "It's not about
fate or curses or destiny. It's about being in the wrong place at
the wrong time and catching a predator's attention."

"Yeah, I guess." He gave himself a shake. "So we've got
Chris's statement. Let's hear your side of the story."

"I've told you everything. I've got a computer friend who
keeps an eye out on the child porn sites. She simply lucked out
and saw the feed, recognized Kailey."

"How did you get Steve's address? It took us some time."

"I'd gotten a lead on him a few weeks ago," I said. "That he
might be molesting little girls again. So I tried to check him out.
Never found anything conclusive. But like I told you, my friend

and I connected him to Jenna after we found out he'd been fired from Philly Fitness. Another coincidence—I'd just happened to see Jenna's sweatshirt when I spoke to her."

"Yet you don't believe in fate."

"No. Luck went our way. That's it."

"I'm not sure there's a difference," Todd said. "You said you didn't have anything conclusive on Steve. Meaning that he was molesting again?"

"No, nothing conclusive."

"What would you have done if you did find something conclusive?"

I'd prepared for this. "Depends on how I found out. If at all possible, I would have been a witness and called the authorities. If not, I would have contacted parents, guardians, CPS, whatever it took."

"You realize you're way too close to these cases. It won't end well."

Chris's words flashed back to me. He'd been right, of course. There is no happy ending for me. But at least I will save some kids in the process.

"You're probably right," I said. "But I can't live with myself if I sit back and do nothing."

"I'm painfully aware of that."

"What about Steve?"

"He's been questioned all day. Looks like Kailey isn't the first child he's sold. We're working on getting his connections. Technicians are tearing apart his computer."

We studied each other for a moment, and despite Todd's wary expression, his eyes were warm. He understood, at least a little. I decided to offer the olive branch. "I know I've been a pain in your ass. But all of it was done with Kailey in mind."

"That doesn't excuse the fact that you interfered with the investigation. Repeatedly. And don't tell me that you saved the kid. Doesn't excuse what you did. Things could have gone very badly, for everyone."

"I won't argue that."

"Good, because it's a waste of your breath."

"Look, arrest me if you feel you have to." I spread my hands wide in submission. "But leave Chris out of it. He's got enough to deal with right now, and he went to protect me. I called the shots."

"He said he was a willing participant."

"Because I was going to do it with or without his help," I said. "Did you get the DNA results back? Or identify the bodies from the fire?"

"We're working on the identification. The medical examiner's established the child was a female between the ages of twelve and twenty. Other body was a male." He let the words sink in.

I gritted my teeth. "Mother Mary?"

"In the wind. Crime scene techs combed the property. There's evidence Mary—Martha, whatever the hell she goes by —was up to her old tricks. Holding teenaged girls. There are a few missing persons cases in the state that fit the female victim. No sign of other bodies, though. We don't know if she was running a prostitution ring or buried them somewhere. But there's fairly fresh blood in the barn."

Evil never ends. "So, what, she killed the man and the girl and then set the place on fire?"

"We think so, yes. She's a big woman, probably snuck up on them. There's signs of blunt force trauma on both skulls."

"So who was the man in the fire?"

"We assume another patsy, just like Chris's dad."

"Is his dad talking?"

"No," Todd said. "He's loyal to her, and I don't pretend to understand why."

"So Mother Mary is still out there. She's been free all these years." My stomach clenched. "Justin was an innocent kid."

He nodded. "I wonder if being incarcerated saved his life, though. She hated him. I always guessed it, but I didn't realize how deep her hatred of Justin went."

"Maybe. But his life isn't great. And I didn't help the matter." I felt ashamed. "I hope he can start again. For a second time."

"Yeah well, his brother's going to help with that."

"Chris? It's definite, then?"

"It is. Chris's uncle—the assistant district attorney—is going to file a case to get Justin's name cleared. We're filing charges against Mary, and we're going public. Justin's terrified, but he wants the truth out there."

I managed to smile. "Good for him."

"Speaking of the ADA, he's waiting for you. Along with his nephew."

"To file charges?" I prepared myself to accept my fate without argument. "Against Chris too?"

"To take you both home." Todd looked irritated. "Chris used his one phone call the right way. ADA Hale came in here two hours ago and made it clear we weren't pressing charges against Chris. Apparently his nephew's got some pull, because the ADA pled your case as well."

I exhaled, the resulting ache in my chest indicating I'd been more tense than I'd realized. "I've never met him."

"You will in a few minutes." Todd leaned back in his chair, studying me with intensity. "I wasn't going to charge you, anyway. I knew it would be tossed out and result in nothing but paperwork. But at least I made you sweat it out."

"You did. I was nervous." I stood up, anxious to get out of the cardboard box of a room.

Todd ran his index finger along his mustache. "There's just one more thing to discuss."

I swear I heard the creaky wheels of the lethal injection table rolling into the room. I sat back down.

"Brian Harrison was found dead in a parking garage early this morning," Todd said. "Preliminary autopsy shows he died in a manner very similar to his brother."

The hairs on the back of my neck spiked. I swallowed hard, forcing my voice to remain neutral. "Really?"

"Yep. Medical examiner said it's likely a heart attack brought on by years of drug use. He also had fairly fresh tracks on his arms."

"I'm sorry to hear that, but I'm not sure why you're telling me."

"You know exactly why. Brian Harrison pointed the finger at you for his brother's murder. Suddenly you've got information he might be a suspect in Kailey's abduction. I know you talked to Hank about the girl Sly Lyle claims he saw being attacked."

"So?" My skin grew clammy, my mouth dry. I licked my lips and immediately regretted it.

"So, we recovered Brian Harrison's computer. There were a lot of pictures of little girls on it. One of them was Josie, the older girl who walked Kailey home. We think she's the girl Lyle saw with him."

"Get her some help, then." The hammer was about to drop. Let it. Kailey was alive, and I'd taken more than one predator off the streets.

"Brian Harrison's neighbors witnessed a redheaded woman and a man with a baseball cap near his residence the day before he died."

"Again, why are you telling me this?"

"You know why," Todd snapped. "Since Harrison's dead after saying you killed his brother, I think it's pretty easy to put two and two together."

I laughed and hoped it didn't sound panicked. "You're

saying I caused both men to have heart attacks? I can be a bitch, but I'm not that bad."

"Other things can present like a heart attack. Things that go undetected unless a cop can convince his boss to look deeper. But the brass are telling me Harrison's a convict with no family and a drug addict. Seems open and shut, and the state doesn't want to spend the extra money for more tox tests. I'd say whoever killed him is getting a reprieve."

A sliver of hope bloomed in my chest. *Maybe there's such a thing as luck after all.* "It sounds like you're the one who's too close, Detective. I think the Harrison boys just lost out to the white devil."

He smirked and shook his head. The tension flamed between us, shimmering like a blazing fire against the night sky. "You're something else, Lucy."

"What do you want me to say? I'm sorry for anyone affected by the Harrisons' deaths. But for their loss? The streets are safer without those men." I shouldn't have said that.

"Exactly," Todd said. "I think somehow your dedication to help kids has brought you to a very dark place."

"You're probably right." I stood once more. "That's why I left Child Protective Services."

Todd stood as well. He stepped toward me, pulling my chin to force me to look into his eyes. They were quite pretty. I'd always been too busy pondering at the mustache to notice them. "I believe the Harrison brothers were murdered. By someone who knew what they were doing to kids, and I'm afraid that someone might be you. I can't prove it, but I'm going to be keeping an eye out. More cases like them crop up, I'll have to start investigating them. You get my drift?"

"Sure. But I think you're overworked and a little overdramatic." I pulled away, stepped around him, and reached for the door.

"Lucy, listen to me. Despite all of your antics, I like you.

Your dedication to help kids is really admirable, and you're brave. But if you keep this up, you'll self-destruct. And the law will catch up with you."

Of course it would. Hadn't I known that all along? I just didn't think the reality would be so hard to accept. "Duly noted. Will you promise me one thing, though?"

He looked at me incredulously. "I owe you a favor?"

"Not me. Josie. Please make sure she gets help."

"I will. But don't forget what I said."

FORTY-ONE

Chris stood when I came into the station's waiting area, followed quickly by a distinguished-looking man with silver hair in a matching gray suit. Sitting beside them was Justin. He stood up too.

"ADA Hale, I presume?" I offered my hand. "Thank you so much for speaking on my behalf. I'm in your debt."

"Not at all." The ADA's grip was firm like his nephew's. "The way Chris tells it, without you, we would have never put things together with Mary's crimes."

"Detective Beckett told me you're going to help Justin." I smiled at the boy whose crush I had yet to address. He grinned.

"I'm going to do everything I can."

"Thank you. He deserves that." I glanced at Chris, whose sky-colored blue eyes were pale with weariness. "At least you know the truth. And maybe you and Justin can be friends."

"Maybe."

ADA Hale patted Chris on the shoulder. "I'll get the car, and then we'll head over to impound and pick up Lucy's vehicle. Then you can both get home and get some rest."

I waited until he disappeared around the corner.

"Thanks," I said to Chris. "For everything. Can I talk to Justin privately?"

Chris looked surprised but nodded. "I'll wait outside."

Clearly a bundle of nerves, his hands in his pockets and head down, Justin danced from foot to foot.

"Hey." I touched his arm. What did I say to this boy whose new life I'd nearly ruined? It would be easier if he hated me.

"Hey," he said.

"Listen, about what you said at your mother's house? In the upstairs bedroom?"

"Yeah." He flushed crimson, which only made him look younger. "I'm stupid. You wouldn't be interested in me."

"It's not that. At all. But I'm twelve years older than you. Considering everything I stand for, it's inappropriate. I'm not going to give you the whole, 'sex is about love' thing, because it isn't always. But between two people with the kind of history that there is between us? It could ruin any sort of friendship we might have. And I don't want that."

His eyes were watery. "You want to be my friend?"

"Of course I do. If you'll have me."

"I can deal with that."

I smiled and linked my arm through his. "Then let's get out of here."

Justin left, promising to meet ADA Hale in the morning. ADA Hale dropped Chris and me off at the impound lot, and I thanked him again.

"You could have gone on home with your uncle," I said after I'd paid for my car. Chris and I wandered the massive lot, searching for my Prius. "I'll be fine."

"I'd rather go with you." He slung his arm around my shoulders. The gesture felt comfortable, easy. In so many ways—the ones that mattered—we were the same. "So Slimy Steve was selling kids. He'll have fun in prison."

"At least he'll stay there this time." But Steve was just a cog in an ever-growing machine. How many other children were being trafficked while I celebrated? I leaned into his embrace and told myself it was because of fatigue. "You know what I meant back there, right? When I said 'for everything'?"

"I kept you out of jail."

"You kept me from killing Steve. I had the cyanide. If you hadn't been with me, I would have done it. And I would have been arrested."

"I know."

We faced each other, faces close, body heat mingling. "I *will* take care of Mother Mary."

"I have no right to ask you to do that. I never should have mentioned it."

I laid a hand on his chest, over his heart. "You are a good person. You have an aunt and uncle who love you—who have dedicated their lives to helping you prosper. I will not let you throw that away. I won't let you sink into my dark place."

Because it would make me feel guilty, and I don't like what that says about me.

His heart beat against my hand, its steady rhythm calming me. I patted his chest. He took my hand in his and held it close.

"I won't let you live in the dark place by yourself."

My throat tightened; a swell of emotion rose in my chest. I swallowed it down. "See? Not a sociopath. Honestly, you're not even good at pretending to be one."

He smiled. "If you say so."

"Just calling it as I see it."

"That's what I like about you." Still holding my hand, he pointed to the southwest corner of the lot. "There it is."

A huge yawn tore through me, and I gave him the keys. "You drive. I'm taking a nap."

Inside, the car was warm, and I sank into the seats, my eyes suddenly heavy. "You know the way to my place from here?"

The corners of his mouth twitched into a grin. "Of course I do."

"Creepy stalker."

He laughed, pulling out into traffic. Comfortable silence embraced us, and I slid toward sleep.

"Lucy?"

I closed my eyes, longing for the warmth of my bed and the sound of Mousecop's relentless purring. "Yeah?"

"My mother is dangerous."

"I know."

"We have to stop her."

"We will, I promise."

I thought again of Kailey on the auction site. Of the predators huddled in front of their computer screens in darkened rooms, waiting to buy a child. Of the masses of kids with no chance of being saved. The police knew what Mother Mary was capable of now. If Todd had his way, all of Philadelphia PD would recognize her on sight.

But what about all the faceless predators with money to burn?

We would look for Mother Mary eventually. But for now, I had other targets in mind.

A LETTER FROM STACY

Dear reader,

Thank you so much for reading the Lucy Kendall series. It's still hard to believe how much readers have bonded with her! I have so much fun writing the books and I hope you enjoy reading them just as much. If you want to be notified about new releases in the series, just sign up at the link below. Your email address will never be shared, and you can unsubscribe at any time.

www.bookouture.com/stacy-green

One of the best parts about storytelling is hearing from the readers. If you loved the book, please take a moment to leave a review.

I love hearing from readers, and you can reach me on Facebook, Twitter, or Instagram.

Stay safe and healthy,

Stacy

KEEP IN TOUCH WITH STACY

www.stacygreenauthor.com

 facebook.com/StacyGreenAuthor

 twitter.com/StacyGreen26

 instagram.com/authorstacygreen

ACKNOWLEDGMENTS

Lucy Kendall is the tiger mommy in all of us and a character near and dear to my heart. I self-published the series in 2014 and it did modestly well, but I always knew Lucy deserved a bigger audience. I am so thankful to Bookouture and my editor, Lydia Vassar-Smith, for believing in the series and bringing it to new readers.

My mom, Teri, loved the Lucy Kendall series. We lost Mom in 2017, so it is bittersweet to work on the series again. Without Mom, there's no me. She was the best person I knew, and wherever she is, I hope she knows I would have crashed and burned at this writing thing if she hadn't been in my corner.

Thank you to Lisa Regan, Teresa Russ, Maureen Downey and Jo Ann Willard for their support of my writing and friendship. To Rob and Grace: your endless support means everything to me.

Many thanks to Dr. D.P. Lyle (*Howdunit Forensics: A Guide for Writers*) for his patience and willingness to answer my numerous questions on cyanide, its effect on the body, and its presence at autopsy. Thanks to William Simon for his expertise in computer programming and police procedure. Thanks to the Philadelphia Police Department and the National Center for Exploited and Missing Children for guiding me through the search for Kailey Richardson. Special thanks to Heather Cathrall for being my virtual eyes and ears to the city of Philadelphia.

To Kristine Kelly, thanks so much for your support of my

writing and your honesty. Annetta Ribken edited the original series and her tough love helped bring the story to another level.

I'd also like to give a heartfelt thank you to all the survivors of sexual abuse—both childhood and adult—who share their stories so that others may learn from them. Without their bravery, the subject matter would have been even more difficult to handle correctly.

If you or someone you know is the victim of sexual abuse, the National Sexual Assault Hotline is confidential and available 27/7. Chat at online.rainn.org or call 800-656-4673. Rainn.org includes support opportunities for Spanish speakers and male survivors as well.

Made in the USA
Las Vegas, NV
28 May 2023

72651327R00177